in the
blink of an
eye

BOOKS BY KATE HEWITT

in the
blink of an
eye

KATE HEWITT

bookouture

Published by Bookouture in 2024

An imprint of Storyfire Ltd.
Carmelite House
50 Victoria Embankment
London EC4Y 0DZ

www.bookouture.com

ISBN: 978-1-83790-295-8
eBook ISBN: 978-1-83790-294-1

Dedicated to Cat and Amanda,
who have shared with me something of the uneasy dread of the
school gate,
and to Jo, who so wonderfully embraces it! You are all an
inspiration
and I will miss you very much!

PROLOGUE

It's not my fault, even though I know that's what everybody thinks. I see how they all look at me, with their squinty eyes and pursed lips. They're suspicious, I know it. They think I did something wrong. They've been *waiting* for me to do something wrong, all this time. That's how everyone is here—just waiting. Wanting it, even. If they can point their fingers at me, then they feel better about themselves. They think I don't know that, that I can't understand it, but I do. I see every time someone slides me a sideways look or cocks their head. They're thinking, *you're the guilty one. Not me, just you.* And it makes them feel so smug.

The truth is, though, I know who is to blame for what happened, although I'll never tell. Some secrets are worth keeping.

ONE

NATALIE

Six weeks earlier

"*Everyone?*"

I repeat the word with a lightly skeptical laugh, because really? Invite *everyone*? Twenty-odd rambunctious seven- and eight-year-olds, running around and screaming? Even for Eleanor, this is ambitious.

I am curled up on one corner of her family-room sofa, sipping a mug of herbal tea, although I'd rather have a glass of wine. It's only four-thirty, though, and Eleanor and I have a rule, explained to anyone who asks, that we don't open a bottle until after five.

"Yes, *everyone*," she replies, whirling around me in a blur of movement.

After four o'clock, Eleanor can never keep still; that is, until she flops on the sofa and decides to take a five-minute breather. Now she darts and weaves around me as I sit and sip—picking up toys, checking on the undoubtedly healthy casserole bubbling away on top of the massive Viking stove in the adjoining kitchen, then a quick glance to her phone to thumb a reply to a text. Eleanor is on a million committees, and she chairs most of them. I'm the vice-chair, but only when she asks.

"But they're turning eight now," I point out. Connecticut is one of the few states that has December rather than September as the cut-off date for school, so Bella and Freya are both on the younger side of the year, but third grade still feels like a big step, halfway through elementary.

I glance out the French doors to where Bella and Freya are both playing. Bella, with the same tumbling, blond hair and big hazel eyes as Eleanor, is holding court by a wooden outdoor kitchen Eleanor's husband, Brian, built last summer, complete with taps that turn on and off, hooked up to a rain barrel, so not only is the play kitchen made completely of sustainable materials, but it is eco-friendly. Naturally.

Freya is observing her, as quiet and watchful as always, her brown eyes wide and solemn behind her glasses, her dark hair in thin braids that hang down on either side of her face. She is waiting for Bella to give her a cup of rainwater tea that she will obediently pretend to sip.

"What does it matter if they're turning eight?" Eleanor replies expansively, so the comment is generous, rather than a point of contention. I turn back to her, and my own cup of tea. "Class parties are meant to be *inclusive*." The way she says this, I can't tell if she's being gently sarcastic or genuinely earnest. That's often the case with Eleanor; we've been best friends since Bella and Freya were both in diapers, but I can't always read her.

And I know she can't read me, even if she thinks she can.

I take another sip of tea while I organize my thoughts. Why should I mind if Eleanor throws a class birthday party for Bella? As Bella's best friend, my daughter Freya would be invited regardless, and the party will undoubtedly be amazing in the non-showy way that Eleanor has perfected, but still makes many mothers in the girls' class grit their teeth, at least a little. It won't be as cringingly ostentatious as the ridiculous stuff you read about on the moms' forums online, like iPhones in party bags, four-tiered birthday cakes, or renting out an entire fire station for the six-year-old who's obsessed with fire engines. I mean, is that even safe or *legal*?

No, Eleanor is the queen of the lovable homegrown party, while still managing to make it seem elite, which is exactly the vibe of our small town of Wetherby, Connecticut: be amazing but don't look as if you're trying too hard, or at all.

Tucked up in the northwest corner of the state, we're too far from Boston or New York to be truly suburban, but we're not quite rural. Most people here are either townies (although no one uses that word, of course) or ex-urbanites who have come to Wetherby for the "community," aka, the cheaper house prices. We're gentrified while pretending to be authentic, and if I sound cynical, it's probably because I am, especially since my husband Matt left me three months ago. I'm a townie, one who made good, although no one would ever use those words, either.

"It's just," I tell Eleanor with a little, smiling shrug, "that I thought by third grade people weren't doing the big class parties anymore. I mean..." I hesitate, because while this hasn't been an unwritten rule, I feel like it's more or less been mutually agreed by most parents now their kids are just that little bit older. I think of the conversations I've had in the schoolyard so far—half apologetic, half defiant. *Brody's having only a few friends over this year. Chloe just wanted a special time with one friend for her birthday.*

Surely, by this time, no parent *wants* to organize and supervise the dreaded class party—with all its ensuing noise, chaos, and tears? I think of the twenty-odd party bags that children rabidly hunt through, chucking aside the colored pencils and strawberry-shaped erasers to find the Starbursts or Hershey's Kisses. The devastation of torn wrapping paper and birthday cake ground into the carpet, if you have been brave, or maybe just foolish, and had the party at your home.

Although a party at a venue, whether it's a swimming pool or a trampoline park, can feel even more overwhelming. The noisy clamor of not just one party, but usually two or three, held side by side, so not only do you have to deal with the kids *you* invited, but all the other kids there, as well.

"It's a lot, isn't it?" I conclude. "And by this age, boys and girls often want different things for a party, anyway."

"Yes, but that's exactly why I *want* to have a class party," Eleanor replies, stopping for a second in her relentless tidying up to gaze at me with her usual endearing mixture of earnestness and certainty. She's wearing a long, patchwork skirt that would look far too hippyish for Wetherby, save for the fact that it's made by some new ethical designer and is paired with a simple and expensive white T-shirt. Her hair falls in tumbled waves about her shoulders, with perfect streaks of platinum and honey blond.

I know for a fact she doesn't dye her hair, the way I do, to cover the gray, even though at forty-three, she's four years older than me. Eleanor hit the jackpot in so many areas of life, but I schooled myself a long time ago not to feel envious. It's enough, I've told myself, to be her friend.

I raise my eyebrows. "So why do you want a class party, exactly?" I prompt.

"Because you're so right, Nat," she effuses, coming to flop down next to me on the leather sofa in their sprawling family room. With its huge stone fireplace and vaulted, skylit ceiling, it looks like a cross between a hotel and a ski lodge, but somehow Eleanor makes it feel homely. There are hand-crocheted throws draped across chairs, mixed with designer pillows and a Navajo area rug that I *know* cost five figures. In winter, there would be a fire crackling away in the fireplace, but on this sunny September day, the French doors are thrown open to the balmy breeze.

"Boys and girls *do* want different things," she continues, "and there probably won't be many more class parties, if any, after this one." She lets out a small, nostalgic sigh as she slumps back against the sofa. "Remember Bella's circus party in kindergarten? That was so fun."

"Epic," I agree. Eleanor had hired several circus performers to entertain the kids in the backyard, while Brian had donned a full ringmaster's outfit to supervise the proceedings. There had been an old-fashioned popcorn cart, as well as a cotton candy machine, and a couple of clowns.

"I just want one last celebration, before they get too big," Eleanor explains. "You know Lizzy doesn't even want a party this year?"

Lizzy is Eleanor's older daughter, and she turns fifteen six days after Bella's eighth birthday. They've always been too far apart in age to have joint parties, and so, in past years, Eleanor has had a crazy rush she calls "birthday season," putting on one low-key extravaganza after another. Not this year, though, it seems.

Eleanor's expression, full of whimsy and wistfulness, clouds briefly. "She just wants to go out with her friends, without us. She asked Brian to drop them off at the mall in Farmington and come back in a couple of hours to get them. I don't even know who she's inviting. She refuses to tell me. She won't tell us *anything* these days. I feel like she's turned into a different person."

"Yes," I remind her with a gentle smile. "A teenager."

I can understand why she's taking Lizzy's secretiveness hard; Eleanor and Brian have elevated the concept of family time to an exalted status—movie nights every Friday, family hikes on the weekends, dinner every evening around the table, holding hands for a blessing. They have the photographs to prove it all—one on each step going up the stairs, candid shots and artful poses—Bella on the rope swing, blond hair glinting gold in the sunlight; Lizzy on a sailboat on the nearby Twin Lakes, a look of concentration on her face as she takes the tiller.

And then there are the ones of Brian and Eleanor, that would be cringily sentimental if they didn't seem so sweet—arms around each other, staring into each other's eyes, Eleanor looking as if she's about to laugh, Brian radiating love and contentment. Put all the photos together and it looks like a magazine spread, or one of the ads the pharmaceutical company I work for runs that flash on TV—*take Rinvoq for your arthritis or psoriasis and your life will turn into a dreamy montage of Instagrammable moments!*

And yet that's how Brian and Eleanor's life actually seems. They're not even smug about it, just *certain.*

"So what kind of party are you thinking of, then?" I ask as Eleanor gets up to tidy papers into piles and then stir the casserole in the cobalt blue Le Creuset pot.

She glances at the wall clock above the massive table of country oak, and I know she's counting down the minutes until Brian arrives home. Eleanor has a bit of a 1950s housewife thing going with Brian; she likes to have everything tidy and peaceful for when he comes home, "to create a welcoming space," as she's explained to me. They usually share a glass of wine before dinner, their "quiet time." It's a nice routine, really. Who knows, maybe that kind of thing could have saved my marriage, but often I don't finish work until after six, and dinner is usually something straight out of the freezer.

"Something classic," Eleanor states firmly. "Nothing over-the-top at all. I was thinking of having it here, in the backyard—outdoor games, maybe an entertainer. Just someone who makes balloon animals, that sort of thing. I'll bake the cake."

"Really?" For Eleanor, this is genuinely low-key.

"Oh, and pony rides," she says, and I smile. *Of course.*

"Sounds pretty great," I tell her.

"Well, I'm expecting you to be my second-in-command," she replies, wagging a playful finger at me.

"Absolutely," I answer, as I always do. I don't even hesitate.

Eleanor glances at the clock again; it's after five and I know this is my cue to go. No wine today, although, admittedly, it's a Tuesday. We save the wine for the weekends, or the rare occasions when Brian is working late.

"So when are you thinking of having the party?" I ask as I rise from the sofa. Eleanor is putting a bottle of Sancerre in the fridge for her and Brian's quiet time.

"Last Saturday in September," she replies. "It should still be warm, right?"

"I should think so. And the leaves will have started to turn, which will be beautiful."

Eleanor has an amazing backyard—well over two acres, with a pasture for the pony rides and a lovely little pond at the bottom, fringed by maples and birches. I picture their leaves deepening to red and gold by that time, children running through the rippling grass underneath their boughs as the sun shines benevolently down. It will be like something out of a picture book, or maybe an Instagram feed.

Eleanor turns to me with a bright smile, and one clearly of farewell. "Yes," she agrees, "that's what I thought."

I walk to the French doors; Bella and Freya have moved on from the kitchen and are now playing hopscotch on a grid made in bright pink chalk on the patio. Bella is hopping nimbly on one leg, while Freya watches, her skinny arms wrapped around her waist. Something in me tightens at the familiar sight.

"Freya!" I call. "Time to go, honey."

She turns to blink at me for a second before glancing back at Bella, almost as if she is asking for permission.

"So everyone in the class," I muse to Eleanor as I wait for Freya. "What is that, twenty-seven kids now?"

"Twenty-eight. Don't forget Kieran." Eleanor's smile is determinedly overbright as I try to suppress a grimace and fail.

How could I forget Kieran? He's new this year, his family having moved here from New York City, and just two weeks in, he has already completely disrupted the peaceful equilibrium of the third-grade class. Freya recites his daily infractions with a monotone matter-of-factness—*Kieran had to go to the principal's office three times in one morning; Kieran ripped up Jackson's coloring sheet; Kieran had to stay in at recess because he'd spoken rudely to Miss Stoviak.*

"You're sure you want to invite Kieran?" I ask a little dubiously, and Eleanor grimaces again.

"A whole class party... how can I not?"

I concede the point with an answering nod. And maybe he's not *that* bad, just the usual overactive little boy.

"Okay, I should go," I say, beckoning to Freya, who is still watching Bella complete the hopscotch grid. "See you tomorrow?"

"Yes, tomorrow," Eleanor agrees.

We see each other every day, at school drop-off, and two days a week, when I finish work early, I often come over here like I did today, for a cup of tea—or glass of wine—and a chat. For the next few weeks, I imagine those afternoons will be filled with prep for this birthday party, and something in me wilts a little at the thought. I don't really want to help Eleanor stuff twenty-seven—*twenty-eight*—envelopes with invitations, or fill twenty-eight party bags with moderately expensive junk, or do any of the other things that a "classic" homegrown party will require, but I know I will. I always do.

Freya comes into the kitchen and silently slips her hand into mine. I squeeze it gently, drawing reassurance from her presence.

"All right, then," Eleanor says chirpily, in a voice more suitable for talking to a toddler. "Bye bye, Freya." She waggles her fingers at Freya, who simply blinks back at her. I squeeze her fingers again, my signal that she needs to say goodbye out loud. Freya has always been a bit quiet, but we're working on these social niceties.

"Bye, Mrs. Dalton," Freya says dutifully, her monotone making Eleanor's smile falter. I know she sometimes finds Freya a little odd, so different from her own bubbly Bella-bee— Eleanor and Brian's nickname for her—and yet the two girls have been firm friends since preschool.

"Did you have fun with Bella?" I ask Freya as we get in the car. It's what I ask her at the end of every playdate.

She stares at me for a moment, as if she's wondering why I ask the same question when she always gives the same answer. Or maybe I'm the one wondering that.

"Yes," she says, and turns to face the window.

"I saw you were playing hopscotch," I remark as I reverse out of the Daltons' drive. "Or at least Bella was." I keep my voice light. "Did you get a turn?"

Freya is silent for a moment, so I wonder if she heard me.

"Frey...?"

She keeps her face to the window as she answers in her flat monotone. "Yes," she says. "I got a turn."

"So, this birthday party, huh?" I remark, as we turn off Wetherby's Main Street, with its artisan bakeries and hipster cafés, interspersed with the more classic small-town staples of a post office and hardware store. "That sounds fun."

Freya just shrugs, and I decide to drop this as a topic, too. I'm not looking forward to a class party, with all its chaos, especially now, when my work as a pharmaceutical sales rep is more pressured than ever as senior management is obsessed with profit margins and I'm still trying to figure out what this separation—and maybe looming divorce—means for me, as well as for Freya.

Not that Eleanor would understand any of that—she's not

divorced, and she doesn't have a job. She has plenty of time, and help, and money, to throw the biggest birthday party in the world.

As I pull into our drive, I tell myself this party doesn't have to be a big deal. Of course, Eleanor's parties are always big deals, but I'll just show up and do what I'm told, the kids will be hyper and then they'll go, and three hours later it will all be over.

What could possibly go wrong?

TWO

ELEANOR

A sigh escapes me as Natalie leaves, and I'm not sure if it's one of disappointment or relief. Maybe a bit of both. I enjoy her company, I absolutely *do*, but friendships can be so complicated. Natalie has been a great support to me, there's no doubt of that, but she can also be a little... negative, especially since Matt left her, although, as far as I'm concerned, good riddance to him. Not that I'd express that to her, of course, or tell her what I know about him that she obviously doesn't. It would only hurt her, and I'm not great at confrontation.

But even before her separation, she's always been a bit... bemused... by my over-the-topness, like she finds it a little bit too much, maybe even ridiculous. I'm the mom who not only brings in the cupcakes iced like pumpkins for Halloween, but who even writes each child's name in glittery sparkles on top of the icing. I'm the mom who hand-sews the Halloween costumes, who changes the wreath on the door to match the season, who has a scrapbook of family photos per *year*. I'm not ashamed of any of it, but I know how it sometimes looks to everybody else. Like I'm trying too hard. Like I think I'm superior.

I laugh at myself when I'm with other moms, admitting my excessiveness like it's just a quirk rather than a commitment, and usually they laugh along, although I've seen the occasional look exchanged between them, like an internal eye roll, and I get it, I do. Motherhood is a competition, even when you don't want or mean it to be.

But maybe I'm being paranoid. God knows I've got enough reasons to doubt myself. It's hard work, being this way; I might try to make it seem effortless, but it isn't. And I don't think Natalie is *inherently* negative; it's just that her separation from Matt has sharpened her a bit, taken away some of the softness. And I can hardly blame her for that, no matter what a jerk I now know he is. He walked out on their marriage, their *family*, with barely a word. If Brian did something like that... well, I can't even imagine it. It feels impossible.

In any case, I did my best to help Natalie through the heartbreak—having Freya over as often as I could, making casseroles, offering wine. We got through it, and now Matt is in Danbury and Natalie and I are closer than ever.

I glance at the clock again and then go to the French doors that Freya left open to call to Bella. She's abandoned the hopscotch, pink chalk scattered across the patio, to play on the rope swing hanging from the big oak tree that Brian made when Lizzy was just a toddler.

"She should never play on this without supervision," he reminded me, a little severely, as he secured the thick knots on the huge branch high above. "You never know what could happen."

Brian has a thing about any potential danger—the swing, the pond. It took ages to convince him to get a trampoline, and we have a safety net, as well as a strict rule of only one child on it at a time, which somewhat limits its capacity for fun. I get why he's like this—because his childhood felt so unsafe, and also because he wants to be the best, kindest, most careful dad in the world. It's both sweet and a little sad, but occasionally it can also be the *tiniest* bit tiresome, not that I would ever say as much. I'd much rather have a husband who cares too much about his children's well-being than not enough.

"Bella!" I call now. "Please come and clean up the chalk."

Bella has just pushed off with her feet, so the swing goes high up into the air, her blond hair flying out behind her, her toes pointed like a ballet dancer, her face suffused with expectation and joy. The sight of such lovely, childlike freedom makes me feel a mix of wistfulness and gratitude. I must have been like that once, although I can't honestly remember. I grew up with parents who had Expectations, with a capital E, at least in relation to my twin older brothers. I managed to start disappointing them with my averageness pretty early on—mildly dyslexic, not athletic or ambitious in any way. I was popular, simply because I was pretty, but I think my parents would have far preferred me to be smart.

"Just one push?" Bella calls to me, giving me a hopeful smile, her whole face lighting up, and, as ever, I can't resist. There's always time for just one more push.

I walk across to the swing, enjoying the mellow late-afternoon sunshine. It's early September, but it still feels like summer, even though in this part of New England, the leaves are already touched with crimson and gold, giving a wistfulness to the season that I both love and dread.

Time always feels as if it is slipping through my hands—first with Lizzy, starting high school and now so querulous and distant, and already with Bella. *Eight* in just three weeks. How did that happen? I feel like if I turned around, I'd see her toddling toward me, two years old and hands outstretched, blond ringlets haloed by the sun. Or even as a darling baby, with her rosy cheeks and gummy smile.

Whatever her age, Bella is *beautiful*. I know I'm her mother, and so I'm understandably biased, but everyone acknowledges it. From the time she was a newborn, people would stop me in the supermarket, hands pressed to hearts as they gazed down at her lying like an angel baby in her baby seat. "Isn't she *gorgeous!*" This wasn't just the usual, kindly coo over a baby; they sounded amazed, as if they were looking upon some sort of miracle, Helen of Troy or Venus de Milo. And I understood it, because she *was* gorgeous, and she still is. My golden girl, so longed for, so cherished. We had to wait six years before we were able to have her.

Now I place my hands on her back and gently push, sending her soaring. She lets out a laugh as clear as a bell, and I smile, so grateful for my girl. I know some people think I am a little smug about my good fortune—my beautiful family, my handsome and involved husband, my gorgeous house—but I'm *not*. I'm just so very thankful for it all, and I will work as hard as I can to keep it—and everything—exactly as it is.

I push Bella a second time, and as she tilts her head back, she laughs again, the sound so sweet and clear, and my heart lifts as I lift my face to the last of the summer's sunlight.

"One more!"

"No, sweetheart, you need to clean up the chalk." I am kind but firm as I grasp the rope handles of the swing and slow it to a stop, Bella's sneakers scuffing through the dirt as she lets out a good-natured sigh. "Then you can have half an hour on the iPad while Daddy and I have our quiet time before dinner," I add.

This is a ritual we never break, and Bella knows it. She skips off to gather the chalk and put it back in its tub, and I head to the kitchen to make sure everything is as it should be. The chicken and tomato casserole is bubbling away on the stove, and there is fresh bread baking in the oven, scenting the air with its yeasty goodness. The table is already set with glossily glazed pottery plates and crisp linen napkins, and the family room is tidied up. I glance in the mirror in the hall and smooth my hair, pinch my cheeks for a bit of color.

I know Natalie thinks I'm ridiculous for being like this, and I can almost hear her dryly affectionate remark. *June Cleaver called and she wants her life back.* I can picture my embarrassed laugh, my reciprocal eye roll. *All right, yes, Nat, this little ritual is a bit old-fashioned, I do recognize that, but it works.* Not that I've explained it to her, but the truth is, I've learned to stick with what works, because why wouldn't you?

Bella has finished cleaning up the chalk and she slips through the French doors, a blissfully expectant look on her face as she anticipates thirty minutes of uninterrupted screen time. I take the iPad out of our tech drawer in the kitchen and hand it to her with a smile.

"Only half an hour, okay, sweetie?"

She nods, knowing the drill, and once again my heart swells with love for my little girl. Maybe it's sappy to feel this way about your children, but I do. I am so very grateful for both her and Lizzy.

As Bella retreats to the den off the kitchen, the front door opens as if Brian was responding to a cue. "I'm home!" he sings out, and yes, that's a bit *Leave it to Beaver*, too, I know, but I love it. I love how he makes me feel—safe and happy and appreciated, and most of all, *loved.*

I take a deep breath and then turn to face him. "Hey, honey." My smile is wide and welcoming, and as Brian comes back into the kitchen, his face creases into an answering smile and his eyes light up, the way they always do. A sweet rush of relief runs through me at the sight of him and he holds out his arms.

"How was your day?" he asks as I step into them, pressing my cheek against his broad shoulder, and close my eyes. He smells of sunshine and his Tom Ford cologne and I breathe him in, savoring the scent of him that is so wonderfully familiar.

"My day was good," I answer, as I always do. Even if I've had a stressful day, even if something hard or downright horrible has happened, I don't tell him about it here, at this first greeting, when he's shrugging his world from his shoulders, and I am welcoming him into the domestic tranquility of mine. I might not tell him about it at all, depending. I've learned what Brian needs to know about and what he doesn't. It's being smart rather than sneaky; Brian is a wonderfully hands-on dad, and I don't need him getting stressed about things I can handle by myself. I slip out of his arms and head for the fridge. "Glass of white?" I ask lightly, and he nods as he removes his jacket and loosens his tie.

We are so familiar with this routine, it's like a script we follow without needing even to glance at our lines; they're imbued within us, unspooling like a golden thread and anchoring us in this moment.

"How was *your* day?" I ask as I pour us both glasses. From behind the den door, I can hear the beep and trill of some game Bella is playing on the iPad, and I make a note to myself to tell her to turn it down before we head into the living room.

"Fine, the usual. Where's Lizzy?"

I hesitate because this is a slight deviation off our well-known script. Lizzy should be up in her room doing homework, or maybe at an after-school club—field hockey or lacrosse, depending on the season.

"She texted me to say she was hanging out in town with some friends until dinner," I tell Brian.

He raises his eyebrows, and I can't tell if he's pleased or worried by this change. Since starting ninth grade two weeks ago, Lizzy has become so much more of a *teenager*. Of course, she was one before; she's almost fifteen, after all, but in middle school she seemed sweeter, more open and innocent—like Bella, but bigger. She gave me spontaneous hugs and was always up for blueberry pancakes and an extra side of bacon with Brian for a Saturday morning breakfast at the old-fashioned diner in town.

Now she seems to always be sidling into rooms or giving us sideways glances, angling her phone—which we only relented to buy for her at the end of eighth grade—so we can't see the screen. Of course, we've got all the parental controls and locks on it, but *still*. I don't like my little girl having secrets from me, even though I know, intellectually anyway, that it's all part of growing up. Becoming a teenager, just like Natalie said.

"Friends, huh?" Brian asks as he takes the two wine glasses from the counter. "Do we know who they are?"

"I haven't met them," I admit. Wetherby High has a wide catchment area, and it would be impossible for me to be familiar with all the kids in Lizzy's class, unlike in Bella's little elementary school, which just serves the town. When I pressed her for their names earlier, she fired a terse text back that I didn't know them.

"Hmm." I can tell Brian isn't all that pleased about this. I should have got the names, but I was distracted by Natalie and Freya being here, and the whole thing around the birthday party. Natalie didn't seem thrilled by the idea, but I know she'll come around. She always does.

"Shall we go into the living room?" I suggest. "Or the patio?" It's still warm out, although the sun is starting to sink behind the fringe of maples at the bottom of the yard, sending its last long, slanting rays across the grass, turning everything to Technicolor.

"Let's go outside," Brian replies. "It's going to get cold soon enough."

"Not too soon, I hope," I reply, deciding this is probably the best time to mention the birthday party I'm planning. "I want to have Bella's birthday party in the backyard on the twenty-eighth."

"Here?" Brian asks in some surprise as we step outside.

"Yes, *here*, that is where our backyard is," I tease.

We move over to the L-shaped rattan sofa by the firepit and

settle in, Brian on one end and me on the other. I tuck my feet up underneath and take my first sip of crisp, white wine, closing my eyes to savor the taste. This is probably my favorite moment of the whole day.

"It's just a lot of kids to have over here," Brian replies with a musing sort of frown.

I take another sip of wine and wait for more, because usually he likes having kids over at our place. We're certainly set up for it, with the huge yard, the swing and the trampoline, the basement playroom with a million toys, as well as a ping-pong and foosball table, the giant flat-screen smart TV. We are the house, the *family*, other kids gravitate to, which is how Brian always wanted it, because it was so far from his own deprived and chaotic childhood—an absent father, an alcoholic mother, moving around every few months, never much food in the fridge or money in the bank.

"I'm just thinking about the logistics," he explains. "What about the pond?"

"We won't go down near the pond," I promise. "And, of course, we'll have adults around at all times." Natalie and me, anyway. "Besides, at this time of the year the pond's little more than sludge, anyway. I don't think the kids will want to touch it."

He frowns. "It's probably two or three feet deep in the middle."

"True," I agree, because what else can I say? Should we not have Bella's birthday party in our yard simply because we have a pond? We've had events in our yard before—summer barbecues, fall evenings around the firepit, and Bella's fifth birthday, when I brought in all the circus stuff. The difference is that back then, the pond was fenced off. We took down the fencing this summer because it had started to rot, and we haven't replaced it yet. Brian has been pricing out various options, but it seems to be a decision that takes some time.

Still, I'm not worried. I can't imagine any kid would want to even get close to the pond—it's filled with mulchy leaves and thick, oozing black mud, and while it looks pretty from a distance, it's not the kind of pond anyone would want to wade into. "We'll be careful," I promise, and slowly, giving his assent, Brian nods.

"Maybe I'll look into getting it fenced off before the party," he muses. "When did you say it was?"

"The twenty-eighth."

"How many kids?"

"The whole third grade."

Another frown. "Isn't there some troublesome kid in the class now?" he asks.

I *might* have mentioned Kieran once last week, when I was feeling annoyed after reading with his group and he kept flinging everyone's books onto the floor, including Bella's.

I volunteer in the classroom twice a week, moving around reading groups. I usually love reading with Bella's group, but Kieran made it almost unendurable. He wasn't even being silly about it; he did it methodically, taking each book, throwing it on the floor, like it was a job he had to get done. I had to grit my teeth as I spoke to him in that pseudo-sweet voice I think all parents reserve for when someone else's kid is driving them crazy. It didn't work.

"I think you probably mean Kieran," I tell Brian. "He's a handful, it's true."

"Are you sure you want to invite him?"

"You can't have a whole class party and not invite one child," I protest, although, admittedly, I did think about it, briefly. The prospect of Kieran tearing through our backyard makes me tense. "Besides, he's new. He probably just needs to settle in, find his feet."

"What are his parents like?"

Brian is a great believer in kids being mini reflections of

their parents, which is a little ironic because he would be the first to admit that his parents were complete disasters, and yet somehow—really, thanks to a sheer force of will—he turned out okay. More than okay.

I shrug. "I don't really know that much about them. They moved from New York, and I think they both work. I've never seen the dad, though. I get the sense he might be a bit... out of the picture." Although I'm not sure why I think this; it's more that Kieran's mother, Joanna, always seems so *alone*. She's forty-ish, tall and dark-haired, always dressed in expensive separates and looking very pulled together and reserved. Very New York.

"You've never seen the dad?" Brian repeats, sounding a little bit censorious, although with work he only does the school pickup himself once in a *very* blue moon.

"School did only start two weeks ago," I remind him. "And if he's working..."

"Isn't there a meet-and-greet thing soon?"

I glance toward the kitchen, where the chalkboard wall calendar takes up a good four feet of wall space. Even though I can't see it from here, I can picture the meet-and-greet written in my careful cursive for this Friday at 7 p.m. Wine and cheese in the school gym, chitchat and humble bragging.

"Yes, maybe we'll meet him then," I say in the manner of someone soothing an anxious child, although Brian doesn't seem *that* worried. It's just this habit I have, like I have to smooth everything over, all the time.

I'm not sure when I started feeling like I had to *manage* Brian; probably sometimes between Lizzy and Bella's births, in the blur of those years of babyhood and deep disappointment, when we went through four miscarriages and then three rounds of IVF. It was utterly grueling, and Brian struggled even more than I did. He'd always wanted a big family; at the start, we talked about minimum three, preferably four children, who knew, maybe even five... *Crazy!*

We stopped talking like that after the third miscarriage.

And ever since then, I've felt protective of Brian, or maybe just of what we have together. It feels fragile, even though I know it's not. Everyone in Wetherby is always exclaiming about how amazing our marriage is, how great we are at making time for date nights and weekends away, which we do, religiously. And our marriage *is* amazing; I have no doubts about that. But I still have this ingrained need to keep all the plates spinning, all the balls in the air... without Brian even knowing that I'm doing it, or how much effort it takes.

I unfold my legs from under me as I drain the last of my wine. "I think the casserole should be ready," I say brightly.

As I come into the kitchen, I see a blur of movement heading out into the hall and I realize it's my oldest daughter.

"Lizzy!" I call, filled with relief that she's home but also a bit worried by how fast she's moving, almost as if she's trying to avoid me. I hear her steps on the stairs, and alarm gives way to exasperation. "Lizzy," I call again, and the footsteps still.

"What?" she asks in a surly voice from the stairs.

When, I wonder, did I become the bad guy, and more importantly, why? It feels like about three weeks ago I was still the nice mom Lizzy liked to cuddle with while we watched *Gilmour Girls*. Now, suddenly and without any apparent reason, I've become the enemy.

"Can you come in here?" I ask, trying to pitch my tone between interested and teasingly exasperated. "I want to hear about your day."

"Yes, Lizzy," Brian calls as he comes into the family room, closing the French windows behind him. "Who are these friends of yours you're hanging out with all of a sudden?" He speaks jovially, but I tense, and from the kitchen we both hear Lizzy groan.

"Nobody, okay?" she says, and then she hurries up the stairs while I go to take the bread out of the oven.

"Why won't she tell us?" Brian asks. He sounds endearingly perplexed.

"Because she's almost fifteen and it's no longer cool to like your parents," I tell him. Despite my own hurt, I speak in a voice of relaxed authority. I've read enough parenting books to know what's going on; that doesn't mean I have to like it.

From the den, I hear the ping of the iPad. I forgot to tell Bella to turn the volume down, but in any case, now I need to tell her to get off it. After that, I'll put the dinner on the table and then supervise a hopefully pleasant and cheerful mealtime conversation. Then it will be getting Bella into the bathtub, and negotiations about snacks, and bedtime stories, while also checking the parental controls on Lizzy's phone to make sure everything's okay there and also making sure that she's doing her homework.

Brian will be part of this whole process; he really is an involved dad. Still, over the years, I've discovered that what defines an involved dad is not the same as a mother of any stripe. An involved dad hands the mother the diaper, but she's the one who changes the baby. An involved dad swoops in for a bedtime kiss and a tickle that makes their child squeal with delighted adoration; the mother is the one who reads the four stories, picks up the dirty clothes, and turns out the light.

But Brian will be on hand for the party, I tell myself. Potentially troublesome kids aside, he loves being the maestro of a children's birthday party. With him and Natalie there, it will be fine. It will be great.

"Eleanor?" Brian asks, frowning, and I realize I am standing in front of the oven, staring into space, while upstairs Lizzy's door slams shut, and another electronic trill sounds from the den.

"Yes, all good," I reply, an answer to the question he didn't ask, and I give him a reassuring smile before I turn back to the bread, which is now just a little bit burned.

THREE

JOANNA

"I'm not going."

Tim manages to sound both apologetic and defiant as I frown at my reflection in the hall mirror. We're due at the Wetherby Elementary third-grade parents meet-and-greet evening in fifteen minutes, and the babysitter I hired off an internet childcare site is due here in five. And now my husband tells me he's not coming?

Unfortunately, I'm not even surprised.

I purse my lips and try not to sigh. "*Tim...*"

"I'm sorry, Jo." In the mirror's reflection, I see him slump onto the sofa and fold his arms, looking both dejected and obstinate. "I just can't face it."

I stare hard at my reflection, noting the fine lines fanning out from my eyes, the deeper ones carved from nose to mouth that weren't there a year ago, the strands of gray threading my dark, shoulder-length hair and catching the light. I'm forty-four, but I feel older. I look it, too.

I take a deep breath, letting it out as slowly as I can. Count to three, just in case. I am trying to be patient, heaven knows, but sometimes, like now, it feels impossible. "I know it's hard to go to new things, meet new people," I tell Tim as I turn to face him. "But we want to make a new life here. For ourselves as well as for Kieran. And we can't do that if we don't try."

"Kieran's not going," Tim replies, his chin now tucked in toward his chest, and I have to press my lips together to keep from snapping that he sounds like a child.

"But meeting the other parents in his class will help his experience at the school," I say instead, my tone deliberately mild.

I know we have not had the smoothest entry into the Wetherby Elementary community. It's been just over two weeks, and I've been called into school "to talk about Kieran's behavior" three times already. That's in addition to the four conversations I've had with the teacher, Miss Stoviak, at pickup. I recognize the look on her face perfectly—strain only just covered by patience. I fear it's the same look I now have on my face as I talk to my husband.

"*You* can go," Tim says, as if he is offering me some sort of concession. "We need someone to stay home with Kieran, anyway."

I bite down on my lip hard enough to send a pang of pain shooting through my mouth. "I booked a babysitter." He knows this, of course. How could he not? I glance pointedly at my watch, hating that we're having these kinds of conversations, that everything has become adversarial, when what I really want to be is sympathetic. I was understanding for *months*, but now I need Tim to try just a little bit harder, or even at all. "She's going to be here in less than five minutes," I tell him. "And I'll have to pay her for her time, whether she babysits or not."

Tim shakes his head. "You know Kieran doesn't do well with sitters."

Kieran doesn't do well with a lot of things, which is another point of contention between Tim and me. How did we get here,

I wonder, far from the first time. Here, to Wetherby, a place I'm not entirely sure of yet, but also *here*, to this place between Tim and me. Like work colleagues who pretend to get along, every conversation a negotiation. That's not what a marriage is supposed to be. It's not what our marriage *was*... until six months ago.

"If you change, and then shave," I suggest, as gently as I can, "you might feel better. Up to it, I mean. And meeting people... it could help, Tim." He's barely left the house since we moved here a month ago, and that can't be good for anyone's mental health, and especially not for someone who is already struggling with depression.

Tim shakes his head. He can be so stubborn, in a way he never used to be before his breakdown.

I hate that word—*breakdown*. It makes me think of a broken car, a flat tire. Something that needs to be fixed, but, more importantly, that *can* be fixed, with a little time, money, elbow grease, maybe a few spare parts. There's a hope in the phrase, a suggestion that it is temporary.

Tim, however, didn't break down; he exploded. Or maybe imploded. Really, he just *stopped* everything—work, family, marriage—and became this... this *being*, who could only focus on how he felt. In the space of what felt like a moment, our whole life upended, imbalanced, and I was left feeling like I was alone in a room all the time, even when he was right there. I'm scared there's no way of getting our life together back... especially if Tim won't even try.

But I can't think like that now. This move from Manhattan to Wetherby was meant to be our fresh start. A new school for Kieran, space and time for Tim to continue to heal and recover. And me? Well, I'm just trying to keep everything going.

A growl of frustration from the playroom has both Tim and I tensing. I hear the sound of the iPad being flung down and I hope and pray that the screen hasn't cracked—again.

Tim and I exchange knowing glances, and then, with a sense of resignation, I leave to find our son.

Kieran is sitting on the playroom's sofa, his arms folded, his face crumpled into a scowl, although it evens out to a defiant stare as he looks at me, his blue eyes, just like Tim's, narrowed, his blond hair rumpled and messy.

"Everything all right, bud?" I ask lightly. The iPad is face down on the floor, but at least it fell on the carpet. I pick it up and exhale in relief that the screen is not cracked. We've repaired this thing four times in the last year. Four times too many, I know so many sanctimonious parents would say, rolling their eyes and wagging their fingers. *What you really need to do is set boundaries and then keep them.* So very easy to say when it's not your kid.

Kieran doesn't answer, and I force myself to continue, even though I know it might spark a tantrum—although that doesn't even begin to describe Kieran's sudden rages. He can be the calmest kid in the world, utterly even-tempered to the point of seeming indifference, and then suddenly it's like some devil got inside him and he goes berserk—screaming, punching, throwing things, destroying whatever is in his path, like a four-foot five tornado. The mercy is these rages burn out quite quickly, leaving us limp with emotional exhaustion, but relieved.

We've taken him to a couple of different therapists over the years, mainly to help him manage his anger, but we have both been reluctant to go further than that in search of an actual diagnosis. Labels don't always do children any favors, although I have forced myself to consider what labels could be applied—ADD? ADHD? Autism?—but none of those usual suspects seem to fit with Kieran's range of symptoms. He can be aggressive and angry in short bursts, but mostly he's calm, even detached. He avoids physical affection, but he loves watching TV with Tim. He always says sorry if you ask him to, but he hardly ever sounds like he means it. He often seems almost indifferent to people, but can become fascinated, even obsessed, with some activity—a puzzle or building something out of Lego. Nothing I've read online seems to fit all his symptoms, but I am starting to wonder that if we did manage to get a diagnosis, then we might get some help in how to handle—and help—him. Because the parenting books I've devoured, the websites I've studied like academic texts, the well-meaning friends who don't have a clue... none of it has helped so far.

"Kieran," I tell him now, my voice firm but gentle, "using technology is a privilege, not a right. If you throw the iPad and treat it disrespectfully, then I'll have it to take away."

Fortunately, Kieran doesn't kick off; he just glowers, but in some ways that's worse, because he looks so *cold* then, in a way that takes me aback. I tell myself I'm overreacting because everything about our new life is strange right now; Kieran is adjusting, as Tim and I are. This is how he reacts to stress, and it's not too dissimilar to the way I react, closing myself off emotionally. Maybe Kieran's behavior unnerves me because in some ways it's so close to mine.

"Fine," he says, with a shrug. "Take it. Those games are stupid, anyway."

"All right, then." Unfortunately, I've backed myself into a corner, because now I have to follow through—all part of setting those boundaries and keeping them—but Kieran without tech- nology can be much harder to deal with. "You can have it back tomorrow after dinner," I say, which isn't much of a punishment because it's near his bedtime anyway, and he's only allowed the iPad in the evenings.

Kieran must realize this because his mouth twitches in something like a smirk before he shrugs again, seemingly indifferent.

"Why don't you get your pajamas on?" I ask him as I put the iPad in a cupboard, too high for him to reach.

Silently, Kieran walks out of the playroom and up the stairs.

I breathe a sigh of relief. He can be obedient, I remind myself. He can be pleasant and even fun. The other day, we went to pick apples at a nearby farm and he was fascinated by the whole process, delighted in filling the burlap sack we'd been given. We enjoyed ourselves—that is, until he chucked an apple and hit another kid in the head. But that was an accident. The child wasn't really hurt, and Kieran did say sorry. Besides, what seven-year-old boy wouldn't be tempted to throw an apple? The trouble is, parents can be so *judgmental*. Do their angels never act out? I wonder. Or do they just not see it?

Back in the living room, Tim is still slumped on the sofa, and now the TV is on a baseball game. I stare at him for a moment, fighting a swamping sense of futility.

"Are you really not coming?" I ask, trying not to sound too accusing.

"I told you, Jo, I'm just not up for it. Please don't give me a hard time, okay?" His gaze doesn't waver from the screen as he trots out this line as he has, in one form or another, a dozen times before over the last six months.

There's no point discussing it, I know. This is not a battle I'm going to win, and there isn't the time to fight it, anyway. As if to prove my point, the doorbell rings. It's the babysitter, and I'm going to have to pay her forty bucks just to go away.

I do, and she seems more annoyed than relieved, as she's had to drive twenty minutes to get here, but I give her a flurry of apologies before closing the door rather firmly in her face. If I don't hurry, I'm going to be late.

I turn back to Tim just as Kieran comes downstairs, dressed in his pajamas. His hair is ruffled from pulling his top over his head and his expression brightens when he sees Tim is watching baseball.

"Who's playing, Dad?" he asks as he scrambles onto the sofa and scoots into the corner, even though Tim's arm is outstretched along the back of the sofa, ready for him to snuggle in. Kieran's never been a cuddly kid, even as a baby. I'd pick him up when he was crying, and he'd arch away from me, crying all the harder. Even as a toddler, when I gave him a hug, he'd simply stand there and submit to it, rather than throw his chubby little arms around me. But maybe I shouldn't be that surprised; I've never been the most physically affectionate person, either, preferring smiles to hugs or even handshakes.

Tim gives Kieran a quick smile. "The Phillies."

Their favorite team, since Tim grew up on the Main Line, outside of Philadelphia.

Kieran grins back at him, and my heart suffuses with love for them both. As hard as things have been, I still want them to work. I want our family to recover, to *thrive*, here in Wetherby, Connecticut. So maybe I need to go to this event alone. If that's what it takes...

I can hope, anyway.

"All right, guys," I say as lightly as I can. "Lights out at eight, Ki, okay?" I say this mostly for Tim's benefit, as a reminder. In the past, he's forgotten, and I've come home from some work event at ten or eleven at night, and Kieran's light is still on. "I should be home by nine."

"Sure thing, have a great time," Tim says, his gaze back on the screen. He makes it sound as if there had never been any discussion of him going, as if he never intended to. I remind myself that this is a battle I am *not* going to fight, and then I step out onto the porch, closing the front door behind me.

Outside, the pine trees loom up darkly all around the little Cape we're renting out on a lonely country road until we've found something we want to buy closer to town. We've got plenty of money from the sale of our two-bedroom apartment on the Upper West Side, but there's no reason to rush. Still, I'm not entirely thrilled with living in what essentially feels like the middle of a dark and somewhat claustrophobic forest, although Tim was keen on the privacy. It's the kind of area where people buy their homes and stay in them for seventy years, which was what attracted us. That, and the commuting distance to Hartford, where my company's head office is, and the excellent school district for Kieran.

I take a deep breath and tilt my head to the sky, which is a deep, velvety indigo, with the first stars just starting to glimmer. The only sound is the whisper of the wind high up in the trees, and I tell myself to enjoy the peace, the solitude, the beauty. This was a good move for us. It will be. I'll make sure of it.

I fish my keys out of my bag and then head to the car. It's a ten-minute drive to Wetherby Elementary, and I already know I'm going to be late.

Sure enough, I'm the last one into the gym as I slip into the back row. I thought it was more of a mingling thing, but it's set up like an assembly and Mrs. Bryson, the principal, is standing at the front, along with Miss Stoviak, the third-grade teacher. She's only thirty or so and talks in the earnest edu-speak of modern-day educators: inspiring communities, dedicated learners, safe spaces. I always nod along and pretend I buy into it all, which I do, really. I mean, I *want* to, but I just can't quite keep from wondering if it actually *works* the way they seem to believe it does. It doesn't seem to with Kieran.

A dozen people glance at me as I come in and then look away. I don't meet anyone's gaze, so maybe I miss their welcoming smiles, but I *feel* the lack of them. I know a few people have already complained about Kieran's behavior. Maybe they think I'm oblivious to it as well as to them, but I'm not. Miss Stoviak made it clear, in her careful way, that some parents weren't happy with how Kieran had been acting out, although she didn't say it as bluntly as that.

Kieran's behavior is proving to be challenging for the rest of the class. I picture her strained smile, the way she worded everything so politely without actually *looking* at me, and then my own response—the stiff smile, the understanding nod, the inward, mingled shame and fury.

Yeah, I know parents aren't happy. *I'm* not happy. I just don't know what I can do about it. There are no simple fixes when it comes to your children.

Now I slip my purse under my chair and fold my hands in my lap, adopting a friendly, attentive look as Mrs. Bryson launches into her welcome speech, redolent with insider knowledge.

"I know you're all old hands at this"—there's a murmur of chuckles—"but welcome to another year at Wetherby Elementary. We are so pleased to have your children learning with us again this year."

Am I being paranoid, or is she deliberately not looking at me? I'm the only one in the back row, and the principal's gaze skims right over me. As she continues in the same vein about this "familiar community of learners," I feel my cheeks start to burn.

It's *not* a snub, I tell myself, just because Kieran is the only new child in the class this year. But I blush all the same, because it *feels* personal, like she's not-so-subtly reminding me that I'm not just the newbie, but the outsider.

Tim and I knew Wetherby was a tight-knit community when we arrived; it was one of the things that attracted us to it— a historic and eminently strollable Main Street, a school where parents linger in the schoolyard, chatting. Fall festivals and winter fun days and town parades and picnics, like a Norman Rockwell painting come to life. It is what we want, but as participants, accepted and even beloved members, not strangers standing on the outside, longingly looking in.

Mrs. Bryson continues, with smiling nods for various parents, and a particular shout-out to someone named Eleanor, who sits in the front row with her self-assured husband. His arm is draped along the back of her chair, revealing the glinting links of his Rolex on one muscular wrist, and she is leaning into him a little as they both look around, nodding graciously.

I feel my stomach start to cramp. I don't want to be here, and we haven't even started with the mingling yet. What made me think—made both Tim and me *believe*—that we could start over in a small, close community like this, with all these smugly satisfied parents whose children don't seem to step a toe out of line? What arrogance or naivete—I don't know which—possessed us to try?

Because sitting in the back row, looking at all the parents smiling and nodding, tilting their heads toward one another to murmur something that makes the other person smile and nod back, I don't think I'll *ever* be part of this group. Not with Kieran the way he is... and not with me the way I am.

I realize that I've completely tuned out the rest of Mrs. Bryson's welcome speech, and most of Miss Stoviak's chirpy monologue about what they're all going to learn this year. I manage to catch something about a unit on the indigenous peoples of North America which they will cover around Thanksgiving, and another unit on exploring impressionism that they will cover in spring—or was it surrealism? I'm not sure. I've lost track, because I'm so consumed with trying to *look* as if I'm listening, that I've forgotten to actually take any of it in.

I wish Tim was here—the old Tim, before his breakdown. That Tim would murmur dry remarks into my ear, making me smile and have to cover my mouth to hold in the laugh. That Tim would make me feel like we were in this together, the two of us against the world, whether it was the intense, career-driven parents of Manhattan or the smug, holier-than-thou parents I'm prejudging here. Either way, I would have felt like I had someone in my court, on my side. Instead, sitting by myself in the back row, I feel completely alone.

Miss Stoviak's speech comes to a halting close, and around me people are rising from their seats with a scraping of chairs against the gym floor. Two parents, including the indomitable Eleanor, have gone to a folding table set up on the side to start pouring wine and offering platters of Triscuits topped with slices of oozing Brie or orange cheddar, adorned with a couple bunches of grapes. Nearby, someone bursts into laughter, and someone else squeals. The chatter has become a low, intent hum around me, vaguely threatening, like the buzzing of bees.

If I leave right now, how bad will it be? For me, but, more importantly, for Kieran? Surely not *that* bad, because I can already tell that nobody here is going to talk to me. I'll spend fifteen minutes standing by myself, clutching a glass of cheap, lukewarm Chardonnay, wishing I was just about anywhere else.

Surely I can miss *that*.

Then, to my surprise, I hear a voice address me—warm, dry, with a thread of humor running through it.

I turn to see a petite, dark-haired woman standing near my chair. She has dark eyes and a faint, bemused smile, almost making me think she's observing this microcosm the same way I am. She looks to be in her late thirties, and has clearly come from work, dressed in a slightly creased button-down blouse in pale pink and pair of basic black bootcut trousers, also wrinkled. I tense, because I think I see judgment, or at least assessment, in her gaze, even though she's smiling. Has she come to corner me about Kieran? She wouldn't be the first parent who has done so.

"Hi," she says, her smile quirking up a little more. "I'm Natalie, Freya's mom. You're Kieran's mom, right?"

FOUR

NATALIE

For a second, Kieran's mother looks shocked, maybe even terrified, by my greeting. She's elegantly pulled together, in that effortless, expensive way all New Yorkers seem to manage. Her hair is pulled back into a tight bun, and she's wearing a pair of tailored trousers in navy, matched with a short-sleeve white T-shirt that is also tailored, and clearly designer and very expensive. She's also very thin; a Cartier watch dangles loosely from one bony wrist, and diamond studs twinkle discreetly in her ears. She looks to be mid-forties, judging from the lines around her eyes, which are a deep blue, although her hair is dark, with barely any gray.

"Umm, yes." She offers a brittle laugh along with her hand. "I'm Joanna Walters."

"Natalie West." I transfer my wine glass to my other hand to shake hers. "Pleased to meet you."

"Likewise."

She looks at me with such obvious apprehension that I can't help but feel sorry for her. It can't be easy, being the mother of the boy in class everybody seems to love to hate, and only two weeks in. Sometimes I find it hard to be Freya's mom, with her little oddities and quirks that other kids don't always get, but I suspect Kieran might be next level.

"How are you finding Wetherby?" I ask. "You moved here recently, didn't you? From New York?"

"Word gets around in a place like this, I guess." Joanna gives another laugh, this one even more brittle, as she touches one of the diamond studs in her ears, a nervous gesture.

"It does," I confirm with a wry smile, and then wait for her to answer my question. I realize I feel sorry for her, and of course I want to be friendly, but I'm also curious. Is she one of those helicopter moms who always feels the need to justify her child's behavior? *People don't seem to understand that Kieran is a very sensitive child...* Or is she a career woman, so focused on her ambition that she neglects to give her child the attention he needs, so he ends up acting out in a desperate bid for affection? Or something else?

Of course, I recognize that these possibilities are incredibly judgmental, assuming Kieran's behavioral issues must stem directly from his parents... but *come on.* Don't they? There aren't *bad kids,* per se, are there, those who are difficult from the get-go, from the womb? There has to be some kind of explanation for Kieran's behavior.

"We're still settling in, getting to know the place," Joanna answers finally. Her gaze is darting around the gym, as if looking for escape routes, and she's still fiddling with one of her earrings. "I couldn't really say how we find it just yet... it's only been a few weeks."

"Is it just you and Kieran?" I ask, a little abruptly it's true, and Joanna looks startled by my nosiness. The truth is, I'm half-hoping that she's divorced or separated, just so I'm not the only one. It would be nice to meet someone who gets where I'm coming from. Of course, there are a couple of other divorced parents in the school—Wetherby isn't *that* wholesome—but their kids aren't in Freya's class, and I'm not friends with them.

And in any case, no matter how many of us there are, people around here act like divorce is catching.

In any case, Joanna shakes her head, and that barely thought-out hope, selfish as I know it was, dies a swift death. "No, my husband Tim is..." She pauses, and then finishes a bit uncertainly, "At home. In Wetherby, I mean."

Her hesitant tone makes me want to ask more questions, but I don't. "Well, I hope you all settle in quickly," I say with a smile. I think I need to stop with the semi-inquisition. "Wetherby is a really friendly place... too friendly, in some ways, with everyone all in your business, but they mean well."

"Do they?" Joanna asks, wrinkling her nose, and I am surprised by her undisguised cynicism. It makes me like her more.

"I like to *think* they do," I reply with a smiling shrug, "but who knows?" I step closer, lowering my voice to explain in a confiding manner, "My husband and I separated three months ago. Sometimes it's felt like it was happening onstage, and the entire town was the audience, holding the popcorn."

I make a rueful face, expecting, or at least hoping, for some sort of conspiratorial look back, a moue of sympathy or a grimace of understanding, but Joanna goes all stiff and formal. "I'm sorry to hear that," she says politely, and takes a step away.

Ouch. Okay, maybe we won't be united in our disdain of gossipy, small-town culture. Never mind.

I shrug as I take a sip of my wine. "It happens."

I glance around the room, looking for someone to draw into our conversation, but everybody else is standing in tight little clusters, practically shoulder to shoulder, catching up on the summer and frankly seeming very unapproachable.

In truth, I'm not really that good friends with any of the other mothers in the class. I smile and wave hello in the school-yard, and I chat with them at birthday parties and school functions, but my position as Eleanor's second-in-command takes up

all my social energy, and, for a reason I can't entirely understand but at the same time sort of get, has made other friendships feel difficult, like a division of loyalties, or maybe just too
much effort.

I glance at Eleanor, who is holding court at the drinks table,
handing out plastic glasses of wine and telling people in her
generous, effusive way, to try the Brie. "It's from Costco, but,
honestly, you would *not* know it." Cue the friendly eye roll, the
trill of laughter as she thrusts the platter toward another parent.

She clearly doesn't find having other friendships difficult,
although I don't know if any of the other mothers in the class
would genuinely call themselves her friends. They're in thrall
to her, certainly, but is that really friendship? Sometimes I'm
not sure I know the difference, but maybe I'm just being cynical. Since Matt left me, it's been hard not to feel jaded about
almost everything. If you can't trust your husband to stick by
you even when things have gotten tough, why trust anyone else?

"I'm sure you'll settle in quickly," I tell Joanna for the
second time, as if repeating it will somehow make it true. "And
Kieran, too." I pause because I'm not sure whether to mention
Kieran's behavioral issues. It must be obvious to her that
everyone knows about them, talks about them even, amongst
each other, but it feels like the elephant in the room we're meant
to politely ignore, even as it cavorts and stampedes all
around us.

"Thank you," Joanna replies, and now she sounds like she
can't wait to be rid of me. Then I notice the tremble of her lips
before she presses them together, and I feel a rush of sympathy
for her. It's got to be hard walking into this crowd alone, especially when you know your child's been labeled the difficult one
in the class. She must realize I know what's going on and am
simply not saying anything, which maybe makes it worse. I feel
bad, and yet I know there's nothing really that I can do about it.

Unless...

"Eleanor Dalton's daughter Bella is having a birthday party in a couple of weeks," I tell her impulsively. "All the children in the class are invited. It might be a nice opportunity for Kieran to get to know the other kids outside of school..." I trail off because she looks startled by the idea, like it was just about the last thing she expected... or wanted.

"Maybe..." she allows cautiously. "Thank you for letting me know." She hitches her bag higher up on her shoulder, her gaze darting around in that way that makes me think she really is longing to get out of here. I can't say I blame her, and I decide to put us both out of our misery and move along.

"Hope to see you around sometime," I offer with a farewell waggle of my fingers, and then I head to the drinks table for a refill on my glass of wine.

"How are you holding up?" I ask Eleanor. She is handing out drinks and snacks like she's hosting the event, which, in a way, she is. Although she's as put together as normal in that effortless, slightly bohemian way she has, in a flowing batik print dress that probably cost close to four figures, I can't help but notice she looks a little tense. "Brian's working the room?" I query with a wry smile.

I glance around and see him chatting easily with a few other dads, hands deep in the pockets of his pressed khakis, hips thrust out, head tilted back. When our kids started kindergarten, Brian formed a group of dads whom he got together with regularly for beers out and the occasional Saturday morning breakfast at the local diner, or even a paintballing session or baseball game. He easily inhabited the role of the maestro who organized everyone, acting as the genial host even when he wasn't actually hosting the thing... just like Eleanor.

"I'm fine," she says in that firm way she has, like she doesn't want to argue the point. She tucks a strand of hair back into her loose updo before she hefts the bottle of white. "More wine?"

"Yes, please." I hold my glass out. "I was just talking to Kieran's mom," I tell her as she pours some cheap Chardonnay into my glass. "I don't think she's really gotten to know anyone. I told her about Bella's birthday party."

To my surprise, Eleanor's expression clouds as she puts the bottle down. "Oh, I wish you hadn't," she says, sounding unhappy, which surprises me.

I take a sip of lukewarm wine. "Oh? Why not?"

"Well..." She sighs and shakes her head. "There's been a bit of an *issue* between him and Bella." She says "issue" with hushed emphasis, like I should know exactly what she's talking about, but I don't, maybe because I was at work right up until this event, thanks to the ever-increasing pressure from my boss to "show up for myself" at work, which translates to make your sales targets by the end of the month or else.

"Specifically?" I ask Eleanor. I am a little surprised that there's been any issue; Bella, golden child that she is, gets along with everyone. As far as I have seen, Kieran has been acting out against the other boys, who can be rough, but not quite as rough, as he is.

"Yes, in their reading group." She drops her voice to a hushed murmur, full of import. "Kieran's been grabbing her book, throwing it on the floor, that sort of thing."

I nod as I take another sip of my wine. "Okay..." To me, it sounds like fairly average seven-year-old boy behavior, but I know Eleanor—and Brian—would both find it upsetting.

"But then this morning he did something worse," Eleanor confides, dropping her voice another octave as she leans over the table toward me. "He pulled her *chair* out from *under* her." She says this like Kieran punched Bella in the face, or pulled a knife on her, but I make a suitably shocked expression, because that is a little more serious than throwing a book.

I shake my head. "Poor Bella. Is she okay?"

"Yes, I think so." She grimaces. "Fortunately, she fell on the carpet, so I don't think she was too badly hurt, just a bit bruised on her tailbone. Brian wanted to get an X-ray, though, just to make sure, so that's where we've been all afternoon, practically right up until this evening. Nothing's broken, thank goodness." She lets out another sigh, this one long and resigned. "But Brian doesn't want Kieran coming to Bella's party."

"Oh..." I absorb this fact, along with what I told Joanna about everyone being invited. "So, you mean you're going to just go with inviting the girls or something?" I ask, and now I am speaking in the same hushed tone as Eleanor. Birthday party invitations—or lack of them—is, I know, a sensitive topic, and I am conscious of all the mothers circulating around me, ears undoubtedly pricked, wondering who has or hasn't made the cut.

"I don't know," she admits with another unhappy sigh. "I told enough people that I can't *not* invite them, you know?" She shakes her head. "I suppose I'll just have to convince Brian to let Kieran come and then watch him like a hawk."

Which means, I suspect, that *I'll* be watching him like a hawk. The thought makes me grimace inwardly—three hours of chasing after a hyper seven-year-old bent on bedlam. Wonderful.

"Sorry if I messed up things with Joanna," I say, admittedly a halfhearted apology, because I don't really think this is my fault. Eleanor was absolute about it being a whole class party three days ago.

"It's all right." She manages to sound magnanimous. "I'll figure it out."

Another mom approaches the drinks table, gushing about something or other, and I decide this is my cue to leave. Eleanor won't want for company, and I've enlisted my neighbor, Mrs. Simson, to babysit Freya and she likes an early night.

But as I get in my car, I feel a now familiar weight settle on me, making my shoulders slump.

Three months on, and I'm still not used to it. The quiet. The *loneliness*.

In moments like these, I feel as if I'm existing in an isolation tank. Last year, Matt and I went to this event together. Our gazes kept meeting over the heads of other parents, sharing a joke we didn't even need to explain. We've both shared the same good-natured cynicism about the state of helicopter parents in the middle-class microcosm that is Wetherby, although, if I'm honest, we both capitulated to the societal pressure often enough. If you *aren't* actually a helicopter parent, act like you are, anyway, to avoid the judgment. But even that we could laugh about... couldn't we?

Sometimes I worry that I've cast my marriage into the rose-tinted glow of remembrance, without truly acknowledging just how tense things between Matt and I had become. And if I want to pinpoint a time when they started to become so, it's probably when I went from working three days a week to full-time, when Freya was in first grade. Matt argued that we didn't need the money, so why do it, and I fired back that *he* was full-time, so why shouldn't I be?

"But, Nat," Matt had exclaimed, clearly exasperated, "you don't even *like* your job that much."

I couldn't argue that point, and neither was I willing to explain that it wasn't about liking my job or not; it was about not being dependent—on anyone. Not having my life revolve around my husband's, the way my mother's had, to her own endless sorrow and pain.

In any case, now that I'm on my own, I fear my cynicism is no longer good-natured; it possesses a serrated edge that draws blood. Instead of feeling wry, I am scornful, superior. I didn't want to become this person—cold, contemptuous, jaded. Most of the time, I manage—I think—to cover it up, to fake my cheerfulness and optimism, but not always. And maybe, in truth, that cynicism was always there, latent and hidden, and all it took was one deep disappointment in life to bring it to the fore.

My cell phone rings, interrupting my gloomy thoughts—it's Matt. I put him on speaker as I drive out of the school parking lot.

"Hey." My voice comes out a little flat.

"Hey." Matt's voice is warm. "How was it? Interminable as ever? Hopefully there was wine."

I think of the Chardonnay now fizzing unpleasantly in the pit of my stomach. "There's always wine."

"Mrs. Bryson gave the same spiel about Wetherby's 'inspiring community of learners'?"

A reluctant smile tugs at the corner of my mouth. "Of course."

Matt chuckles softly, and the sound steals through me, making me ache with a longing I have been trying to school myself not to feel. I don't want to want him, certainly not now, and maybe not ever. Not that much, anyway. "I'm sorry I wasn't there."

"You aren't, really, though, are you? Considering what you got to miss?" I speak lightly, because he'd meant to be there, except for some work meeting. I acted like it didn't matter either way, and, in truth, I wasn't sure which one I wanted—Matt coming, and having it be painfully poignant and awkward, or Matt staying away, and me feeling lonely, like I do. People would have gossiped regardless, that much I know.

"Is Freya okay?" he asks and I force my mind back to the current conversation.

Freya responded to Matt leaving with stony silence, as she has done with any stress, retreating into what the pediatrician calls "selective mutism"—a serious-sounding diagnosis I try to avoid, because, really, she's just *quiet*. It's not like she's *actually* mute.

Matt and I both tried to talk to her about our separation, but our attempts at explaining the situation just made her shut down further, and how can we explain something like that, when Matt wasn't even able to give me a real reason?

"If you can't see it, I'm not sure there's any point explaining it to you," he'd said to me wearily, which was just about the most unhelpful remark ever. Yes, I knew things had become stressful between us; I just wasn't sure on the *why*, and maybe that was part of the problem. Why did I feel like Matt was always disappointed in me? Why did I insist on constantly proving myself, like I was in a contest with someone neither of us could see? They are questions I've only started asking in the last three months, and I still haven't come up with any satisfactory answers.

As for what he said to Freya... *Your mom and I just need to take a little break, to make sure we know what we want.* I didn't know what that meant, never mind Freya. In any case, I am hopeful that she'll regain some of her usual cheerfulness eventually, but three months on she is still quieter than usual, wary and watchful.

"She's fine," I tell Matt as I drive down the darkened Main Street, all the storefronts shuttered, the whole town seeming empty.

"I'll pick her up on Saturday?"

"Yeah, that will be good." We've worked out an informal custody arrangement—Matt sees her every Saturday and every other Wednesday, when he takes her out to dinner at a pizzeria on Main Street. It's not nearly enough, considering how hands-on he was before, but it's all either of us can manage for now, considering the distance. Why he had to move to Danbury, I still don't really understand, along with so many other things.

"How about you, Nat?" Matt asks. "How are you holding up?"

The gentleness of his tone makes me grit my teeth even as my eyes sting. *You don't have the right to ask that kind of ques-*

tion anymore, I think, but don't say. No one else is asking it, that's for sure.

"I'm fine," I reply shortly.

"I know this is hard." He makes it sound like it's something that just happened to us, an illness or a tragedy, rather than something he chose, willfully, deliberately, without explanation.

"Yeah, well." My throat is tight with emotion, but I sound impatient, because I can't deal with these tender moments he tries to orchestrate. *You left, Matt*, I want to shriek at him. *Why are you acting this way now? Just to hurt me? Twist the knife in a little deeper?* "I've got to go," I say abruptly, and I disconnect the call before Matt can even say goodbye.

A shuddering breath escapes me, and I blink hard as I turn into the driveway of our family home. I don't know how long I'll be able to afford the mortgage; Matt's and my salaries don't really extend to two homes, but we've been making it work so far, if only just. Neither of us wants Freya to have to move.

I can see Mrs. Simson sitting on the sofa in the living room, watching the QVC channel as she always does when she comes over, the blue light flickering over her face. I sit there for a moment, struggling to compose myself, because, in truth, I feel like howling. I won't, though.

I square my shoulders as I walk out of the car, into the house. Mrs. Simson turns to me with an owlish smile.

"Hey, Mrs. Simson."

I've known Mrs. Simson for most of my life; I grew up only two streets away, although my parents retired to a condo in Daytona Beach three years ago, where my father plays golf and my mother flutters around him, anxious as ever, while he does what he damn well pleases. My older sister lives an hour away in Norwalk, and my younger one in New Haven. It amuses me, in an unfunny sort of way, that out of the three of us I'm the one who ended up in Wetherby, when I consider how I was definitely the one who most wanted to leave.

"Was it a nice evening, dear?" Mrs. Simson asks as she gathers her bag and her knitting, her book of crossword puzzles. She always brings lots to do, and then ends up watching QVC the whole time.

"Yes, great." I'm not about to go into it. "Thanks so much for watching Freya."

"She was as good as gold. Not a peep out of her." Mrs. Simson smiles at me, and I smile back, even though, suddenly, I feel almost near tears. I can't have these conversations with Matt, like everything is normal and fine. It's not fine. *Nothing* is fine. "Goodnight, dear," Mrs. Simson says, and I nod and watch her go with a lump in my throat.

Right now, alone in my house, the emptiness yawning all around me, I don't care about Kieran or Joanna or Eleanor or Bella's stupid party. I just want my life back, the one I had with Matt and Freya that I took for granted without even realizing it, that I was scared to trust in case it was taken away. Now it has been, and I have no idea how to get it back.

FIVE

ELEANOR

"I don't want him to come." Bella pushes her lower lip out as her golden-green eyes swim with tears, turning them luminous.

Everything else about this moment is perfect—we're sitting at the kitchen table together in a puddle of golden sunshine, the party invitations fanned out before us, the smell of freshly baked chocolate chip cookies scenting the air. Dinner is in the oven, the wine cooling in the fridge, and Lizzy is home, thankfully, doing her homework upstairs. I can relax, *breathe*, except...

"Everyone's invited, sweetie," I remind Bella.

It's been a week since I first floated the idea of the birthday party, and she's spent the last hour uncomplaining as she writes out the party invitations in her careful script, with the promise of a chocolate chip cookie when she's finished. I think it makes it so much more personal, when the child writes out the invitations, rather than the parent, but now we've come to Kieran's invite, and we've run into trouble.

"I don't want him to come!" Bella says again, stubbornly. She stares down at the invitation she has yet to fill out. "He's mean."

I hesitate, trying to think of the right words, to find the patient, understanding tone with the necessary, underlying firmness. Usually I can pitch it just right, but today it's taking effort, maybe because I'm just so *tired*. Lizzy still seems as if she speaks to me only on sufferance, and Brian has pulled a few unexpectedly late evenings at work, which puts the burden of bedtime solely on me. And then there's this party, and all the accompanying pressure to make it perfect, fun and safe.

"You don't have to spend the whole party with him, Bel," I reassure my daughter. "But it would be unkind not to invite him, when everyone else is invited."

She keeps staring down at the invitation, and then a fat teardrop splashes onto the paper.

"Oh, Bella." I rest my hand on her shoulder. I don't want to invite Kieran. Admittedly, at the start I was committed to the idea, to the inherent fairness and generosity of it, but after the furore on Friday, I don't feel like doing anything for that little punk.

I know that's not the right way to think about a seven-year-old child, but patience and understanding take you only so far. Bella did nothing to him. *Nothing*. And he pulls her chair out from under her, sends her flying onto the floor? I'm still fuming, Brian even more so.

He drove into school, closeted himself with Mrs. Bryson for half an hour, talking about duty of care and hinting at lawsuits. It was all blowing smoke—mostly—but he was even more furious than I was.

"She could have broken her tailbone," he fumed at me after we returned from the X-ray. "Or had a serious injury to her back. There was a girl in my high school who had that happen to her—in that case, it was onto concrete, but she needed *spinal* surgery."

I murmured something placating, although I'm not even sure what I said. What could I say? This was not something I'd been in control of, and yet I felt guilty. If I'd volunteered that morning... if I'd talked to Miss Stoviak about my concerns about Kieran... if I'd asked for Bella to be moved to a different reading group...

But, I reminded myself as I waited for Brian to calm down, nothing terrible actually happened. Bella has a bruised bottom, true, and her feelings had been hurt, but in the grand scheme of things, we were all okay.

Eventually, Brian realized that, as well, mostly; he calmed down and agreed, admittedly with deep reluctance, to let Kieran come to the party, or at least be invited. He didn't like it, but I think he saw how rude and ungenerous it would look, to exclude just one child from the class, even if I think most, if not all, the other parents in the class would understand—and agree with me. It's not what I want to be known for. It's not the kind of person I want to *be*.

So poor Bella will just have to put up with it.

"I'm sorry, honey," I tell her, "but it's the right thing to do, and I think you know that."

I squeeze her shoulder, and she draws a shuddery breath before she begins to write, in her careful, rounded letters, Kieran's name. I press a kiss to the top of her golden head. My kind and beautiful girl.

We get through the rest of the invitations, with Bella painstakingly writing each one out and then putting them into their envelopes. We both breathe a sigh of relief now that the job is finished. As promised, I reward Bella with a fresh cookie, and she goes outside to enjoy it, in the last of the day's light.

There are still twenty minutes or so before Brian comes home, so I decide to take a cookie and a glass of milk up to Lizzy in her room, although we usually have a no-food-in-the-bedroom rule. I don't want to be the kind of parent who can't bend when necessary, and Lizzy is still seeming distant, a bit sullen compared to the smiling, affectionate child she was just a few short months ago. Maybe the cookie will help.

I tap once on her door and then open it; she's not sitting at her desk doing homework as I'd thought, or at least hoped; rather, she's lying on her bed, pouting into her phone.

"Lizzy." My voice comes out too censorious. "You know you're not allowed your phone in your bedroom." I can't believe I didn't check when she went upstairs, but I'm still operating under the way things used to be, when Lizzy would be diligent about leaving her phone on charge in the kitchen, tearful with remorse if she forgot.

"Oh, Mom, come *on*." Her gaze does not waver from her phone's screen; she makes a duckface before finally lowering her phone to glare at me. "Does that rule really apply anymore? I'm in *high school*."

"You're fourteen."

"Almost fifteen," she shoots back. "None of my friends have this stupid bedroom rule. *None*."

"That may be," I reply evenly, "but we do not make these rules lightly, Lizzy. There is absolutely no need for you to have your phone in the bedroom." And many dangers in allowing her to. I've read the parenting articles, the horror stories, about sexting and naked selfies, cyberbullying and self-harm sites. We haven't dealt with any of that yet, thank God, but I am not about to open the door wide to such temptations and pressures. I put the cookie and milk on her desk and then hold out my hand. "Give me your phone, please."

Lizzy draws back, grabbing her phone and clutching it to her as a look of horrified disbelief comes over her face. "Mom, you aren't serious—"

"I am." Even though I wish I didn't have to be. I came up here to bond with my daughter, not pick a fight.

She shakes her head, golden hair flying. "You can't just *take* my phone..."

"Lizzy," I tell her, my voice comes out stern and firm, "we gave you your phone and we can take it away. Give it to me now, please." I keep her gaze, my hand still stretched out.

Lizzy still looks like she wants to refuse, and it alarms me. How, after just a few months of having this device, can it mean so much to her? I realize, with a sense of both shame and shock, that I thought my daughter was above this sort of unhealthy, teenaged obsession. I thought my parenting was good enough, even foolproof, to protect against these sorts of dispiriting arguments.

She still hasn't given me the phone.

"Lizzy."

"Fine." She practically hurls the phone at me, slapping it hard into my hand so it stings my palm. "You are *so* lame," she spits. "And so *unfair.*" She flops onto her bed, drawing her knees up and hunching her shoulders so she is curled up into a ball, her back to me. "I hate you," she says, her voice muffled against her knees.

"Enough, Lizzy." My voice trembles because her words hurt, even though I tell myself not to let them. She's just angry, that's all, and yet Lizzy *never* talks this way to me. How did we get here? Is it really all because of this stupid, stupid phone? "I brought you up a cookie and some milk," I tell her, and she just huffs.

I close my fingers around this wretched rectangle of technology, half wishing it had never been invented. And more than half wishing I didn't have to be its enforcer. Where is Brian in moments like these? Except I already know I don't even want him here in moments like these, because then it will seem like I can't handle them.

I know when he comes home, I'll have to tell him what has happened, and then he might go upstairs and pontificate to Lizzy on the dangers of cell phones and how there are *rules,* young lady, but I'm the one who had to face her down and confiscate the thing. He just does a bit of cleanup, and he'll probably sweeten the whole deal by offering to take her out for a father-daughter bonding breakfast on the weekend or something. I don't feel resentful, not really; I just feel so *tired*.

And I feel even more tired when I realize what Bella has been up to in my absence. She finished her cookie and has so very helpfully put the party invitations into a bag for me to take to school and hand to the teacher, which she has left next to her backpack. Something about this thoughtfulness jars just a little, though, and so I count the invites to make sure they're all there, and sure enough, they're not. One is missing, and I know whose it is.

"*Bella*." Her name comes out in a groan. I don't have the energy to fight battles on multiple fronts, and yet I know I have to because that is what a good parent does. I just wish Brian was here, to take up some of the slack.

There's no reply, but I hear the ping of the iPad from the den.

"Bella," I say again as I open the door to see her curled up on one corner of the sectional sofa, her face lit up by the electric glow of the screen. "I didn't tell you that you could have some screen time."

She looks up from the iPad, her eyes wide and so very clear. "But I always have screen time when Daddy comes home."

"Yes, but I still need you to ask me, sweetie." I decide not to press it any further, for both our sakes. "Also, what did you do with Kieran's invitation?"

She bites her lip. "I don't want him to come."

"Bella, we talked about this." I soften my voice as I come to sit down next to her. "Besides, sweetie, how would you feel if you were the only one not invited to a party that every other person in your class was? Wouldn't that make you really sad?"

She presses her face into my shoulder as I stroke her hair.

"Yes..." she admits in a suffocated whisper. "But I still don't want him to come!"

"I know. And, like I said, you don't have to spend time with him." I hesitate and then add carefully, "I know Kieran can seem unkind, but we don't know what's going on in his life or what has made him the way he is. Let's try to be understanding, okay?"

Bella lifts her head, her face blotchy from holding back her tears. "What do you mean?" she asks. "What's going on in his life?"

I actually have no idea what is going on in Kieran's life, although there has certainly been some speculation about it between the other mothers. No one, it seems, has seen his father, and some people are wondering if he actually has one. "I don't know, I'm just saying, something might be," I tell her. "Who knows if he's having a hard time at home, or he misses his dad..."

Bella frowns. "Misses his dad? Why would he miss his dad?"

"I don't know," I say hurriedly, not wanting to stoke speculation. "I just haven't seen him around. I thought maybe... he worked a lot or something. Where's the invitation?"

"In the trash."

I sigh. "Let's go get it together."

Bella hesitates, and then with a sniff, she uncurls herself from the sofa.

The invitation is resting on top of the trash; my daughter isn't sneaky enough to have hidden it beneath the carrot peelings, thank goodness. I brush it off and add it to the bag. Disaster averted, at least for now.

Bella gives me a watery, wide-eyed look. "I'm sorry, Mommy," she whispers. "I'll try to be nice to him."

"Oh, honey." I put my arms around her and draw her close. "Thank you."

She squeezes me tight for a second, her head buried in my stomach, and then I release her, so she skips back to the iPad. I put Lizzy's phone into our tech drawer—and lock it. Then I take the bottle of wine from the fridge and pour myself a glass, even though Brian won't be home for another five minutes. Right now, I don't care. I just need a moment's respite.

I leave the half-full glass on the counter while I check on the casserole and set the table. I manage to restore my sense of equilibrium with these little tasks; I am recreating the family life that we have, that we need. I decide to light a Diptyque candle just to add to the ambiance, breathing in its scents of jasmine and orange blossom. Candlelight always calms things, doesn't it? I want to feel calm.

I take another sip of wine as I survey the scene and let a feeling of contentment creep cautiously over me, start to settle. *This.* This is what I am working so hard for.

A few seconds later, Brian opens the front door. "I'm home!" he sings out, activating our familiar script.

I close my eyes briefly. "Hey, honey!" I call back.

Brian comes back to the kitchen, already loosening his tie, an expectant smile on his face. His dirty blond hair is a bit rumpled, his blue eyes bright, his shoulders as broad and strong as ever. He's so handsome; I know I'm very lucky. Then his gaze zeroes in on the wine glass I'm still holding.

"Starting early?" he asks lightly, and though I know he meant to sound teasing, I hear a thread of censure running through his voice. Brian's mother, Christina, was an alcoholic and spent most of his childhood in a semi-inebriated state, often forgetting to buy food or pick Brian up from school; he cut ties with her over twenty years ago. I understand why he might be sensitive, even paranoid, to see me drinking alone. The only alcohol he drinks is carefully controlled—a glass of wine before dinner, a beer on the weekends with the guys. Nothing else, ever.

"Yes, I thought why not?" I reply as casually as I can, putting my glass down on the counter.

Brian frowns, and I feel like I gave the wrong answer.

"It's been a tricky afternoon," I tell him, and his expression manages to clear a little even as his frown deepens. This is an acceptable reason, I suppose, to crack open the wine before he comes home, just this once.

"What's happened?" he asks as he takes off his tie.

"Lizzy had her phone in her bedroom and Bella didn't want to invite Kieran to her party," I explain with an insouciant shrug, not wanting him to worry. "It's all fine now. I've confiscated Lizzy's phone and Bella has agreed to invite him." I manage a smile as I reach for my wine once more. "So everything's all right."

Brian's frown settles on his face, his forehead creased, his mouth in a downturn as he opens the fridge. "I can't blame Bella for not wanting to invite that kid," he remarks as he pours himself a glass of wine. "He seems like a real piece of work."

"Maybe," I allow, wanting to be generous, "but who knows what's going on at home, or why they had to move?"

Brian turns to me. "What do you mean? Have you heard something?"

"No," I answer slowly, "but no one has seen his dad around at all. And his mother—Joanna—seems kind of cagey about it. I think there must be something we don't know." Not that I've actually spoken to her, but she always looks so *furtive* on the schoolyard, darting away as quickly as possible.

When Miss Stoviak has had to talk to her after school about Kieran's behavior, she always has a pained look on her face, as if she can't wait to get away. That's understandable, I suppose, but people have noticed—and wondered. Shouldn't the dad be coming to some of the drop-offs or meetings at the school? And shouldn't Joanna at least *try* to seem like she's making an effort to deal with her child's issues—for everyone else's sake, if not her own?

"Hmm." Brian takes a sip of his wine. "And he didn't come to the meet-and-greet thing, did he? I'm not even sure I saw the mother."

I don't miss the extra note of judgment there. Of course *the mother* has to come to these things.

"She was there for a little while," I tell Brian. "I think she left early." Maybe because of the whole chair-pulling incident, but I don't want to bring that up now.

Brian shakes his head. "What is it with these parents? Mothers who can't be bothered and deadbeat dads..."

"*Brian.*" I can't keep from sounding scolding, even though I know he's speaking from his own personal history and pain, with his mother was drunk for most of his childhood, and his dad coming in and out of his life at random. "We don't know if either of those things are true in this case. Joanna works, which is *fine*, and her husband..." I trail off.

Brian raises his eyebrows, as if to say he's proved his point. "His dad? Does he even *have* one?"

I press my lips together. "Maybe it doesn't matter."

"It always matters," he replies, and I wonder if he's even aware of how he sounds. *He* didn't have a dad around very much, and yet he turned out fine. Why couldn't the same be true for Kieran? "You'd better watch him like a hawk," he warns me.

"You'll be the one watching him like a hawk, I think," I reply teasingly, only to see Brian tense. I realize that I knew what was coming even as I made that remark. "Brian...?" I prompt, my eyebrows raised.

He lets out a sigh, his gaze lowered. "I'm not sure I'll be able to make it to the whole party," he admits. "Although, of course, I'll do my best. You know I love being there."

I'm both surprised and unsurprised at the same time. I think

I knew by his tone that something like this was coming, and yet Brian *always* makes the girls' birthday parties. He loves them, loves being a part of them. "How come?" I ask, unable to hide either my surprise or dismay. "It's a Saturday..."

"I've got clients flying in for the weekend," he explains, glancing away. "Big ones."

And he didn't think to tell me this before? Brian started his own investment management a couple of years ago, after working for one of the big firms in the city. He often has clients coming to be wined and dined so they'll be convinced to let his company manage their assets. Baseball games, golf tournaments, cigar bars, Michelin-starred restaurants in the city—it's all part of the job. But he's never missed a birthday party before.

Instinctively I glance toward the bag of invitations, so painstakingly written out by Bella. "We can change the date," I tell him, although I dread the thought of Bella having to write all the invitations out again.

"No, no," Brian says quickly. Too quickly? I can't believe I feel uneasy, even suspicious... and yet I do. At least, some small, scared part of me does. This isn't the way my husband operates. This isn't how *we* operate, as a team. "You've already made the arrangements," he tells me. "It would be a shame to have to rearrange everything, and really, when is there ever a good time? It's fine. I'm sure I'll be able to slip away for at least part of the party. Be there for the cutting of the cake or something."

I nod slowly, and yet I still feel unsettled. Brian has never missed a party before, and right now he's not meeting my gaze. What could my husband possibly be hiding?

SIX

JOANNA

Nearly a month into the school year, I am starting to get used to the prickle between my shoulder blades every time I walk into the schoolyard. It's not a nice feeling, and it takes a lot of effort to hold my head up as I pass through the friendly, outdoorsy-looking gates of red cedar. Although the yard itself is just the usual rectangle of concrete, the school has made it more appealing with a few playground spaces on softer tarmac scattered around. Parents all have their positions—kindergarten by a set of tree stumps children can hop across; first grade in the middle, by a carved bench and sensory board. Third grade is right in the middle, by a picnic table. A few mothers are standing around it now, shoulder to shoulder, as impenetrable as a brick wall. Not one of them throws me so much as a grimace of acknowledgment, never mind an actual smile.

Is this what I am always going to have to expect in Wetherby? Kieran's school back in New York was so much more understanding about his issues, but then it was a small, private progressive school with its fair share of "problem" kids. Not that I want to label my son that way, but it seems like everyone else already has, even after less than a month.

Admittedly, Kieran hasn't made it easy for himself—or for me. In addition to the usual infractions of throwing books, talking back, and just generally misbehaving, we had a "major incident", as Miss Stoviak told me so gravely, the day of the parents' meet-and-greet. I didn't find out about it until Monday morning, because the teaching assistant had handled pickup, but apparently Kieran pulled the chair out from under his classmate Bella, the very girl whose party he's going to be invited to, according to the woman, Natalie, whom I met that night. No wonder it felt as if other parents were looking at me a little funnily; had everyone known what happened except for me?

"We take this *very* seriously, Mrs. Walters," Miss Stoviak informed me that morning, sounding more upset than angry, as if she was taking this all very personally... just as I was. I felt as if I was the one who had done something wrong, and maybe I had. It certainly seemed to be the silent yet entirely felt consensus of every other parent in this place. Kieran's misbehavior is my fault. "We do not tolerate our learners behaving in such a violent manner," she continued. "And of course we have a zero-tolerance policy toward any form of bullying or harassment. Because Kieran is new and still adjusting to our community, Mrs. Bryson is willing to be lenient in this one instance. However, if something like this happens again, I'm afraid Mrs. Bryson will need to hold a meeting with you and your husband to consider what measures will have to be taken to ensure all our learners can feel secure and assured that they are thriving in a safe and protected environment."

Who actually talks like that, I thought in exasperation, even as I felt my cheeks start to burn.

"Yes, yes, of course," I murmured, doing my best to keep my head up, even though I felt like scurrying away. Did Miss Stoviak really need to have this conversation in full hearing of at least half of Kieran's class and their parents? Not that the kids were paying attention; they were racing around, laughing and shrieking, but I could tell that the parents noticed—and were straining their ears to overhear the scolding I'd just received. "Thank you," I told Miss Stoviak, as humbly as I could, a penitent.

I looked around for Kieran, and breathed a silent sigh of relief that he wasn't doing any damage. He was standing by the schoolyard fence, his arms folded, a look of bored indifference on his face. Better than causing trouble, I told myself, and I nodded toward him and got out of there as quickly as I could.

Now, three days later, I am still feeling as if I am on high alert. I am both trying to meet other parents' eyes and trying *not* to, which means my gaze moves around like a pinball in the proverbial machine.

I want to make friends, for Kieran's sake at least, but I'm afraid of the judgment I'm pretty sure I'll see in everyone's eyes. As far as I know, Kieran hasn't made any friends in his class yet, although there are a couple rough-and-tumble boys that don't seem *so* far removed in terms of their behavior. Still, it feels like everyone has singled Kieran out, maybe because he's new, or because I am.

Wetherby is way more of a close-knit community than I expected; I thought, based on its location, it would be more of a haven for ex-New Yorkers, but it feels like we're the only ones who came from the city. Everyone else acts as if they've been here for decades. Centuries.

The schoolyard is the same every day—parents positioned in little conversational clusters near the doors of their kids' classes. That was one of the things I liked about Wetherby—a school in walking distance of most people's houses, although, admittedly, not ours, so there are lots of parents at pickup. Only a handful of kids take the school bus, and while Kieran is eligible for transportation, I decided that was a battle I didn't want to face. Who knows how he would act, in the back of a bus with little to no supervision? I don't trust my child, and I don't know if that's common sense or cowardice.

I'd also hoped that dropping off and picking up Kieran every day would help me to form my own friendships with the parents, but that was clearly a delusion. Only Natalie, at the parents' evening, has said so much as hello to me, and, quite honestly, I'm not sure I want anyone else to.

The truth is, I've always struggled to make friends. I am the third child of five, the quiet one in a large and boisterous family, everyone jostling to be heard and seen, and most of the time I've *liked* feeling invisible. At home, I was the kid everyone forgot was there, and when I wasn't, it took them ages to look around and ask in surprise, *wait a minute, where's Jo?* I was usually upstairs reading, away from the noise.

The few friends I have were formed after decades of knowing and trusting them, and I can count them on one hand, without using all my fingers. I miss those few people now, when I feel so alone, standing to the right of the third-grade door by myself as other parents gossip and whisper by the picnic table.

They're not necessarily talking about me or Kieran, I tell myself as I keep my chin up. *Don't be paranoid, Joanna.*

I catch the gaze of a mother with platinum blond hair and icy blue eyes. Her penetrating gaze jolts into mine for a single second and then hers moves deliberately on. It's hard not to feel stung. I glance away, feigning indifference, wondering why I care so much. Is it just the sense of public humiliation played out on this particular stage, or do I actually want these women as my friends? Natalie was nice enough, I suppose, but the others?

I've never been the kind of woman to want to be in the center—or even on the fringes—of some kind of girly crowd. Even during my school years, I wasn't the type to squeal and throw my arms around another girl, or gossip about the latest scandal, fad, or heartbreak. I liked my own company, the few friends who were similar, and then, of course, Tim.

Tim. I left him sleeping, another afternoon nap that makes me struggle not to grit my teeth, because six months on from his breakdown, he surely does not need to catch up on sleep. He needs to get *going* again, find a purpose, but if I so much as hint at that kind of thing, he shuts down all the more. I feel like we're in a doom spiral of nothingness.

I have no idea what will get Tim up and going again—in work, in life, in terms of us. I don't even want to think about when the last time we touched was. We've been existing like roommates, or even acquaintances, for the better part of a year. Maybe that's why I care what these women think; I do want them as friends because, self-sufficient as I usually am, right now I feel *lonely*.

The classroom door opens, and I straighten, trying not to tense. Please, *please* let Kieran not have got into trouble today. A few other parents straighten, as well, looking toward the door, and then the children emerge. One by one, I watch them run to their parents, trailing papers and lunch boxes, excitement lighting up their little faces. I glance at a few of the parents, crouched down with arms outstretched. All around me, happy reunions are taking place, as if parents and children have been separated for six days rather than a mere six hours. I know when I see Kieran, he'll just fall into step alongside me without saying much at all.

I tell myself that it's okay, that I don't need to compare myself to how other parents are with their children. Kieran has never been physically affectionate, but then, neither have I. It's *fine*.

And then he emerges, hair rumpled, shirt untucked and covered in splashes of mud, a streak of dirt on his cheek. It's all good, I tell myself. It means he's been active. *Happy.*

I smile as he walks toward me. "Hey, bud." I rest a hand briefly on his shoulder before removing it. "Good day?"

He shrugs, and I take that as an adequate reply.

"All right, let's head home." I pause to glance around again at the little clusters of parents dotting the schoolyard, willing someone—*anyone*—to meet my eye and smile, just once. I just want a *connection*, even if I semi-dread it, but it's like we're invisible.

Then I notice that all the kids around me are waving bright yellow envelopes, taking out pieces of paper decorated with colorful balloons and gleefully showing them to their parents. They're *invitations*, I realize with a plunging feeling of dread, and it looks like everyone in the third grade got one. Everyone but Kieran.

I look back at my son, his face set in a mask of indifference. Did Bella hand out all the invitations to each child, I think with a spike of anger, and just *skip over* Kieran? And everyone was okay with that? How did it make him feel? Kieran always acts as if he doesn't care what other kids think, but what if he does? What child *doesn't*?

I look around again, checking to make sure every single third-grader that I can see is holding one of those brightly colored invitations, and sure enough, they are. I cannot see a single child in Kieran's class who isn't waving the yellow envelope or hasn't already torn it open.

The spike of anger I felt is turning into a slow, steady burn. I'm almost positive that Kieran is the only child in the entire class who didn't get an invitation, and that makes me furious. Worse, it *hurts*. Devastates me, in fact, but I hide it behind anger because that feels so much stronger.

"Kieran..." I turn to my son. "Did you get an invitation to Bella's birthday party?"

He blinks at me, his expression more bored than perplexed. "No."

"But she handed them out today?" I press, trying to keep my tone matter-of-fact and upbeat, like it doesn't matter that much either way.

He shrugs.

I take a deep breath. The rational part of my brain is telling me to drop the whole thing, slink away, and forget about the stupid party. I'm not even sure I'd want Kieran to go; Natalie framed it as an opportunity for him to make friends, but it's just as likely—if not more—that it's an opportunity for him to get into some kind of trouble and alienate his classmates in the process.

But... a *party*. A party everyone else gets to go to, except for my son.

Kieran shifts his weight from foot to foot, expelling an impatient breath. "*Mom*. Can we go?"

"Yes..." I glance around again. I don't know exactly what I'm looking for, only that I want to find some evidence that Kieran isn't the only one who was not invited. But all I can see are happy children and smiling, benevolent parents, invitations fluttering in the breeze along with the laughter.

Then I see her—Eleanor Dalton, Bella's beautiful mother. She's standing just a dozen feet away, chatting to a few other mothers, or, really, holding court. They are clearly hanging on her every word, and she just as clearly relishes it.

At five eleven, I usually tower over most people, men and women alike, but Eleanor looks to be only an inch or two shorter than me. Everything else about her is unlike me, though; while I am wearing tailored trousers and a crisp, button-down shirt, she is dressed in a pair of flowing linen pants and some kind of kaftan top. While I am stick-thin and bony thanks to a fast metabolism and a Manhattanite's view of what a woman's body should look like, Eleanor is generously shaped, curvy in all the right places without looking remotely fat. And while my hair is dark and poker-straight, hers is tumbling and blond, piled on top of her head in an artfully messy bun and glinting with a dozen shades of gold.

But none of that matters right now, because it's the expression on her face that tips me over the edge. It is generous and expansive, confident and so very assured. Eleanor Dalton is utterly secure in her world. She doesn't care at *all* that she willfully excluded one lonely child from her beloved daughter's party. I watch as she tips her head back and laughs, a tendril of long, blond hair falling against her cheek, and something in me, uncharacteristically, snaps.

I stalk over toward her, surprising Kieran, as well as myself. I am *not* confrontational. And yet here I am. I stop right in front of her, breathing a little too hard.

Eleanor stops mid-sentence to look at me with a startled frown. Slowly she tucks the tendril of hair behind her ear. "Oh, hi, um..." She pauses, clearly trying to formulate her greeting. She knows who I am—everyone does because of Kieran's behavior—but I can tell she's wondering if she should admit to it, considering she's never said boo to me before. "You're... Kieran's mom, right?"

"Right." My voice sounds harsh and grating, and I know—I *know*—I'm making this a thousand times worse. Even now, I am telling myself to stop and slink away. Surely that is the safest option. The *sanest*. But I don't, because I've been at this school for three whole weeks, and no one, save for Natalie's half-hearted attempt at the meet-and-greet, has been nice to me. No one has even said hello. Not that I have, either, but *still*. What kind of place *is* this? What kind of woman invites every single kid to her daughter's birthday party except the new one?

"I saw you sent all the invitations out to your daughter's birthday party," I remark flatly, and Eleanor's hazel eyes widen. "Umm... yes..."

"And you didn't think it was a little rude, a little unfriendly and even *cruel*, to exclude just one child from the party? The child who's new, who doesn't know anyone yet?" My voice rises, breaks. I'm not speaking in that passive-aggressive, pseudo-pleasant voice that so many mothers use.

"What?" She stares at me blankly. Next to her, two mothers have fallen utterly silent and are watching this exchange with undisguised avidity. I will be the subject of Wetherby's gossip for the foreseeable future, although I'm pretty sure I already was. Still, this is much worse. "Um... Joanna..." She fishes for my name like she doesn't know it, but she does. They all do. "I'm not sure what you mean? Because Bella invited Kieran."

I stare at her as her words penetrate my high dudgeon, my moral outrage. My mouth is dry, my heart thudding.

I open my mouth, but for a second, no words come out. "Kieran says he didn't receive one," I finally say, faintly. I have a horrible, creeping fear that I have got this completely wrong. I feel dizzy and faint as my body catches up to what my brain just did. I confronted the queen bee of the third-grade class. I *shouted* at her.

"Well..." Eleanor screws her face up in a parody of concentration, although who knows, maybe she's being genuine. "Miss Stoviak put the invitations into all the backpacks herself," she explains.

This could be why Kieran didn't know he'd received one. I stare at her, unable to form a single word as she continues, her voice the perfect mix of earnestness and accusation.

"Maybe check his bag?"

Yes, that would be a good idea, I think numbly. It would have been a *particularly* good idea before I came storming over here like some kind of avenging harpy. If Bella's invitation is in Kieran's backpack, I know I am going to want to disappear. I will want to leave Wetherby and never, ever come back, because, clearly, I have ruined my social prospects, as well as my son's, in this godforsaken town.

I swallow. Nod. "Yes..." I can't manage a smile. I turn to Kieran, who is standing mutely next to me, looking like he's more bored than embarrassed. "Can you check your backpack, bud?"

He gives me a *why-on-earth-would-I-do-that* look, and I plead with him silently, willing him, just this once, to obey me without protest or complaint. Mercifully, he does. Eleanor and her friends—one of them is Natalie, I realize—watch silently as Kieran slowly undoes the zipper. The very air feels taut in a way that part of me acknowledges is utterly ridiculous; we are talking about a birthday party invitation from an almost eight-year-old girl, but it feels like Kieran is about to defuse a bomb. One that, if it actually exploded, would perversely save me a lot of face.

He roots around among his spelling book and lunch box, and sure enough, there it is, a bright yellow envelope slipped inside. I swallow again; my throat is so dry, the movement hurts. I have no idea what to say.

"Oh..." is all I manage before Eleanor takes control of the conversation.

"Oh, I'm *so* glad we figured that one out," she says in an overly cheerful voice, like we'd just put our heads together and problem-solved. "Can Kieran come to the party, do you think? It's on the twenty-eighth."

"Um..." I can't think. I still feel faint. "I'll have to check," I manage in little more than a whisper. "But thank you... for the invitation." I stuff the envelope back into Kieran's backpack and zip it up. Every single second under these women's gazes feels agonizing. "See you," I force out before, with one hand on his shoulder, I steer Kieran toward the school gate.

Some sixth sense has me glancing back, and I see Natalie

rolling her eyes at Eleanor, who frowns and shakes her head. I don't know if that little interaction makes me feel better or worse.

I hightail it out of there as fast as I can, and I don't look back again.

SEVEN

NATALIE

The day of Bella's birthday is perfect weather-wise, as if Eleanor ordered it. Bright blue skies, warm, lemony sunshine, a faint breeze that holds a hint of summer even though it's just two days before the start of October.

I get to Eleanor's two hours before the blessed event, to help with the setup. I've spent the last few weeks helping with the prep for this party—filling party bags, choosing decorations, endlessly discussing options for food and party games with Eleanor. Yesterday, I helped her frost three dozen chocolate cupcakes, although Eleanor is such a perfectionist when it comes to these things that all I ended up doing was showering them with sprinkles and putting them in Tupperware while she created perfectly swirled whorls of chocolate buttercream.

At least after today it will all be over.

I slip out of the car, going to the back for the dozen mylar balloons decorated with sparkly number eights that I picked up for Eleanor in town before I came, and which, somehow, I am supposed to keep secret from Bella. Freya obviously knows about them; she runs ahead to knock on the front door while I attempt to keep them all together in the breeze.

"Oh great, you're here!" Eleanor opens the door with her usual, wide smile, although her tone sounds a little tense. I suppose she's not immune to pre-party jitters. She looks as lovely as ever, in a pair of flowing linen pants and a patterned top, her hair in its usual artfully messy bun.

"With balloons, as promised," I answer cheerfully.

Freya slips past Eleanor, who calls after her.

"Bella is up in her room, honey!" She turns back to me. "I'll hide these in Brian's study, and we can bring them out with the cake."

"Where is Brian?" I ask as I come into the house. There is a smell of lavender furniture polish in the air, along with fresh coffee, but it feels curiously empty.

Eleanor lets out a gusty breath as she closes the study door on the balloons. "Unfortunately, he had to work today." She purses her lips for a second before she continues in a determinedly cheerful tone, "Clients have to come first."

This is so unexpected, I can't keep from doing a double take. Clients *never* come first with Brian; Matt used to grumble a little bit, wondering how he could be so successful, when he was always able to be home at five-thirty and never work weekends. Matt, like Brian, is in finance, although in Matt's case it's a mid-level job at a mid-tier firm in Hartford. He's generally good about clocking off on time and not bringing his work home—unlike me—but he certainly doesn't have Brian's expansive flexibility. Brian opened his own business right here in Wetherby a couple of years ago, after logging the long hours for JP Morgan in New York, and as he would assure anyone in a jocular tone, he's "never looked back."

"Really?" I manage after a few seconds. I follow Eleanor back into the kitchen. "How come?"

"What do you mean, *how come?*" Eleanor sounds tetchy, which is so unlike her that I almost do another double take, but I keep myself from it. "I told you. He has clients visiting for the weekend."

"Yes, sorry," I backtrack quickly, "I just meant, I thought he would have cleared his schedule..."

Eleanor presses her lips together. She's got one hand flat on the counter, the other on her hip, and she looks like she might either burst into a temper or tears, I'm not sure which. I've never seen her so rattled. "Sometimes these things can't be helped. He's going to try to make it in time for the cake."

Her tone makes it clear this is not something she wants to discuss.

"Okay, well..." I manage a smile. "How can I help?"

We spend the next hour getting everything ready for the party—laying out forks, plates and napkins, positioning party bags on a tray, going through the yard and setting out various lawn games—beanbags toss, hula hoops, giant Jenga. Eleanor really did mean it when she said she was going classic and homegrown; this is the most basic party she's ever thrown, even though it still feels like a lot of hard work to me.

"Where's Lizzy?" I ask as we lay out a few blankets on the grass for the kids to picnic on. Eleanor is serving what she calls "childhood classics"—hot dogs (all beef and organic, of course), mini pizzas—with gluten-free options, naturally—and jam sandwiches, made with Eleanor's homemade raspberry jam. Homemade cupcakes for dessert, along with the birthday cake. It's all a far cry from the wood-fired pizza truck someone brought in for a birthday party last year.

I wonder what has made Eleanor do things so differently this year; in the midst of all the organization, I somehow didn't clock just how countercultural she was being. I assumed *homegrown* meant Eleanor's version of it—curated like an Instagram feed to look effortless and easy while actually requiring a level of meticulous difficulty and preparation. Instead, it does really feel homegrown. *Normal.*

"Lizzy is out with some friends," Eleanor tells me, and her tone is the same one she used about Brian. End of discussion.

What is going on, I wonder, *with my usually fabulous friend?*

"Is everything okay?" I ask after a moment, and Eleanor shoots me a look of surprised suspicion.

"What do you mean?"

I never ask Eleanor if she's okay. I never need to; I never even think about it. But now I do, and I can tell she resents the inference.

"Just... that with Lizzy, and Brian..." I'm not sure what I'm trying to say. So Brian has to work, and Lizzy is out with friends. Those are totally normal and expected occurrences, nothing alarming at all, for the average person. But why then does Eleanor look so tense? "I don't know," I finish with a shrug, because I really don't.

"I'm *fine,*" Eleanor assures me shortly. "Just ready for this to be over, you know. And, honestly, I'm a little worried about Kieran. After the whole chair incident..." She shakes her head.

"He hasn't done anything too bad in the last few weeks, has he?" Truthfully, I feel kind of bad for Kieran, and even worse for Joanna, after that cringingly awkward showdown in the schoolyard a couple of weeks ago. Parents were talking about it for *days,* and the poor woman looked absolutely mortified at the time. I admit, I found it a little ridiculous at first, but Eleanor just seemed troubled, and then I felt guilty for being amused by someone else's misfortune for so much as a millisecond. I don't want to be that kind of person; it feels like another way I've become too cynical.

"He hasn't been *too* bad, I suppose," Eleanor replies slowly. "I mean, he's definitely continued with the acting out, a bit of rambunctiousness, but no... major *incidents.*"

"I wonder if he's become a scapegoat," I venture tentatively as we walk back inside. "I mean, throwing reading books onto the floor, pushing a kid occasionally, talking back... I know it isn't great, but it isn't anything our kids haven't done, right?"

Eleanor draws back a little. "Bella certainly hasn't done any of those things."

Of course she hasn't. "Right, yes, I know, but I mean the boys in the class. At this age, they're all a little hyper, aren't they? A little wild?"

Besides the usual naughtiness, there are two boys who were diagnosed with ADHD last year, and another two who are on the spectrum. They each have their own issues, and the school is generally pretty good about supporting them, with parents being understanding, for the most part. There are a few mean girls in the class, as well, who were given their own iPhones and are already on social media at seven years old. Bella might be a little bossy with Freya, but at least she's not on Snapchat.

In any case, my point is, it's not a class of perfect little angels, by any means, even if Eleanor seems to think it is.

"I don't know," she replies with a sigh. She sounds like she doesn't want to talk about it. It feels like there are a lot of no-go areas this afternoon, which is weird. "Anyway." She lets out another sigh as she shakes her head. "It will all be fine." It's as if she's trying to convince herself. "How are you?" she asks me, turning the brightness up in her voice.

"I'm all right." Work is crazy with end-of-the-month sales targets, my boss is breathing down my neck even more than usual, Matt is missing today's visit with Freya because of this party, and my sister invited me over for dinner next weekend, to show off her perfect family, no doubt. In any case, I don't tell Eleanor any of this. She got enough of my drama when Matt walked out and I don't particularly want to give her any more, especially when she already seems to have her own right now... whatever *it* is.

By one-thirty, just half an hour before the party starts, we're finished. The house is immaculate, the sun is shining down, and the girls are playing outside on the swing. At least, Bella is on the swing; Freya has been pushing her. Part of me wants to go out there and ask, nicely, if Bella can give Freya a turn, but I know it will annoy my daughter, so I don't. I watch them, though, out of the corner of my eye, waiting for Bella to slide off the swing. She doesn't.

"Right," Eleanor says briskly, like she's about to make an announcement.

I glance back to see her frowning at her phone before she shoves it in a drawer. She and Brian have this concept called their "tech drawer," where they lock all devices away, including their own, during meals, in the evening, et cetera. I think she read it in a parenting book, as so many of us have, but she's the only one I know who follows through. Everyone talks about it, admits it's a good idea, but to *do* it?

"Shall we have a drink?" she asks, and I raise my eyebrows. We carted a big, old-fashioned glass drinks dispenser filled with homemade lemonade with lemon slices floating on top outside onto the patio, but from her tone I don't think that's what she means.

Sure enough, she stands on her tiptoes to open the cupboard high above the fridge, where I know she and Brian keep their liquor. She withdraws a bottle of Tanqueray with a defiant waggle of her eyebrows.

"Just a small one, before the party starts?" she suggests. "I feel like I'm going to need it."

This is definitely not Eleanor's usual. Yes, we enjoy a glass of wine—or two—occasionally in the evening, if Brian isn't home and the kids are occupied. But a G&T twenty minutes before twenty-eight kids descend on you for a birthday party?

Bring it on.

"I'm definitely going to need it," I tell her, and she grins and goes to the fridge for the tonic and lime.

In this moment, I am reminded how we became such good friends, when Freya and Bella were in preschool. Back then, Eleanor was still earnest and intense, but not quite as earnest and intense as she's become since. She liked a good laugh, a night out, a drink. We used to roll our eyes at the sanctimonious mothers who prepped their eighteen-month-olds with Baby Einstein flashcards and gave them raw broccoli for a *treat*. What, after all, was wrong with twenty minutes of *Peppa Pig* and a cup of goldfish crackers? Or grapes cut into quarters, if you felt you needed to be healthy?

Because, you see, as much as we liked to roll our eyes at it, we weren't really renegades. We just liked to act as if we were, but we followed the unspoken rules the same as everyone else; we bought into the belief that a good mother would never put a pinkie toe wrong. We shopped organic and monitored screen time and read the parenting books that made us feel like failures even as we followed all their advice assiduously. And I did this on top of a full-time job, so sometimes it felt as if I had no space in my brain, save for trying to show everyone how I had it all, I was doing everything right... even if I pretended to be cynical about it.

And now I really am.

As for Eleanor... between then and now, she has become much more intent on achieving that impossible perfection, like she's being graded on her performance as both mother and wife. Maybe that's how she feels; maybe that's how we *all* feel. But it has, I've come to realize, made her less fun to be around, so I'm glad she's willing to unwind a bit now, even if it might not be the smartest thing to do right before a children's birthday party.

But, whatever. It's just one drink, after all.

Eleanor splashes a generous measure of gin into two glasses before adding tonic.

"I'm not doing this again," she announces firmly as she drops a slice of lime into each glass and hands me mine.

"Not doing what?" I ask, raising my eyebrows over the rim of my drink, which goes down smoothly but is definitely heavy on the gin.

"Having a class party. Or any party. Bella isn't bothered, so why should I be? It's so much effort, after all, and for what? They'll all be disappointed with their party bags and hyped up on sugar, and probably fall apart the minute they get home, if not before."

I stare at Eleanor in undisguised surprise, because, once again, this is so unlike her. She might as well be speaking Mandarin or Portuguese; this is absolutely not her language. It's far more... *mine*.

"Cheers," Eleanor says, a little defiantly, and we clink glasses.

I wonder—again—what might be going on, but I don't ask.

"So, what's the plan for the party?" I say instead. "Are parents staying?" Having parents stay for a party is a bit of a mixed blessing; it can be useful, to have more hands on deck, but sometimes the mothers need as much managing as the kids, if not more. At one party last year, I recall, a parent complained that his son hadn't won at musical chairs, and why didn't everyone get a prize just for playing? Judging from the looks on other parents' faces, he wasn't alone in his grievance. The frazzled hostess ended up handing out extra party favors to all the kids, her expression one of ill-disguised resentment.

"No, no parents staying," Eleanor replies, tossing back more of her G&T. "I can't deal with any of them right now."

Yet another very un-Eleanor thing to say. I am mystified, but I am also concerned. What on earth has happened to make her act like this?

"It might be helpful," I venture. "Especially if Kieran is such a handful."

"What is the deal with him, anyway?" Eleanor asks abruptly. "Do you know what's going on with the dad?"

I frown. "The dad?"

"Have you even *seen* him?"

"No..." I tense, because with Matt now living in Danbury I'm not really in the mood for a diatribe about absent fathers. Eleanor came down pretty hard on him for leaving, hinting at what a waste of space he clearly was and maybe I was better off without him, and for some reason, it annoyed me more than a little. *I* can rant about Matt, but I didn't really want Eleanor doing it, especially if Bella or Freya were around. And he isn't anything close to an absentee father, anyway, even living in Danbury.

"Well, I just wonder if he even exists," Eleanor replies with a shrug. "I mean boys without fathers... they act out, right? That's, like, a known. If a father isn't around—"

"There are plenty of families with single parents," I reply a little sharply, "and anyway, Joanna told me he is around." At least, I think that's what she was saying, back at the meet-and-greet.

"Well, still," Eleanor insists. "I think there's something going on with Kieran's dad. Something doesn't feel right."

The sound of footsteps in the hall has us both stilling guiltily, drinks in hand.

"Bella?" Eleanor calls, and for a second there is only silence.

"It's me," Lizzy replies.

Eleanor swallows the last of her drink. "Great, Lizzy," she calls. "I'm glad you're back. You can help with the party."

In reply, Lizzy grunts and heads upstairs.

Eleanor grimaces. "She used to love helping out at these things."

I'm not entirely sure about that; Eleanor has often corralled Lizzy into helping with Bella, assuming her oldest daughter loves taking care of her younger sister as much as her mother does, and maybe she does, but sometimes I see a look on Lizzy's face like she's not quite on board with all the Bella adoration.

I know both Brian and Eleanor dote on their youngest; she came after multiple miscarriages and rounds of IVF, their desperately longed for second child. It's understandable that they feel the way they do, and it isn't like Lizzy doesn't get her fair share of attention, but... I can see how, for an almost fifteen-year-old, her parents' pandering to Bella might be a little tiresome.

"Anyway," Eleanor resumes, "I thought you could be outside supervising the games, and I'll do the food in here."

Inwardly I wilt. That is so *not* the job I want.

"Are you sure?" I ask. "I can do the food..." I would *rather* do the food, in the peace and quiet of the kitchen, while twenty-eight children run amok outside.

"No, no, it's okay," Eleanor says quickly, like she's giving me the better job. "And remember, the balloon guy will be out there. He can help manage the kids." She glances at her watch. "He should be here by three, I think."

Since when did a *balloon guy* help with the management of twenty-eight overexcited children? And what about the first hour when I'm on my own?

"And the pony rides?" I ask. It reminds me that this party isn't that basic, after all. But it will keep the kids occupied, at least.

"Oh, I didn't go for those, in the end," Eleanor replies, a bit vaguely. "Too much effort."

Since when did that ever stop her? I don't ask, of course, just accept that it's going to be me, the nameless balloon guy, and twenty-eight children.

"It'll be fine," Eleanor assures me. "They'll play the lawn games, use the swing, the trampoline... there's plenty to entertain them. And Lizzy will come out and help, I'm sure. Just keep an eye on Kieran, okay?"

I force a smile as I nod. I know Eleanor depends on me as her deputy, but this feels like too much. Still, if she's going through something, and it seems like she is, I want to help. Today I'll have to be the Eleanor-like one, I guess. I tell myself I can rise to the challenge, for my friend's sake.

I am tossing back the last of my G&T as the doorbell rings. The first guest has arrived, and the party is about to start.

EIGHT

ELEANOR

I turn my smile up to maximum wattage as I open the front door to Polly Phillips and her daughter Casey.

"*Hi.*" My voice is effusive.

As Polly comes in for an air kiss, I press my lips together, afraid she'll smell the gin on my breath. What was I thinking, having a drink right before the party? Still, I can't regret it. With everything currently going on in my life, as well as the stress of this birthday party, I needed that little bit of unwinding.

Bella skips down the stairs, skidding to a stop before the door, followed by Freya.

"Happy Birthday, Bella," Casey says rather dutifully, and hands her a present wrapped in sparkly pink paper.

I go through the usual assurances and niceties with Polly— *no, no parents don't have to stay, pickup is at five, yes, yes, have fun!* Trill, trill, wave, wave. I close the door with an audible sigh of relief, and then turn to see Natalie looking at me strangely.

Admittedly, I am acting strangely. I am not acting like myself; I am not *feeling* like myself. Ever since Brian told me he was going to miss Bella's party, I've been on high alert, noticing little things that I'm afraid are not so little... the texts he glances at over dinner, even though we have a hard and fast no-phones-at-the-table rule. I've watched him frown as he reads the messages and then swipe quickly away, before putting his phone face down on the table, right by his plate. There have been the nights he's been late home, without telling me he was going to be. Half an hour might not seem like much, but in our carefully orchestrated and guarded family life, it *is*. The air of distraction he has about him, like he's not really listening when I launch into our usual, beloved script. The lines are familiar, I know, but Brian has always been fully present for them. Lately I've felt like half his mind is elsewhere... maybe with someone else.

A few days ago, I broke down and tried to check his email while he was in the shower. I tiptoed down to his study and opened his laptop; we've always known each other's password, PINs, whatever. That's the kind of couple we've been, we *are*, but when I typed in the password to Brian's computer, it didn't work. The blank little box gave an accusatory jerk and warned me I had three more attempts before I'd be locked out for an hour. And, recklessly, I used those three attempts just in case I'd mistyped or had the caps lock on or *something*. None of them worked. Clearly, Brian had changed his password without telling me... and I don't know why.

I can't believe he's having an *affair*; I can't let myself believe it. It feels so cringingly clichéd, but worse, *far* worse, is the question that thunders through me—if Brian is having an affair, what have I been doing with my life? What has been the point of parties like this one, or the carefully curated photo albums going up the stairs, or the nightly glasses of wine together, or *any* of it, if none of it was real? I feel like I've been living a lie, and I've only just realized it.

The doorbell rings again, and I find my smile. I'm going to have to do this twenty-six more times. I long for another G&T, but I know I can't succumb to that temptation. I need to be *on*, with the megawatt smile, the gushing tone, the air of assurance, even if I no longer feel like doing any of it. *Being* any of it. But if I'm not that, what am I? It feels like far too existential a question for me to grapple with when I am slightly buzzed, and minutes into my child's birthday party.

Within ten minutes, most of Bella's classmates have arrived. I've ushered them outside and they are now inspecting the lawn games Natalie and I laid out, looking, I can't help but notice when I duck into the kitchen to check through the French windows, fairly unimpressed. These are kids who have grown up knowing basically from birth how to swipe a screen, expect everything to be streamed instantly, and are used to the entire world being at their childish fingertips.

As for birthday parties... the last class birthday party had a spy theme, complete with decoder rings, invisible ink pens, and a privately hired laser tag venue. The whole thing was run by two professional party planners from New York who dressed like James Bond and Miss Moneypenny, even though seven-year-olds hardly knew who those characters were. They still managed to whip them all up into an ecstatic frenzy, although by the end of the party, they were all already becoming bored by it all.

Still, beanbag toss and homemade lemonade undoubtedly pale in comparison.

The doorbell rings again, and suppressing the huge sigh I feel like giving, I go to open it, stopping short when I see who it is. Joanna and Kieran.

The smile that normally springs so readily to my lips falters and slides away. I know I should—I *know* it—but I cannot smile at this woman or her son. Not after everything that has happened... Kieran pulling the chair out from under Bella, Joanna having an absolutely hissy fit over the invitations. When she stalked over to me and accused me of not inviting Kieran, I had a split second of terror that Bella had somehow confiscated his invitation—again—without my knowing. I realized it was perfectly possible, and yet perversely, that made me feel more self-righteous, and act all the more certain that the invitation was in his backpack. Thank God it was.

Now I try for a smile again, and this time I find it, if only just.

Joanna stares stonily back for a few seconds before she seems to realize how she looks, and then she forces a smile just like I did, both of us standing there with rictus grins.

"Hi, Eleanor," she says politely. Her hand is on Kieran's shoulder, as if to anchor him in place. "Thank you for inviting Kieran."

"Yeah, thanks," Kieran mumbles. He's clearly been schooled to say this.

Something in me softens. Kieran, really, is just a seven-year-old boy, like any other seven-year-old boy. He's moved recently, and I'm starting to feel pretty sure there's something amiss with his dad, so there might be some understandable behavioral issues. I need to cut him some serious slack. I feel a rush of guilt, along with good will. I am going to be more welcoming to Kieran... and Joanna.

"Of course, of course," I assure them, a bit too effusively. I stand aside so they can come in. "I'm so glad you're here, Kieran," I tell him, which might be a *bit* of an exaggeration, but in that moment, I feel like I mean it.

I glance at Joanna, whose lips are pressed together, her eyes narrowed. She looks decidedly skeptical. I wonder if she can smell the gin on my breath, and I press my lips together, too.

"Do you need help during the party?" Joanna asks. Her voice is an unsettling mix of eagerness and courtesy. "I'd be happy to stay, if you like." She glances, maybe without meaning to, at her son.

For a second, I am tempted. If Joanna stays, she'll probably dog Kieran's heels the whole time, and I won't have to worry about him so much. And yet... the thought of spending the next three hours under Joanna's beady eye is enough to have me groaning aloud. I can't cope with it.

"That is *so* kind of you," I reply as I cock my head and smile, my hand still on the knob of the front door, "but we should be fine. It's not like they're all that little anymore, anyway, is it?" I let out a laugh that Joanna is meant to echo, but she doesn't. She just gives me exactly the sort of beady-eyed stare I'd expect from her. I made the right decision. I wait it out.

"If you're sure..." she says, and she sounds regretful, like she really wants me to change my mind. What kind of mother wants to stay at these things? I did, once, but all my expansive bonhomie has gone right out the window. I only feel flat, and I know that this party is going to be challenging enough without having to deal with Joanna's prune-faced presence.

"I'm sure," I reply, smiling. "But again, thank you." I hold her gaze along with my smile as I wait for her to go.

Kieran hasn't said a word or even moved a muscle. Joanna glances at him again, looking torn, and I almost relent. Normally I would let any parent stay who wanted to, especially if they were worried about their child, although, in truth, even the most relentlessly whirring helicopter parent usually can't wait to escape the chaos of a children's birthday party.

"All right," Joanna says at long last. She rests a hand on Kieran's shoulder, ever so briefly. "Have fun, bud, okay?" Her voice is soft, even tender, and something in me stirs. No matter how difficult Kieran might be, I know Joanna loves her son, and right then I feel sorry for her as well as touched.

He nods without looking at her, and then, with one last glance at me which I can't quite decipher, she leaves. I close the door with a silent sigh of relief and then turn to Kieran, who hasn't trotted off to find his classmates the way just about any other kid would. He simply stands there, a blank look on his face.

"Hey, Kieran, everybody's outside," I tell him in my most chipper, jolly hostess sort of voice. "Do you want to join them? There is a lot of fun stuff to do—trampoline, swings, giant Jenga... do you like Jenga?" No reply, and so I continue in the same slightly manic tone, "You can put your present on the gift table in the kitchen. Why don't you do that?" He's holding a rectangle that looks like it has been professionally wrapped in pretty lavender paper, with a card taped to it with "Bella" written in a beautiful, copperplate script. Joanna's work, obviously.

He glances at me then, and although he doesn't say anything, I am taken aback by the almost scornful look in his eyes, like he can see right through my jolly-mommy tone. Or am I being paranoid?

Then, without a word, he walks off, toward the kitchen. Jeez. *Some kid*, I think, and I wait a few moments to make sure Kieran has gone outside before I head back to the kitchen myself, which is mercifully empty of any children.

In a moment of recklessness, I pour myself another sneaky G&T, smaller this time, even though I told myself I wouldn't. I sip it discreetly as I watch the children play outside. Thankfully, they seem to have got into the spirit of the thing, more or less—a couple of girls are taking turns on the swings, and some boys are pelting each other with beanbags, but no one seems to be upset about it. In the middle of all this, Natalie stands, her head swiveling left and right as she tries to keep an eye on everybody.

I take another sip of my drink, and a lovely, liquid feeling of relaxation spreads through me. Swallowing the last of my drink, I decide to venture outside and help Natalie out.

"Controlled chaos," she announces a bit grimly as I stroll across the lawn.

"That's the best kind of party!" I reply, and Natalie gives me one of her looks. Did I slur my words? I wonder with a lurch of panic. No, surely not. I feel relaxed, but not alarmingly so; I'm still completely in control. I think. It's not like I'm *drunk*.

"I don't know how long these games will hold them," Natalie warns me. "When is the balloon guy coming?"

"I think I said three...?"

Natalie glances at her watch and frowns; it's only two-fifteen. The minutes stretch endlessly in front of us.

"It will be fine," I say. "But you know not to let them go by the pond, right? We took the fence down."

"I know." She rolls her eyes, trying to seem wryly good-natured, but she looks tense. "Anyway, it looks like nothing but a big muddy puddle right now. I don't think any of them want to explore it, but in any case, I've kept them up here. No one's allowed down the hill."

I glance toward the bottom of the backyard, which is down a little dip, but I can't see anyone venturing that far. Everyone seems to want to stay by the house, in sight of civilization. Perhaps it's another symptom of this world we live in, where helicopter parents instill such needless fear of danger in their children. *Don't play outside. Don't go around the corner. Don't ride your bike. Don't do anything fun. Don't. Don't. Don't.*

All right, maybe I'm a *little* drunk.

And yet, for a second, I feel stone-cold sober, as I realize just how reckless I am being. I have *sole* charge—with Natalie—of twenty-eight children, including my own. I need to take that responsibility seriously. I take a few even breaths as I glance around, counting heads, relieved when I reach twenty-eight.

I look for Kieran, who is standing by the swing all by himself, observing a few girls who are lining up for a turn. There's absolutely nothing wrong with what he's doing—in fact, I wonder if he looks a little lonely—but for some reason, it still gives me a second's pause. A slight feeling of unease.

I push it away. I've had enough judgmental thoughts about

both Kieran and his parents already. I don't want to be like that anymore.

"Shall we organize a game?" I suggest to Natalie, who looks slightly horrified by the idea.

"A *game*?"

I laugh, a merry sound. "Yes, Nat, like duck, duck, goose or something?"

She frowns. "They're not five."

"They're only eight," I counter, but I take her point. "Okay, how about freeze tag? That one's always a winner, and this is meant to be a classic party, after all."

Natalie's frown deepens. "Eleanor..." she begins, but then she just shakes her head.

I clap my hands and put on my teacher's voice to get the kids all paying attention. It only takes a minute or two to organize them; Bella, as the birthday girl, decides she wants to be "it" and she runs through the grass, her golden hair haloed by sunshine, as children dart and weave away from her, their laughter floating on the balmy breeze. It's a beautiful moment, the kind I want to capture, hold between my hands, and never let go. *This.* This is what I want, and all it represents, all it promises.

Except then I remember Brian and I realize it doesn't promise anything.

I glance at Natalie, who is now frowning at her phone. "Is everything okay?" I ask, and she shrugs.

"It's just work."

Natalie never really talks to me about work, in part because I don't really understand it and, in reality, I'm not all that interested, although of course I haven't said as much. But pharmaceutical sales... is *anyone* interested in that?

"Work on a Saturday?" I return on a slightly hard laugh. *Just like Brian.*

"It's the end of the month, Eleanor," Natalie tells me, and

there is an edge to her voice. "I have to make my sales targets every month, and Monday is the last day. There's been a lot of pressure on sales reps to make their targets." She says this like she's said this kind of thing before, many times, and she probably has.

"Oh." I do my best to give her my full attention, although I'm trying to keep tabs on all the kids. And where is Kieran? I see him sitting on the swing, slowing pushing off with his feet. He's not playing tag; he really does look *lonely*, and once again I feel myself soften toward him. I must make more of an effort with him.

"So," I ask Natalie, "do you think you'll make your targets?"

"Maybe," she answers. "There's one potential customer I'd really like to sign... a HMO in Maryland. I've been waiting for their call since yesterday."

"Would they really call on a weekend?"

"They might," she replies, her tone repressive, and then she slides her phone into her pocket like an end to the conversation.

I know she tries to sell pharmaceutical drugs to various hospitals, doctors, clinicians, et cetera. I know she spends a lot of her time on the phone, or sending emails, and occasionally she has to fly out to see people in person, give them the hard sell. I know all that, but I don't really get it, as a *career*. Natalie is very passionate about her job, defensive but also determined to excel in a way I can't really understand, especially because she doesn't seem to like it all that much. Whenever I ask her about it, she almost always replies with an initial grimace.

"Well, I hope you make them," I say, a bit dutifully, and she nods.

"Thanks."

I glance around at the kids again, racing around the yard. The game of tag feels like it's hovering on becoming boring, a few kids wandering away, others clearly getting overhyped. I should switch it up, have them play something else, but I'm not sure I can be bothered. I feel a wave of exhaustion crash over me, which is not helped by having two alcoholic drinks in the middle of the afternoon.

"I think I'll start getting the food ready," I say as brightly as I can, and Natalie looks like she wants to object, but doesn't. "Give me a shout if you need me," I call back to her, a bit guiltily, because I know I am landing Natalie with the lion's share of responsibility, but I just can't cope with anything more today, and I've certainly paid my dues in that regard in the past. Natalie is usually the one hiding out in the kitchen at these things, not me. Admittedly, they've all been my children's parties, not hers, but still.

As I head back into the kitchen, I see Lizzy standing by the French doors, watching the children race around, an unreadable expression on her face. Relief fills me.

"Lizzy! I'm so glad to see you." I put an arm around her, which she is too surprised to shrug off. "Can you be a lifesaver and go help Natalie with the kids? You're so good at that, sweetheart, and it is Bella's special day." I give her shoulders a little squeeze, and she pulls away.

"If I have to," she huffs, and I tell myself she's just pretending to be reluctant, for form's sake. She's always loved helping out at these things before. She adores Bella. Who wouldn't?

While Lizzy heads out to help Natalie, I get all the food ready—heating up the pizza and hot dogs, laying everything out on platters. Amazingly, half an hour slips by without me even realizing; when the balloon guy knocks on the door, I am startled that he's here already. I direct him out back and the kids cluster around him, eager to have balloons made in the shape that they want. I feel another surge of relief. This is all going *fine*. And, who knows, maybe Brian will be home soon, and he'll apologize for missing so much, and everything will be as it was. At least, I can pretend that it is, which right now feels almost just as good. All I want is to go back to the way things were—even if that's just ignorance or determined naivete. *If we could just go back...*

At three-thirty, I venture outside to set up the food. Natalie is looking decidedly hassled, and Lizzy is nowhere to be seen. The kids surge around me, hungry and restless, their animal-shaped balloons already discarded in the grass, several of them deflated.

"Everything okay?" I ask Natalie brightly.

"I missed two calls from that potential client," she replies in something of a huff. "And these kids are *crazy*. There are way too many of them."

I glance around at the children who are now sitting on blankets, waiting for their food. "They seem okay to me."

"You haven't been here, Eleanor," Natalie replies tersely. I've never heard her use that tone with me. "You've been hiding inside—"

"I haven't been *hiding*," I protest, although that's pretty much exactly what I've been doing.

She huffs in disbelief, and I decide to stop this conversation before it escalates into an actual argument. I can hardly believe that's even a possibility; Natalie and I never argue. But then, I've never acted this way before. And *where* is Brian? What is he doing—and who with?

"Let's bring out the food," I tell Natalie. "It will keep them quiet for a little while."

We work in silent, if rather tense, harmony for a few minutes, bringing out the platters of hot dogs, pizza slices, and jam sandwiches, the bowls of goldfish crackers and apple slices. I really did do homegrown this year, but the children seem to like it.

For the next twenty minutes, we are both busy refilling platters, fetching drinks. I look around for Lizzy, and I see her talking to Bella, which warms my heart. Bella is smiling, and

Lizzy squeezes her shoulder. I love my girls, I think fiercely. Whatever is going on with Brian, I'll always have my daughters.

By four o'clock, the kids are ready to run around again, and Natalie and I let them loose while we do our best to tidy up the detritus of paper plates and crumbled napkins, squashed sandwiches and barely nibbled pizza slices. The balloon guy has long gone.

I heave a sigh as I check my watch; four-twenty. "Home stretch," I tell Natalie, and she gives me a tight smile in return. Again I feel a rush of guilt, that I basically left her to do the heavy lifting all afternoon. "I'm sorry I left you out here. I know I should have been more proactive. I just couldn't handle it today."

Natalie frowns in concern more than displeasure. "Why?"

A sigh escapes me, and for a second, I think about telling her about my fears over Brian. I long to be honest, but at the same time, I don't want to let my mask slip. If I don't have it all together, if my marriage and family aren't as amazing as I've said they are... Where does that leave me?

"It's hard to explain," I hedge. "Things have been a little... tense."

"Tense? Between you and Brian, you mean?" She sounds incredulous.

I shrug, wishing I hadn't said anything. My gaze moves over the yard, mentally counting the number of heads. I think they're all there. I see Bella and Freya together, at least, Bella's blond head close to Freya's dark one. They are whispering, but I can't see their faces. Then I see Freya jerk back; for a second, she is scowling. She looks over her shoulder, and I follow her gaze to see she's looking at Kieran, who is standing a few feet away. Bella beckons to Kieran, who comes over to them with seeming reluctance. Is Bella trying to be friendly? My heart swells with love and gratitude for my little girl. She has always had such a good heart.

And yet... why does Kieran look so closed off, his arms folded, his expression unreadable? It's unnerving in such a little kid. At least, I tell myself, Bella is making an effort.

I turn back to Natalie. "I'm going to put the candles on the cake," I announce. "Can you get the kids ready to sing to Bella?"

Natalie purses her lips and nods.

I go inside, breathing a sigh of relief, although that is quickly replaced by anxiety about Brian. He should be here by now. Outside, the children have gone back to the lawn games, and a few are asking for balloon animals again. Kieran is talking with Bella and Freya; I can see Bella's face and she's smiling, animated. Again, I feel a rush of love. The other children seem a little bored, but we're almost done; singing Happy Birthday, cutting the cake, and distributing party bags will take up the rest of the time.

I turn away from the French windows and go to take the cake out from under its glass cover. Carefully I place eight silver candles on top. It's homemade, three tiers frosted in glittery pink, with *Happy Birthday Bella!* written on it in hot pink swirls. Looking down at that cake grounds me somehow, reminds me of all that is good about our life, all that I've worked so hard to keep.

And I *will* keep it... no matter what. I will do whatever I have to, to preserve what Brian and I built together.

I take a deep breath and then I light the candles.

As I head outside, I see the children are all assembled to sing, but there's no Bella. I feel a stab of irritation; I told Natalie I was getting the cake. Couldn't she have made sure Bella was ready for it? She'd just been there by the swing a moment ago, with Freya and Kieran.

As if in answer to my silent question, Natalie frowns and says uncertainly, "Bella was right here a moment ago..."

A flicker of apprehension wavers through me as my gaze tracks through the backyard—the empty swing, the abandoned trampoline, the discarded balloons. No Bella. Reluctantly yet instinctively, I move my gaze to the short hill that rolls down to the pond. From here I can just make out the glint of water—it really is little more than a puddle—and then a heart-stopping flash of pink. Bella is wearing a pink cotton sundress. My stomach clenches and I start walking, the grass whispering against my bare legs.

"Eleanor?" Natalie calls, and the kids look around uncertainly, unsure what is going on, and why I am walking away with the birthday cake. Its candles flicker in the breeze and the plate is heavy in my hands, as I come to the hill.

I suck my breath in a shocked gasp as I catch sight of the scene below—Bella is lying face down by the pond, with Kieran standing directly over her, his expression as blank as ever.

As my daughter's name is ripped from my lips, the plate slides from my hands, the beautiful birthday cake falling to the ground.

And then I start running toward my daughter.

NINE

JOANNA

I'd been hoping Eleanor would let me stay at the party and help, and when she tells me I'm not needed, I am at a loss. What am I meant to do with three Kieran-free hours? Of course, I can think of myriad things to do—a grocery shop, catch up on work, go home and talk with Tim. Or maybe just walk in the woods that stretches behind Wetherby's main street, a rewilded parkland that runs along a river and leads to the requisite baseball field and bandstand that I haven't yet had a chance to explore.

But I don't want to do any of those things. I was counting on being able to stay, both to keep an eye on Kieran and to try to befriend Eleanor or any other parents who might have chosen to stay. After the walk of shame from the schoolyard, I've avoided just about everyone—and everyone has avoided me. But I told myself that I had to get over the humiliation of confronting Eleanor about the missing party invitation, that there was no reason we couldn't be friends, or at least *friendly*. For Kieran's sake, as well as my own, I needed to make more of an effort. Hence, the offer to help at the party, which was clearly and firmly rebuffed, and had left me wandering through Wetherby, wondering what to do.

I walk through the town, trying not to feel lonely as I look at the various couples and families soaking up the sunshine and browsing the boutiques on Main Street. I end up at one of the town's hipster cafés, its vegan options detailed on a chalkboard outside, and go inside to order an oat milk latte. I left Tim at home watching baseball, and I don't think I can cope with going home and stepping around him, the silence between us deepening by the minute.

As I wait for my latte, I realize Eleanor didn't even ask for my phone number, in case of an emergency. Then I wonder if there is some sort of class text chat that I'm not a part of, and the thought fills me with hopelessness. How will I ever make any headway in this town? But I know I've got to try. Somehow.

I find a table in the back of the café, and I have just taken the first sip of my latte when I am stopped by a hesitant voice as a woman approaches my table.

"You're... Kieran's mom, right?"

I glance up at her warily, not wanting to get drawn into something. "Yes..."

"I'm Rachel, Toby's mom." She's short and smiling, with a round, freckly face and a neat auburn bob. She sticks out a hand for me to shake, which I do. "I think I've seen you in the schoolyard...?"

"Um, yes?" I don't recognize her, but then the other mothers of the third grade have merged into one formless, faceless blob to me. I'm amazed she knows who I am, until I remember Partygate, and realize that probably every parent does, and not in a good way. Rachel, however, seems friendly; in fact, she asks if she can join me and when I give a startled nod, she sits down opposite me with her own latte.

"I've been meaning to say hi," she tells me. "You know, as one mother of a rambunctious boy to another." She offers me a tentative smile, as if waiting for me to reject this label, but I just manage a small smile of acknowledgment back. "Toby was diagnosed with ADHD last year," Rachel continues, in the manner of a confession. "We're still coming to terms with what that means for him as well as for our family. He's been on Ritalin since April, and I think it has helped."

I nod, simply because I'm not sure what the right response is. "I'm sorry" feels insensitive. "It must be challenging," I finally manage, and Rachel nods as she gives a wry smile.

"It's definitely had its moments." She pauses before asking delicately, "Is Kieran...?" She trails off, clearly not wanting to be so crass as to put it into words.

I know what she's asking, of course. Does Kieran have a diagnosis of some kind? Is he on medication? The answer is no to both. But I can't explain to this earnest mother that we've decided to avoid the medicalized route, the assigning of labels, without offending her, so I just demur.

"He hasn't been diagnosed with anything specific," I tell her, and her face falls a little before she recovers herself. Clearly, she was hoping for another member to welcome into her club, and maybe it's one I'll have to join one day, but not yet. Although maybe I *should* join... being part of a club, *any* club, and having a firm friend to fight my corner sounds pretty wonderful just about now. And maybe a diagnosis *would* help Kieran. "We've had a few investigations," I add, hoping this will appease her. "But there's been nothing definitive." I smile. "He just seems like... a very active little boy, I suppose."

"Well, I know it can be hard sometimes, at this age," Rachel says. "Especially when the little girls are all so *angelic*." She grimaces, and this time my small smile is genuine. "Parents of girls don't really *get* boys, I find," Rachel continues, seeming emboldened by my smile, "and how they are... not malicious, just *thoughtless*. Something I wish Miss Stoviak could appreciate a little more."

"I know what you mean," I say truthfully, and she nods gratefully.

We chat a bit more about innocuous things, trading the details of life. I explain how we've moved from New York, that I work as an actuary. No one usually knows what that means, but since we live so close to Hartford, the city nicknamed America's filing cabinet, she at least has an idea.

Rachel tells me about her life too—a part-time job as a book-keeper for a party planning firm, a four-year-old daughter in addition to Toby. I smile and nod and agree with her when it seems necessary, but as much as I want to make a friend, it's hard to keep my mind on the conversation when I am thinking of—and worrying about—Kieran. What if he misbehaves at the party? What if something really bad happens, although I'm not even sure what that could be. He throws the cake on the floor? He pushes another child? None of it is life-threatening, emergency kind of stuff, which should reassure me, but it doesn't.

The truth is, I'm just waiting for something bad to happen... and that makes me feel guilty. Why can't I believe the best—or even just *better*—about my own child? Why am I always living in this tense state of perpetual anxiety?

After we finish our coffees, Rachel says she has a few errands to run before picking up Toby from the party, and we exchange goodbyes. I am both encouraged and a little taken aback by the way she presses my hand, her suggestion that we should meet up sometime, maybe with the boys. It does feel like I've made a friend, or started to, and that heartens me. It's a beginning, which is all I really wanted.

I spend the next hour wandering around Wetherby, in all its whitewashed New England quaintness. There is an independent bookstore with a cat in the window and comfortable armchairs positioned about; an artisan bakery selling apple turnovers that spice the air with their cinnamon sweetness; an old-fashioned hardware store that revels in its history—having been established over a hundred and fifty years earlier—with its bins of loose nails and screws, the space outside its plate glass windows lined with all manner of items—hoes and shovels, coils of garden hose and stacks of plastic buckets, an old rocking chair.

At four-thirty, I decide to make my way back to the Daltons' house. The three-story Colonial, painted a lemon yellow with flower beds bursting with chrysanthemums, almost glows under the late afternoon sun as I walk up the drive. There is the autumnal smell of dry leaves in the warm air that always makes me feel nostalgic for school days. I knock on the front door, but no one answers; they are probably all out in the backyard.

I go around the side, to a wooden gate I'd seen earlier. I try the latch and it swings open. I step through, walking through an archway cut in a laurel hedge to come into the yard itself.

For a second, it feels as if I am observing a tableau—everyone looks frozen in place. Even the air seems to have stilled, like a caught breath. The children are on the patio, assembled for cake no doubt, but no one is moving or even speaking. It's so *strange*, that momentarily I think they must be playing a game of musical statues. Something to make sense of the eeriness. Then I notice that they are all looking toward a small hill that rolls gently down to the bottom of the backyard, and even before I hear the scream—endless and full of anguish—my stomach is cramping with dread, with certainty.

I start striding, and then running, toward the sound. As I crest the hill, I see Eleanor first, running toward a small, shallow pond fringed with maples and birches. She falls down onto her knees and I can't see who or what she is bent over, but she is sobbing, shrieking, asking someone to call 911. And then I see my son, standing just a few feet away. The expression on his face is completely blank.

As I come closer, I almost step in the birthday cake, lying in a smashed heap of pink frosting on the ground. I also see Natalie at the top of the hill, her hand on Freya's shoulder, her face pale.

"Have you called 911?" I call to her. My voice is urgent, but it feels as if it is coming from somewhere else; I am so dazed with shock, I can hardly believe this is real. I reach for my phone, because now I see who Eleanor is bending over. Her daughter Bella, who is unconscious. There is blood in her hair and her face is deathly pale, almost gray. It's also wet, and I realize she must have been lying face down in the water. *For how long?* God, please don't let her be dead. And please, *please,* don't let my son have had anything to do with this... even if he was standing right there.

"I've... I've called," Natalie says as she comes closer, Freya sticking close by her side. Her face is almost as pale as Bella's, her wide-eyed gaze transfixed on the lifeless form of the little girl. *Is* she dead?

I turn to my son. "Kieran..."

Eleanor's head jerks around to face me, and for a second her face twists into a snarling mask of hatred that makes me draw my breath in sharply. "Get... out," she rasps. "Get *out* of here! Both of you! Keep your son *away* from my family!"

I take an instinctive step back, dizzy with shock at the naked hostility in her voice, on her face. "Eleanor..." I begin, but I have no idea what to say. It's obvious she must blame Kieran, and with a sickening churn of fear, I wonder what actually happened. What Kieran might have done. I can't ask; I don't want to know. Not yet, anyway.

"*Get out!*" Eleanor says again, and this time it comes out in a ragged scream before she dissolves into sobs, her body bent over her daughter. "Bella, baby, Bella... come back to me, darling. Wake up, *please...*"

"I think," Natalie says, her voice low and hoarse as she comes closer to me, "that maybe you should just go."

"Do you know what happened?" I force myself to ask, and she gives a little shake of her head. I can't tell whether she's saying she doesn't know, or she doesn't want to tell me.

Children are starting to trickle down the hill, some curious, others afraid. Some hang back, while others edge closer, their faces full of uncertainty and fear. I see another mother come through the gate, her face drawn into a frown of confusion as her gaze darts around the yard. There will be more parents coming, more questions, more concern and horror, more shock and judgment, and my son will be right in the middle of it.

"Kieran," I say quietly. He blinks me into focus. "Kieran, let's go."

It feels like we're running away, but we're not, I tell myself. It's the right thing, or at least the smart thing, to do right now. I reach for his hand, and for once he lets me take it.

I turn to Natalie. "I'm sorry..." I begin, and then stop. I mean to say *I'm sorry this happened*, but I realize it sounds like a confession, and it's not, because I don't know what happened. I'm not sure anyone does.

Natalie shakes her head again, her gaze skating away from mine. Eleanor is still bent over Bella, who hasn't moved. I glance around at the children, a few parents coming down the hill, but no one is looking at me. It feels deliberate, and I realize that Kieran's presence here can only be unhelpful to everyone, especially him. Even though it feels wrong, I think we should go. And so, holding Kieran's hand, I walk out of the yard in a daze.

We walk in silence to the car I left parked a little way down the road. The sun is shining, the birds chirping, the smell of fallen leaves still in the air, tinged with woodsmoke. Wetherby, Connecticut on a beautiful September day. I feel as if I am far away, or underwater, everything happening at a distance, the whole world muted to a silent scream.

We get to the car, and I open the car door for Kieran before going round to the driver's side. For a second, I simply sit in the driver's seat, my hands on the steering wheel, and breathe. Kieran buckles his seatbelt and turns his face to the window.

I am not, I tell myself, going to ask him what happened right now—in the car, alone, already knowing I am unable to deal with whatever he tells me. I breathe out. Start the car. And drive in silence all the way home.

Back at the house, I am grateful, for the first time, for its privacy. The trees looming darkly all around feel like a shelter, a screen, and one I need right now. Kieran goes into the house in front of me, almost seeming carefree. Does he realize what has happened? I wonder. Was he *part* of it?

As I get out of the car, I feel like an old woman, practically hobbling toward the front door.

In the house, Tim is stretched out on the sofa, asleep, the TV showing the ninth inning of a boring baseball game; the World Series doesn't start for over a month. A sudden wave of fury breaks over me. I turn off the TV, wishing it made some noise—a snap or a crack. Instead the room is plunged into silence.

"Tim." I speak quietly for Kieran's sake, but then I realize he's gone into the playroom, closed the door, no doubt with the iPad to hand. "*Tim*," I say again, louder this time, like an accusation.

His eyes flutter open, and he regards me blearily. "Jo...?"

I stare at him and my frustration, my fear, my loneliness from the last six months coalesces into a single, sharp point. I already know I need him present and focused and part of this, for whatever comes next. He cannot check out any longer, simply because work got hard, and life felt overwhelming. Life has just got a whole lot *more* overwhelming, and I know I am not going to be able to cope with this—whatever *this* turns out to be—on my own. I need my husband back.

"Tim," I say for a third time, and now I sound grim, deadly. I just hope no one has actually died. Bella looked so *still*, so pale. Had she hit her head, or fallen in the water, or both? And what could Kieran have possibly had to do with it?

"Jo...?" Tim says again, and I fix him with a serious stare.

"We need to talk."

TEN

NATALIE

Everything was a blur—like one of those movie montages, sepia-tinted snapshots, flashes of color and insight, streaming by way too fast to make sense of them. A shout, a scream, and then I ran. Eleanor was already there; I saw pink icing mashed into the grass.

And Eleanor, bent over Bella, who looked so *still*...

My mind was nothing but pulsing static as I stared at the scene; I saw Bella first, and then Eleanor, and finally Kieran, standing so close to Bella, he was almost looming over her. *Did he push her...?*

Somewhere in the confused mess of it all, I called 911. I can't even remember the details of the call; I blurted out words, an address. Then I saw Joanna, her face pale with anxiety, coming closer. Eleanor screamed at her, and I told her to go. Joanna took Kieran's hand and left; other parents started coming. A child started to cry. At some point, Freya came to stand by me, but I can't remember when.

And now my mind is spinning, spinning.

I walk toward Eleanor because I know I have to. She is

cradling Bella in her arms, weeping. Bella's face is pale, and there is blood on her forehead, in her hair. I'm not sure she is breathing. Should we do CPR? Or not move her because of the head injury? I don't think either of us knows what to do, and if the 911 dispatcher told me, I can't remember.

"Is Bella..." I begin, before I realize there is no good question to ask. "I called 911," I said instead. "An ambulance will be here soon." I'm not sure Eleanor even hears me. "What happened?" I whisper, and she wrenches around to fix me with a glare that makes my heart feel as if it is suspended in my chest.

"Don't you know?"

Thankfully, I don't have the chance to answer that question, because Eleanor turns back to Bella, and some more parents come running. Somewhere, a child is still crying.

"What happened?" someone calls—Jack Reed's mother— and Eleanor hunches away from the voices, the noise.

"I can't..." she begins.

"I'll deal with it," I tell her. "The ambulance will be here soon, Eleanor. It's going to be okay." As if I can promise something like that.

Still, I do my best to take control. I shepherd the kids away from Eleanor and Bella, toward the patio, and I bring out the party bags to distract them. Parents are asking questions, demanding answers, seeming as concerned about how what happened might traumatize their own child as whether Bella is okay. There is, I recognize, an odd sense of relief, or even gratitude, as if, because it happened to someone else's child, it won't happen to theirs. As if there is a cosmic limit.

"Am ambulance is coming," I assure them. "Bella hit her head, but she's going to be fine." I feel like if I keep saying it, it will come true. This won't be the big deal that it feels like right now, looming and enormous. We might even laugh about it later. *Remember how scared you were, for a second, and then Bella was fine?*

I can hope, anyway. I can pray.

As I am handing out the party bags, Freya drifts over to my side once more, slipping her hand in mine. I stop to hug her briefly, tightly, knowing how traumatic this must be for her. Bella is her best friend, her *only* friend, if I'm honest. "It's going to be okay," I tell her, but she doesn't reply.

I am shepherding kids through the side gate when the ambulance finally comes. Four paramedics head toward the pond, while the parents who are still there simply stand around and gape.

"Standard procedure," I explain, almost breezily. "It's fine."

Freya is still holding my hand, and I look around for Lizzy, but I can't see her anywhere. Is she in her room? Has she missed all the drama?

My stomach hollows out as I watch the paramedics load Bella onto a stretcher. She still looks so... *lifeless*. I don't think she's so much as stirred in all this time, and that can't be good.

Freya's little hand squeezes mine hard. "Is Bella going to be okay?" she whispers.

"Yes, of course," I answer automatically. "She's going to be fine."

Eleanor is following the stretcher out, and she grabs my arm as she passes. "I'm going in the ambulance with Bella," she says. "Can you manage everything here?"

I nod, trying to seem capable even though I feel as if I am trembling inside, my legs watery, my insides hollow. "Of course."

"Lizzy..."

I nod again. "I'll talk to her."

"And Brian... I haven't texted him or anything. My phone's in the drawer..." Her face is pale, anguished. "Can you text him?"

"I'll let him know." All these promises I'm making, when all

I want to do is grab Freya and run back to our house, burrow under the covers.

A sob escapes her in a choking sound. "My baby, Natalie," she says. "My precious little baby."

I give her a quick, tight hug. "She's going to be fine, Eleanor. *Fine.*"

She sobs again as she hugs me tightly. I hug her back, wanting to imbue her with a certainty I don't feel, a strength I don't have. I just really, really want Bella to be okay.

For all our sakes.

After Eleanor leaves with the ambulance, parents huddle in knots, whispering, while children drift about, looking lost. No one seems to want to leave, but I need them to. I adopt an appropriately somber yet certain tone as I start chivvying them out, assuring them Bella will be fine, just a precaution, no need to worry at all. I am starting to feel like I am lying.

When they've finally all gone, I breathe a gusty sigh of relief. My stomach is in knots, though, because I can't stop thinking about Bella. What happened to her? Why was Kieran standing so close to her? And where is Lizzy?

I glance at Freya.

"Do you know where Lizzy is?"

She shakes her head. I realize she has not spoken for about half an hour.

"Freya..." I begin, and then stop. Do I want to traumatize my daughter by asking her what happened, pumping her for information? She wasn't at the pond as far as I know, but she almost always sticks to Bella's side. I *need* to know; at least I need to know if Freya knows anything. I don't think I will rest until I do. "Did you see what happened?" I ask. "Freya, honey... how did Bella get hurt?"

Freya's eyes are wide and watchful as she stares at me for a long moment. I wait, unsure what reassurance to give, how to make her talk.

"Freya...?" I prompt as gently as I can, even though inside I feel like screaming, or weeping, or both. "Do you know? Did you see... anything?"

Another long moment passes. Then, finally, she whispers, "I don't know. I didn't see."

I feel relieved, although I'm not sure I should.

"Kieran was nearby," I remark carefully. "Did you see what he was doing?"

Her eyes widen further, and she shakes her head. I can't tell if she's hiding something or not, but why would she protect Kieran?

Kieran. Even after all our worries about him, I still can't believe he might be responsible for something like this.

"Are you sure you didn't see anything?" I press as gently as I can.

Freya shakes her head silently, and I know she won't answer any more questions. Already, she is retreating into herself, chewing the end of one braid, her expression fearful, and I feel too strung out to push her any more. My head is aching, and I feel as if I could either collapse or explode.

"Okay," I tell her, and I pull her close and wrap my arms around her, drawing her to me. "It's okay, Freya, honey. It's going to be okay."

She buries her head against my chest as she hugs me tightly. "How do you know?" she asks, her voice muffled.

I close my eyes as I hold her. The truth is, I don't.

Eventually, I settle Freya in the den watching TV and I go look for Lizzy. I find her up in her room, lying on her bed, hugging her knees to her chest, her face blotchy with tears.

"Lizzy..." I gaze at her, abject, full of pity. She must have seen more than I'd realized. I should have gone looking for her sooner. "Your mom went with Bella to the hospital."

Lizzy sniffs, her chin tucked toward her knees. "Is she going to be okay?"

The question everyone is asking, but, at almost fifteen, I feel Lizzy deserves a more honest answer. "I hope so," I tell her, my voice wavering.

She glances at me, her eyes full of tears. "Did you see what happened? Did that kid Kieran *push* her?"

"I..." I hesitate and then admit, "I didn't see." Which is true, and makes my insides writhe with anxiety. Could I have prevented this?

Lizzy shakes her head slowly. "Why would he do that?"

Because that's the kind of kid he is. It feels like far too mean a thought to think, much less voice aloud.

"He was probably just high-spirited," I say unconvincingly. "I doubt he meant to really hurt her, if he even did it. Maybe it was just an accident." I hesitate and then finish rather lamely, "Maybe it was just one of those things."

She glares at me in disbelief. "*One of those things?* My sister might be, like, in a *coma.*"

A coma? Could it really come to that? For a second, I struggle to speak. I cannot bear to think about comas.

"We don't know that," I finally tell her in little more than a whisper. "She might have just had a knock on the head. She could be fine. *Fine.*"

Lizzy just shakes her head, her face buried in her knees. I reach out to touch her shoulder, but she shrugs me off.

"Just leave me alone," she insists, her voice still muffled.

Feeling like that might be the best option right about now, I do.

Downstairs, Freya is still watching the TV, looking both woebegone and exhausted. There are dark circles under her eyes and her face is paler than usual. "Have you heard anything about Bella?" she asks in a small voice as I come into the room.

"Not yet, but Bella's mom didn't bring her phone, so she can't send me updates." I tuck a blanket around her even though it's not cold and she doesn't resist. "I'll tell you as soon as I know anything," I promise, and I kiss her forehead before I go out to start cleaning up the mess of the party—collecting the lawn games and putting them back in the shed, dumping the remaining paper plates of half-eaten hot dogs and PB&Js into a big black garbage bag. I pick up the ruined cake from the grass, a lump in my throat, and put it in the bag. I even try to scrape the frosting off the grass, to remove any sign that the cake fell, the reason why it did. It's stupid, I know, and yet I do it anyway. I feel a need to.

Back in the kitchen, I check my phone for a message from Eleanor, before remembering that she left her phone here, in the stupid tech drawer. I try to open it, but the thing is locked, and I let out a groan. She asked me to text Brian on her phone, but obviously I can't, and I don't have his number. I'll have to wait until he gets home.

Meanwhile, the third-grade parents' text chat is blowing up with messages about the party.

What happened???

Jesse doesn't know anything.

Olivia said Kieran did something.

Where is Eleanor? Has anyone talked to Natalie?

Clearly there wasn't enough supervision. I offered to stay...

I'm sorry, but something seemed a little off with Eleanor today, even before anything happened.

OMG, what are you saying?! Are you blaming Eleanor?!

No, of course not, I'm just saying something was weird.

Let's all say a prayer for Bella, okay? And leave it at that.

Is no one concerned that Kieran was OBVIOUSLY to blame???

I put my phone down, unable to bear reading anything more. I focus on cleaning the kitchen instead, to Eleanor's shining standard. At least when I am scrubbing and wiping, my mind is almost—*almost*—blank, and I don't feel as if I could come apart at any moment.

Twenty minutes later, the front door opens, and Brian is home. Everything in me tenses as I hear the door close, his heavy footstep. I have absolutely no idea how to handle talking to him, *telling* him. It's seconds away, and I can't even envision it.

"Sorry, hon," he calls as he comes down the hallway. "Meetings went late. These clients..." He gives a wry laugh that rings false to me, although I can hardly dwell on that with everything I'm about to tell him.

Brian rounds the corner, stepping into the kitchen. He's dressed in khakis and a pale pink button-down shirt, his blond hair brushed back from his forehead. His blue gaze widens as he takes in its emptiness, no wife, no adoring daughters—and then me, standing in the middle, probably looking like a scared rabbit, frozen in the headlights of his piercing gaze, mindlessly wiping counters.

"Brian..." I greet him, my voice already faltering.

His gaze narrows as he drops his keys onto the counter with a clatter. "Hey, Natalie. I know the party's over, but... where's Eleanor? And Bella?"

"Um..." I swallow. "I... I'm afraid..."

"Natalie?" He takes a step closer to me, his forehead furrowed, his hand now clenched into a fist at his side, a gesture that seems more fearful than aggressive. "What's going on?"

"There was an accident," I tell him weakly. "Brian, I'm so sorry. Bella..."

His whole body stiffens. "*Bella?*"

"She hit her head. Eleanor has gone with her to the hospital to have it... checked out."

He shakes his head slowly, as if to deny what I've just said. "But... just as a precaution, right? Like with the X-ray. It's not as if..." He trails off, seeming so much like a little boy, hopeful and pleading, that I feel a rush of pity for him. I've always liked Brian, because there's no reason not to, but sometimes I've found him a bit... much. His air of assurance, the oh-so firm handshake, the booming voice. The way he stands, with his feet set apart like he's striding the world. *His* world. There is nothing arrogant or obnoxious about him, which makes me feel guilty for having even the tiniest flicker of impatience at the way he is... and yet I do.

But right now, all I feel is sympathy and sorrow.

"I'm not sure," I tell him. "An ambulance came—"

He gulps, his Adam's apple bobbing in his throat. "An *ambulance?*"

"She was unconscious." I say it like a confession, and it feels like one, because this, and really, *only* this, was what I was there to prevent. Eleanor warned me about Kieran, the pond. I failed her.

And yet if she hadn't insisted on hiding in the kitchen, knocking back G&Ts...

No, I can't think that way, especially now. It's cruel and unfair.

"Unconscious..." Brian's face drains of color and he throws one hand out to the counter, as if to steady himself. "Do you know what happened? How did she fall? Why wasn't someone watching her?"

I stiffen at the implied note of accusation in his voice, even though I know it must be prompted by fear. "I don't know what happened," I tell him. "No one saw, as far as I know. There were twenty-eight kids in your backyard, and it was hard to keep track of all of them, all the time."

Brian stares at me for a moment, as if he wants to say something sharp in return, and then his whole body sags, passing a hand over his face. "You're right. I'm sorry. I'm sorry. I'm just... in shock. *Bella...*"

"I know," I say quietly. "But it might be..." I can't quite make myself say *precautionary*. "I don't know how bad it is, Brian. She might just have had a... a hard knock."

He takes his phone out of his pocket, swipes. "Why hasn't Eleanor called me?" It sounds like another accusation.

"She left her phone here, in the tech drawer," I explain. "She wanted me to tell you, and Lizzy..."

He frowns as he looks up at me. "Where is Lizzy?"

"Up in her room. She's pretty upset."

He nods slowly, absorbing the information without making any move to go see his oldest daughter. "I should go to the hospital," he says as he slides his phone into his pocket. "Do you know which one they went to?"

I shake my head. "Probably Sharon?" It's the closest, but it's pretty small. If Bella is going to need any specialist care, she'll have to be taken to New Haven or Hartford. But why am I thinking that way? This might really be just a bump-on-the-head situation. I can still hope, anyway.

"Okay." He nods slowly. "Okay. Can you stay here? With Lizzy... till one of us gets back?"

I nod, swallow. "Of course."

Brian heads back out without going upstairs to see Lizzy.

I check on Freya again, and find she's fallen asleep on the sofa, even though it's not even six o'clock. My heart aches for her, for all the children, and most of all, for Bella.

I turn back to the kitchen, wanting to do something productive, but I end up just pacing the room. *Oh God*, I pray, *please,*

please let her be all right. I was raised Catholic, but as an adult my faith has been more of a cultural thing; right now, however, I am a true believer. I need to be because I need God to listen to me. I need Bella to be fine. *Fine.*

Because if she isn't... it might be all my fault.

ELEVEN

ELEANOR

Bella doesn't open her eyes for the entire twenty-minute ride to the hospital. I sit in the back with the paramedics, crouched on a little bench seat next to Bella, who is strapped onto a stretcher, trying to stay out of the paramedics' way as they take her blood pressure, her body temperature, her heartbeat. She's breathing, at least, but she is so very *still*.

At one point, they fire a few questions at me. How did she fall? Was she submerged in the water? If so, for how long, approximately?

I don't know the answers to any of the questions. I end up weeping, wiping the snot from my nose with the back of my hand as I explain, wretchedly, that I was inside, bringing out the birthday cake, I didn't see any of it happen. I wasn't there.

I should have been there.

I push the thought away because guilt is not a helpful emotion. I need to focus on staying strong for Bella, on being there for my baby girl, whatever happens next.

And yet I'm so scared of what happens next.

In the hospital, Bella is whisked away from me on a stretcher, into the ER. I am left sitting on a hard plastic seat in the waiting room with a dozen other weary-looking people, some of them coughing wretchedly or cradling what could be broken arms. Hardly anyone speaks.

I am desperately wishing I had my phone. Brian will be going out of his *mind*. Has he come home yet? Has Natalie told him what happened? I need him here with me, talking in his firm, confident way to the doctors, putting his arm around me as he assures me that everything is going to be okay, because he will take care of our family. He *always* takes care of our family.

But he's not here, and I can't even call him, or anyone, and so, sitting there by myself, I struggle not to feel utter despair... as well as wracked with guilt. I should have been there. I should have protected my baby girl. I think of the two gin and tonics still sloshing around in my stomach, my head aching from them, and bile rises in my throat. How could I have been so reckless, so *stupid*? What if my foolishness costs me my daughter's *life*?

After an interminable hour, a female doctor in green scrubs comes out through the heavy, swinging doors. "Mrs. Eleanor Dalton?" she calls out. Her expression is serious, maybe even grim, and my stomach cramps. I wrap my arms around myself as I force myself to stand up on shaky legs.

"Yes..." My voice is a croak.

"You're Bella's mother?"

I nod.

"Why don't we go somewhere a bit more private to talk?"

Oh, no. No, no, no. I do not want to go somewhere *private*. Private means so much more than a bump on the head. Private is the moment in the movie when you see it all silently from behind the glass, the doctor putting a hand on a shoulder, the parent or spouse dropping their head into their hands as they break down and weep.

"Is... is she going to be all right?" I have to force the question out through numb lips, before either of us has moved.

The doctor takes me gently by the elbow as she guides me

around the corner, to an alcove with a couple of vinyl-covered chairs and a vending machine. This, it seems, is as private as it's going to get.

"Mrs. Dalton, Bella's condition is serious," she states without preamble. Her voice is kind yet also unrelenting. I know immediately that she is not going to give me false promises; she is not going to sugarcoat anything, and I realize I want her to. I need assurances. I crave comfort. I'm not sure I'm strong enough to handle anything else right now.

"How serious?" I ask in little more than a whisper. I realize my legs are not going to hold me and I lower myself into one of the chairs. The doctor sits in the other, clasping her hands in her lap.

"She has some swelling on her brain from when she hit her head," she states. "We don't know the extent of the damage yet, but there is the potential for shearing, which is essentially a tearing of the internal lining, tissues, and blood vessels of the brain and can, as you might imagine, result in some permanent brain damage."

Brain damage.

The words feel like gongs being struck, grenades being hurled. There will always, I think, be a before and after; before, when I still hoped she had a concussion at worst, and after, when we are talking about brain damage.

Bella... my Bella.

"The other issue," the doctor continues before I can frame so much as a word, "is that she is suffering from cerebral hypoxia. This is when the brain is deprived of oxygen, which was due to her lying face down in the water." She raises her eyebrows in query. "That is, according to reports, what happened?"

Numbly I nod. "When I... I found her she was face down. But it... it was only a little water, and I don't think it was for very long." I think of Kieran, standing practically right over her, and for a second my hands clench into fists before I force them flat, resting them on my thighs. "No more than a minute or two," I assure the doctor, although, I acknowledge hollowly, I don't really know that at all. How long was I in the kitchen, getting the cake ready? When did Natalie notice Bella wasn't there? Three, four, five minutes? No longer than that, surely. Right now, it sounds like an absolute age. The difference, maybe, between life and death.

The doctor nods in acceptance; I don't sense any judgment from her, but I feel it all the same. *How could you not know?*

"Well, with any case involving brain injury," she tells me in the same, steady voice, "it's difficult to assess the extent of the possible damage until some time has passed, and healing has been able to take place. As we're a small hospital, we're not really equipped to deal with these severe sorts of cases, especially in children. I'm advising Bella be moved to the Connecticut Children's Medical Center in Hartford."

"Okay." My voice sounds papery. "Thank you." I pause to draw a breath, needing air into my lungs. I feel dizzy, spots swimming before my eyes, and for a second, I'm afraid I might pass out.

The doctor looks at me in concern. "Mrs. Dalton... are you all right? Is there someone who can be with you?"

I force a nod, even though I know I'm not remotely all right. "My husband's coming." *I hope.* "Can I please see her? Bella?"

She shakes her head. "I've advised her to be moved as soon as possible to Hartford. I think the best thing would be if your husband met you here, and then you drove together to the Medical Center. When your daughter is stable, you can, of course, see her."

Stable? What is the opposite of stable? I think of *Grey's Anatomy* and *ER*, now sepia-tinted TV shows from my college years and childhood, serious-faced doctors in blood-spattered scrubs coming through the doors. *Critical condition. Life-threat-*

ening. Those are the opposites of stable. But I can't bear for them to be applied to my Bella.

I feel as if I am existing outside myself; I am barely aware of what I am doing as I nod as I knew I'd have to, and then murmur more thanks.

The doctor reaches over to grasp my arm in a gesture of solidarity or maybe just comfort; I can't tell. And then she leaves.

I sit there in the little alcove, feeling utterly adrift and abandoned. For a few minutes, I simply sit, because I don't know what else to do. I long for my phone, to be in touch with Brian, Natalie, the *world*. I suppose I should call my parents, a prospect which fills me with dread. I've always been the disappointment—the semi-dyslexic, unambitious daughter who never had a career or even wanted one, versus Brad and Josh, who were both varsity captains, Phi Beta Kappa, and are now, respectively, a surgeon and a lawyer. No contest. I never even tried.

And this feels like one more way that I've failed. I couldn't take care of my own daughter, my so longed-for child, who came as the biggest blessing ever after years of infertility, disappointment, and even more failure.

Bella. I picture her golden hair, her bright blue eyes, the way her whole face lights up when she smiles at me. How can this be happening? How can I possibly survive it and be strong for my daughter? I cannot see my way through the next five minutes, never mind the next five weeks, months, *years*.

The questions continue to hammer me relentlessly. What if Bella doesn't recover? What if she has ongoing disabilities—or worse? What if she's truly brain damaged? In this moment, I realize just how much I have wanted for my children—not just in terms of happiness, but in terms of health, wholeness, *success*. And Bella might not experience any of it.

And it will be *my* fault.

It is too much to bear. Literally, too much; I sag in my seat, unable to keep upright under the weight of this knowledge, this *terror*, and yet I have to, because I'm a *mother*, and mothers aren't allowed to fumble, fall, *fail*. They can't collapse in fear or sadness; they are implicitly forbidden from showing any weakness at all. That's what has been drilled into me by Instagram feeds and glossy magazines, by well-meaning yet lecturing parenting blogs and books, by every earnest or anxious mother around me, as well as every sanctimonious or supercilious one, including my own, all telling me exactly how amazing I have to be, just to make the grade.

I can picture my own mother, with her perfectly coiffed blond bob and made-up face, the way she'd intone that if I just tried harder, I might make a success of myself. *Really, Eleanor, you have been given every opportunity to succeed. I cannot understand why you don't apply yourself. Look at your brothers...*

But why am I thinking about my own mother? I need to *be* a mother. The realization galvanizes me, and I shoot up from my chair. I need to find a phone. I'll call Natalie, get in touch with Brian. And then I'll go to the Connecticut Children's Medical Center and *be there* for my daughter.

Of course, nothing about this plan is simple. It takes me fifteen minutes to find a pay phone, and then to figure out how to use it, as it doesn't take coins—not that I have any, anyway—but only prepaid cards that I have to buy at the gift shop in the lobby. It feels like a relic from the past, something archeologists will display in a museum of what was once known as modern life. And yet right now I am depending on it.

I call the landline at home and twice it switches to voicemail before, finally, Natalie picks up.

"Hello?" she asks breathlessly.

"Natalie? It's Eleanor."

"Oh, *Eleanor*." Her breath comes out in a tearful rush. "How is Bella? Is she okay?"

No, she's not remotely okay. As I listen to Natalie's questions, I am reminded that *she* was the one who was meant to be looking after my daughter. Maybe I shouldn't have entrusted that responsibility to her—and I certainly feel plenty of guilt—but what was *she* doing? How was Bella able to wander away to the pond, to slip and fall without her noticing? And what about Kieran? I think of how Bella had been beckoning to him right before I went inside—what had that been about? How did they go from that seeming friendliness to a push into the water, to *this*?

The questions jangle in my head, but I don't have space for them. Later, yes, but right now it is taking all my focus, all my energy, to figure out these few next steps.

"She's being transferred to the Children's Medical Center in Hartford," I tell Natalie, my voice strangely toneless. I think it's the only way I can keep it together; to act matter-of-fact, emotionless. "Did Brian come home?"

"Yes, I told him what happened. He's coming to the hospital—"

"Okay, I'll wait for him here."

"*Eleanor*." Natalie sounds on the verge of tears, and for some reasons this causes me a sudden flare of fury. What right does she have, to be so sad? To luxuriate in feelings of grief and sorrow, when I have to keep it all together? Again, *always*? "I'm so sorry..."

And what exactly, I wonder, still feeling furious, is she apologizing for?

"So am I," I tell her flatly. I know I should ask her what she saw—or didn't see—at the party, but I simply don't have the energy for it now—to ask the questions or hear the answers. "How's Lizzy?" I ask instead.

"Pretty sad and worried," Natalie admits. "She's up in her room, but I put in some frozen pizzas for dinner. Freya and I will stay here until you or Brian comes back."

"Thank you." She is being such a good friend, I think, a

necessary reminder. Manning the home front, taking care of my oldest daughter whom I haven't spared so much as a thought for since this whole thing happened. What would I do without Natalie?

Is that a question I really want to answer?

"I'll call you later," I say abruptly, and then I hang up.

Now the only thing to do is wait for Brian. I head for the lobby, where I buy a cheap cappuccino that tastes like the machine it was made in and sip it slowly, simply so I have something to do. It's nearly seven now, and the sky has darkened to indigo, the air possessing a chill that I feel every time the automated sliding glass doors open to let someone into the hospital— a jubilant father with an *It's a Boy!* balloon, an elderly woman walking slowly with a cane, her face filled with weariness. A family, all jabbering excitedly, clearly in a good mood. A woman in a wheelchair, huffing and puffing as she pushes herself by her arms, while a surly-faced teenaged boy walks next to her.

It's like a microcosm of all of humanity, right here in the hospital—birth and death, hope and grief, loneliness and community. I watch it all play out, again and again, and I feel only numb. I don't let myself think about Bella at all.

It's nearly eight by the time I see Brian walking through the doors, and I almost sob with relief.

"Brian!" I call out, and he hurries toward me; I fall into his arms as he hugs me tightly.

"Eleanor. What *happened*?"

"Bella's been taken to Connecticut Children's Medical Center in Hartford. We need to go there."

"The Medical Center?" He releases me even though I long to cling to him, and then rakes a hand through his hair. "That sounds serious."

"It *is* serious, Brian." My voice trembles and I have to wipe my eyes. "The doctor didn't tell me that much, only that they couldn't take care of her here."

"Why not?" His voice comes out with the ring of anxiety, accusation, and I tense.

"Because they're afraid she might have some... brain damage," I whisper. "They're not sure."

His gaze, fixed on mine, widens, and then his whole face collapses as he covers it with his hands. "*No*. No, no, no..."

Seeing his grief is as bad as feeling it myself. Guilt and sorrow rush through, twin rivers of scalding emotion. "I'm so sorry, Brian..."

His shoulders shake for a moment, and then he draws a deep, shuddering breath and drops his hands from his face. When he looks at me, his eyes are dry, his expression determined. "All right," he says. "Let's go."

We don't talk very much for the hour-long trip to Hartford. It's nearing nine o'clock, and I know I should check in with Natalie. She'll have to stay the night with Freya; I should tell her where the clean sheets are, although she probably already knows. And Lizzy... I need to think about Lizzy.

"Did you talk to Lizzy?" I ask Brian. "Before you left?"

He glances at me, gives a little shake of his head. "No. I came straight here."

"We should text or call her. Just check in, you know? Make sure she's all right."

Wordlessly, he hands me his phone. I type in his passcode, only to have it rejected.

"Did you change your passcode?" I ask, and my voice wobbles. I'd put my anxiety about Brian to the back of my mind, but now it comes rushing back. *Why* has he changed his passwords and PINs? It feels like a deliberate way to shut me out... or keep something secret. I can hardly focus on that now, with Bella, and yet it remains a reality. A pressing one, even if I don't have the emotional fortitude to deal with it now.

"Oh, yeah, there was some kind of security breach." He

reaches for his phone, and with one hand on the wheel, puts his thumbprint in. Then he hands it back.

I want to believe him, but I'm not sure I do. I open his messages, and am about to type one to Lizzy, when I see the one at the top, from someone named Tina. *Today meant so much to me.*

My whole body freezes as I stare at it, trying to make it mean something else.

Brian glances over, trying to see the screen, which I have instinctively angled away from him, the same way Lizzy does with us and her phone.

"Just call her, Eleanor," he says sharply, and I swipe off the messaging app.

There is a sour taste in my mouth and my stomach churns. I don't think Brian saw that I read that text, and I don't know if I'm brave enough to confront him about it. I certainly am not about to now.

I swipe for my daughter's number, but despite everything that's happening, all I can think is: *who on earth is Tina?*

TWELVE

JOANNA

On Monday morning, I wake up with dread pooling in my stomach like acid. I don't want to take Kieran to school, but I have to work, and, in any case, he needs some normality after the events of the weekend. Not that I even know what those are, really.

After I got home, Tim and I had talked. He probably thought it was a positive conversation, and who knows, maybe it was. With Kieran ensconced in the den with the iPad, we huddled on the sofa and spoke in hushed voices.

I explained what happened at the party—Bella at the edge of the pond unconscious, Kieran standing over her, Eleanor taking her daughter in her arms.

"She screamed at us to get out," I whispered. "She clearly thought Kieran... *did* something to Bella."

"Okay." Tim absorbed this, seeming surprisingly unfazed. For a man who hadn't been able to drag himself to work for the better part of a year, he was taking this in his stride. I didn't know whether to be annoyed or gratified; I felt a bit of both.

"*Tim*," I said, when he seemed to not need to say anything

more. "Aren't you worried? What if Kieran *did* do something to her?"

Tim gazed at me, nonplussed. "What do you mean? And who's to say he did? Did anyone actually see anything?"

"I don't know…"

"Have you asked Kieran what happened?"

I hesitated and then admitted, "Not yet, I mean, it was all pretty traumatic, and I thought we should both talk to him, together."

"Well, then, let's do that."

He made it sound so simple, but the truth was I wasn't sure I even *wanted* to talk to Kieran. What if he admitted something terrible? He could, I knew; he'd always been unsettlingly honest about what he'd done, even as a small child. *Did you hit William?* I'd asked him in preschool, and he'd stared at me unblinkingly. *Yes, I did.* If he admitted to pushing Bella… what would we do then?

But Tim was determined, and I knew he was right, so we summoned Kieran and sat him down between us on the sofa, and then, in our gentlest voices, we asked him to take us through the events of the afternoon.

"How did Bella hurt herself, Kieran?" Tim asked. "Do you know?"

Kieran sat, blinking slowly, his hands clenched in his lap. He looked so young—the curve of his cheek as soft and round as a peach, his hair as blond as it was when he was a baby, just like Tim's. I felt an ache to hold him in my arms, press him close in a way he has never really let me.

"She fell," he said after a moment, his voice toneless.

"*How* did she fall?" Tim asked.

Kieran shrugged, not meeting either of our gazes, before clarifying, "She fell and hit her head." Which was really no clar- ification at all.

Why, I wondered, was he not answering the question? Was it on purpose, because he was hiding something?

"*Kieran,*" I said, my tone turning a little strident despite my best attempts to keep it gentle. "*How* did she fall? Did she trip, or...do you know if she was... *pushed?*"

He shrugged again, looking away, his hands twitching in his lap. He was hiding something, I was sure of it, and the realization filled me with fear. If Kieran had pushed Bella...

"Was it an accident, Kieran?" I asked, an ache in my voice. Surely a childish accident could be explained?

He glanced back at me, and there was a stubbornness to the set of his mouth, the sudden flash of his eyes. "No," he replied flatly, firmly. "It wasn't a mistake."

That took Tim aback as well as me, and we exchanged uneasy glances, both of us trying to hide our dismay at this rather cold-blooded revelation.

We didn't ask him any more questions after that, mainly because I don't think we wanted to deal with answers we couldn't handle. Kieran went back to his iPad happily enough, and Tim and I sat in a silence that felt frozen, like ice had been poured all over us.

"You know," Tim said after a while, "it doesn't mean that he did it. That he pushed her."

I gave him a look of blatant disbelief. "Tim, he *said* it wasn't an accident."

"I know, but..." Tim shook his head slowly. "Maybe they were playing a game or something?"

Because I wanted there to be another explanation so badly, I actually considered it for a few moments, before I remembered that Kieran and Bella were not exactly friends, and Kieran hardly ever played games with anyone. Still, I felt the need to give the idea some credence.

"Maybe..." I said, so dubiously that Tim scowled.

"Why, Jo?" he asked. "Why do you always think the worst of our son?"

I jerked back as if he'd struck me; it felt as if he had. "What is that supposed to mean?"

"Don't try to deny it. Every single time anything happens, you believe it's Kieran's fault. Automatically. Instantly." His gaze skewered mine, sharp and unrelenting. "No matter what. You *never* give him the benefit of the doubt."

I opened my mouth to argue against this, because it felt phenomenally unfair, but then I stopped, closed it, because I realized Tim had a point... and yet he didn't.

I *did* believe it was Kieran's fault, generally speaking, because it *was*. How could Tim not see that? Every time we were called into school, or the teacher cornered me at pickup, it was because Kieran had done something. There was never any debate about that; Kieran himself didn't deny it. Had we not just kept ourselves from asking him any more questions, because we didn't want to hear his honest answers?

And now, suddenly, this was about *me* and *my* lack of faith in our son?

"This isn't about me giving or not giving Kieran the benefit of the doubt," I told Tim in a level voice. "It's about reality—"

"That *is* the reality—"

"I can't believe you!" I sat back against the sofa, shaking my head. I could not believe he was turning me into the bad guy. Not, of course, that Kieran was meant to be that, but *seriously*. Me? "So what is your alternative interpretation of this particular scenario?" I asked, unable to keep a sarcastic drawl from my voice. "What do *you* think happened?"

"That's not the point," Tim replied patiently. He looked both earnest and disappointed, which was making me start to feel wretchedly guilty. Had I been doing something wrong, all along? Had I been a bad mother, by assuming it was Kieran's fault, all the time? Even when it so obviously was?

"The point," Tim continued, clearly warming to his theme, "is that you make the assumption that it is, and he knows it. How do you think that affects Kieran's behavior? If people are going to have low expectations of you, why try to raise them? Especially if your *parents* are."

"So you're saying Kieran is misbehaving because *I'm* expecting him to," I stated, disbelieving, but also hurt.

"Can you not see how that might be the case? Jo..." He hesitated, and I felt the need to brace myself for whatever came next. "You have such high expectations of everyone," he said quietly. "Can't you see that?"

I knew then that this was far less about Kieran, and much more about Tim. As much as I'd been trying to hide my frustration with his refusal to work or even engage with life, clearly I hadn't succeeded. Maybe I hadn't even wanted to; on some level, I needed Tim to understand how hard his breakdown had been for me. How impossible it becomes, when someone can luxuriate in their own mental health crisis without caring one *jot* about yours.

I rose from the sofa then, went to the kitchen, and started pulling out pots and pans to make dinner. I didn't even know what I was going to make, I just needed to feel busy. And I didn't trust myself to keep that conversation going.

Tim, however, followed me into the kitchen. He stood in the doorway, his arms folded, his expression mutinous. His blond hair was rumpled; he needed a haircut. He'd lost weight, too, I noticed; he'd always been lanky and tall, but now he was looking a little gaunt, despite having gone to the gym back in New York. "Is this not a conversation you want to have?" he asked, a faint note of truculence in his voice.

"Not particularly." My voice possessed its own edge. It felt as if we were on the cusp of an argument, and at a most inconvenient time. I took a deep breath, let it out slowly. "Tim, I think we need to focus on Kieran right now, and what happened at that party."

"We don't *know* what happened at that party," Tim returned, "or even how badly this girl got hurt. It might have just been a knock on the head."

I recalled how Eleanor had held Bella in her arms, her body bent over her. I couldn't really see Bella herself, or how hurt she was... and I so wanted to believe Tim. Believe that this could—and would—blow over.

And yet I couldn't. I couldn't make myself, so maybe Tim did have a point. Maybe I did expect the worst when it came to Kieran.

"I guess we'll find out on Monday," I said heavily.

Tim looked like he was going to say something else, but then he didn't. He walked back into the living room without a word, flopped onto the sofa. A few seconds later, the sound of baseball came on.

I closed my eyes. I was so tired of this hamster wheel we were on. Wetherby was meant to be our new start, but it certainly didn't feel like one. It felt like we were going backward, getting worse... in so many ways.

I grabbed an onion and started chopping. I still didn't know what I was going to make for dinner, but at least it was an excuse to cry.

Now it is Monday, two days after the party, and I am lying in bed, sick with dread. Sunday crawled past; I didn't hear any news about Bella, but how would I? I didn't have anyone's phone number, and no one had mine. Stuck in our house in the woods, I felt as if I had been quarantined, imprisoned.

I ended up going for a walk through the nearby woods with Kieran, who seemed unaffected by Saturday's events. He found a big stick and banged every tree he passed with it while I walked slowly, scuffing my boots through the drifts of dead leaves. There was a hint of fall in the air, the smell of woodsmoke and fallen leaves and crispness. It made me feel sad in a way I couldn't explain; I had a longing for something else, but I didn't know what it was.

I sit up now, swing my legs to the side. Tim is snoring softly next to me, completely asleep. He hasn't woken up to see Kieran off to school since before his breakdown, and it doesn't appear as if Saturday has changed anything. I rise slowly, grab my bathrobe and belt it as I head downstairs. As I spoon coffee into the coffeemaker, I wonder what will greet me at Kieran's school. What—and who—I might have to face in the schoolyard.

An hour later, I find out. My heart is thudding, and my palms are slick as I park a block away from school under the shade of a maple tree, the town as pretty and perfect as ever around me. Parents are heading toward the school; an elderly man is walking his dog. No one, thankfully, is looking at me. I wait for Kieran to climb out of the car. He doesn't seem anxious about what happened or what he might face; it's just me. I hand him his water bottle and adjust the strap of his backpack. I see my fingers tremble, and I tell myself to get a grip. If Bella really did just have a bump on the head, the relief I will feel will be enormous, overwhelming. No one will care that Eleanor shouted at me to take Kieran away, that she so clearly blamed Kieran for Bella's injury.

The second I step into the schoolyard, I know, absolutely, that it was more than a bump. While some parents seem oblivious, the ones of the third grade are standing in a circle, speaking in hushed voices like they're at a funeral. My heart drops down to my toes and then starts beating double time. Oh, no. *Oh, no...*

I rest my hand on Kieran's shoulder. "Let's just wait here, bud," I say quietly. We're still by the gate, for a quick exit, if need be.

One of the mother glances at me, her mouth dropping open

in shock, and then she turns back to the others, whispering furiously.

I feel lightheaded with anxiety, with both fear and humiliation. I keep my hand on Kieran's shoulder, even though I can tell he is itching to run through the yard, head for the big rubber tires he likes to climb on. My heart is thudding slowly, hard, heavy beats that reverberate in my chest. More whispers.

It feels like an absolute age, but is only about two or three minutes, before the door opens, and the kids race toward it and Miss Stoviak. I squeeze Kieran's shoulder. "Have a good day, bud," I whisper, my voice catching in my throat.

I watch him head off, wondering what his day will hold. Will the other kids be talking about it? About him? Does Miss Stoviak know what happened? Does everyone?

I am about to turn toward the gate when a voice, shaking with outrage and accusation, stops me in my tracks.

"Do you know that Bella is in a *coma?*"

Oh, dear heaven. I force myself to turn around even though I am desperate to race away. I don't recognize the mother who has approached me; she looks like so many others—highlighted blond hair, expensive and tight-fitting workout gear, a furious expression.

"I'm so sorry to hear that," I manage in a low voice. "Will... will she be okay?"

The woman huffs. "Did you hear what I said? A *coma.* Are people in comas *ever* okay?"

Well, actually they can be, I think, but of course don't say.

"I'm so sorry," I say again.

I wait, but the woman just glares at me, and so, after a few agonizing seconds, I finally turn away.

"This was Kieran's fault!" she calls after me as I reach the gate. "You know that, don't you? He pushed her! He's a little menace!"

I falter in my step, wanting to come to my son's defense, but

I know instinctively that engaging with this woman right now will not help me or my son.

"The police are going to get involved," she adds, like a taunt. "That's what I heard. Brian Dalton is going to call them and ask them to investigate."

The police? It's not something I even remotely considered. They're *children*; it had to be an accident, no matter what Kieran said. How can it possibly be a matter for the police?

But then I think of Eleanor's husband, who I know from Mrs. Bryson got *very* involved after the chair-pulling incident. He threatened something about the police then, as I recall, and so *now...?* When his daughter is in a coma, and he believes it's my son's fault?

This is not going to go away, I realize. Even if Bella gets better. Even if she makes a full recovery. Brian Dalton will be out for blood, and it seems as if at least half of the parents of Wetherby Elementary might be, as well. The blood of my son.

My head feels light, and my breath is coming too fast; I think I actually am going to pass out. I'm only halfway down the block, but I have to stop, crouching over with my hands on my thighs while I force myself to take shallow breaths as spots dance before my eyes.

After a few seconds, the lightheadedness passes, but the sense of despair doesn't. I long to talk to someone, I need some support, but as I run through my few friends back in New York, I already know none of them are prepared for this. I can't call any of them. Not about something like this. And I don't particularly want to tell my parents or siblings; they all, to varying degrees, find Kieran difficult already.

I take a deep breath and straighten, then keep walking.

Ten minutes later, I am back at home, working in the den. I stare at a screen full of numbers and feel blank inside. Empty. I can't even think.

Somehow, though, I start working. I usually like my work—

assessing risk, offering advice based on solid facts and figures. There are no shots in the dark with actuarial science, no hopeful guesses. There is just assurance, taken from numerical facts. Numbers have always felt safe to me, controllable and trustworthy. But I only work for a little over an hour before my cell rings, and the number is the school.

It's Mrs. Bryson, and she asks me, in a clipped voice, to come to school to "talk about Kieran," which are three words that fill me with dread.

I emerge from my office to see Tim in the kitchen, making some kind of smoothie with about twenty different ingredients. These are the sorts of things he does all day now—watch TV, make smoothies, occasionally work out or listen to a podcast, if he's feeling *productive*. It is enough to make me scream. Where is the motivated, focused man I married? Not that that is something I can dwell on now.

"That was the school," I tell him woodenly. "They want me to come in to talk about Kieran." Belatedly I realize that maybe I should have said *us*.

Tim pauses in his shredding of spinach. "About what?"

"I don't know."

"You didn't ask?"

I grit my teeth. "No. Do you want to come with me?"

Tim looks like he's on the verge of refusal; he has yet to darken the door of the elementary school. "All right," he says at last, reluctantly but with decision, and I am surprised, relieved, and anxious all at once. I realize this meeting—whatever it entails—would actually be easier without Tim. At least without Tim as he is now. The pre-breakdown Tim would have been a stalwart support, but at this point that Tim feels like a figment of my imagination. Still, I can hardly tell him any of that now.

We head out to the car and drive in silence into Wetherby. Now the peaceful Main Street feels mocking; the friendly-looking stores with their cheerful planters full of chrysanthemums a slap in the face. My stomach is a tight, knotted ball of anxiety. Why does Mrs. Bryson need to talk about Kieran? Is this about the birthday party, which is surely outside her jurisdiction, or has he acted out at school... again?

We find out just a few minutes later, both of us sitting in her little office while she stands behind her desk, looking down on us.

"I'm sorry, but you'll need to take Kieran home," she says in the firm voice of someone who has reached a decision and will not be moved. "And I am advising—not insisting, admittedly—that he remain out of school for the rest of the week."

"*What!*" Tim straightens, already looking outraged, while I feel leaden inside. I realize I was expecting something like this. I am not at all surprised.

"Could you please tell us what happened?" I ask, and I am amazed at how calm my voice sounds.

Mrs. Bryson's mouth tightens. "I'm afraid Kieran was violent with several other children. And, as you know, we cannot—"

"Tolerate such behavior," I interject before she can give me a lecture. "Yes, of course, we understand that, Mrs. Bryson." I take a quick, steadying breath. "But can we have a little more context?" Contrary to the popular opinion in this school, Kieran doesn't act out without cause. It's usually because he's frustrated. Either that or he's curious, which is a little harder to explain. When I asked him why he pulled the chair out from under Bella, he told me he wanted to see what happened. In a way, I understand it—a child's natural curiosity—but if you try to say that to a teacher, you don't get very far.

"I'm not sure any context is needed," Mrs. Bryson replies with some asperity. "The other children were not violent to him. As far as Miss Stoviak could tell, he simply lashed out at them."

Somehow, I have trouble believing that. Kieran can be challenging, but he is far from stupid, and he knows how to control himself... generally.

"Did she ask him?" Tim asks, and there is a lethal quality to his voice that makes Mrs. Bryson blink and me tense. I do *not* need Tim to come out swinging here. "Have you even *talked* to him, Mrs. Bryson—"

"Tim—" I begin, and he shrugs and falls silent.

"I talked to his teacher," she says frostily, "who informed me what has happened. And, as I have mentioned before to your wife, Mr. Walters, we have a zero-tolerance policy to any bullying or violence in this school. I was lenient before, because I knew Kieran was adjusting to a new community, but I'm afraid, for the safety of our other learners, I am going to have to be firmer now." She levels us both with a steely gaze. "Kieran is not welcome back to Wetherby Elementary until next week, and then only on a probationary basis. Any more *incidents*, and I'm afraid we will have to consider taking the necessary steps toward expulsion."

Expulsion.

It's just over a month into his first semester. In his three years at his private school in New York, Kieran was never suspended even once. Well, all right, he was *once*, but I still think that was a misunderstanding; a teaching assistant was trying to restrain him, and he hit her in the face by accident.

There seems to be nothing left to say. As we rise from our seats, Mrs. Bryson states, her voice trembling a little, "The Daltons are very respected and beloved members of our community. We are absolutely devastated by what happened to Bella."

There can be no mistaking why she chose to talk about Bella right now. She, and everyone else in this wretched school, thinks Kieran pushed her.

I think Kieran pushed her. Why wouldn't I? He was standing right over her, after all. And yet for once I don't want to let fear be the thing that guides and controls me. I think of how Tim said I always think the worst of Kieran, and I don't *want* to now, but maybe what I need to do is find out the truth.

We collect Kieran from Miss Stoviak, who is doing her best to be civil to my son but is clearly struggling; I murmur my thanks to her although I'm not sure what I'm supposed to be thanking her for. Then, back in the car, when he's buckled in the backseat and Tim and I are in the front, I twist around and stare my son full in the face.

"Kieran," I state in a tone that will brook no argument, no dissembling. "Did you push Bella into the pond? By accident or otherwise?" Next to me, Tim tenses, but he doesn't protest.

Kieran's lower lip juts out as he glares at me. "You think I did it, too?" It's clear from his tone that that was the cause of any violence this morning; the other kids must have accused him.

"I'm not saying that," I state calmly. "I'm just asking. Did you?"

Kieran glares at us both. "No," he says. "I didn't do it. I didn't push her." And then, to my complete surprise, and Tim's too, I think, he bursts into tears.

THIRTEEN

NATALIE

When Eleanor returned from the hospital at seven o'clock the next morning, she looked as if she'd aged a decade. Her skin had a grayish cast, her hair was lank, and worst of all, there was a look of utter hopelessness in her eyes.

"Brian's staying there for now," she told me, her voice lifeless. "I'm going to see Lizzy, have a shower, change my clothes, and then head back..." She shook her head slowly, as if she couldn't believe this was what her life had become.

"And Bella...?" I asked, hardly daring to breathe her name.

"She's in a medically induced coma. It's the safest way of helping her brain to heal," Eleanor explained in the same lifeless voice. "They think there might be some damage—shearing, they called it—from her head hitting the rock at the edge of the pond. Brian always wanted to remove that rock, you know..." Her voice broke on a sob, but she forced herself to continue raggedly, "But I said no. I liked it. I thought it looked *pretty*..." She dissolved into sobs then, and I hurried over to put my arms around her.

"Eleanor, I'm sorry, so sorry..." I kept saying it over and over because I had no other words.

After a few minutes, Eleanor pulled away to grab a tissue to blow her nose. "We won't know how extensive any potential damage is," she told me, her voice clogged, "until they wake her up, out of the coma. That might be days or even weeks. We're not sure." She drew a ragged breath. "And then there's the fact she was face down in the water. They don't know how long that was for, whether her brain was deprived of oxygen for a significant length of time..." Another unruly sob escaped her before she clamped her lips together. "They just don't know."

I felt utterly helpless, along with that stubborn sense of guilt. "I'm so sorry..."

"Brian wants to get the police involved," Eleanor informed me, and my stomach hollowed out. *The police?* Guilt quickly morphed into fear. "They'd have to, anyway, I think," she continued, "you know, any accident, there has to be some kind of investigation... but then there's the question of whether it *was* an accident." She looked at me meaningfully, and for a horrible second, I thought she knew. Somehow, she'd figured out what I hadn't had the courage to tell her. Yet.

"You mean..." I began in a whisper, not wanting to put it into words.

"Kieran," she confirmed, and I was filled with guilty relief. *Kieran*, not me.

"You think Kieran pushed her... on purpose?"

"He was standing right there, wasn't he? Just *looking* at her—"

"We don't know how long he was like that—" I felt morally bound to point out, even though the truth was, it was a lot better for me if Eleanor fixated on Kieran.

"No, we don't, do we?" The sudden sharpness of her tone alarmed me because I thought I knew what was coming next. "Natalie, where were you when I brought out the cake? I mean, I *asked* you—"

"Mom." Lizzy appeared in the doorway of the kitchen, her hair a tangle, her face blotchy. She rushed to Eleanor, who enfolded her in a hug.

"Hey, sweetheart. Hey, hey." She stroked Lizzy's hair as she sobbed on her mother's shoulder.

"Is Bella... is she...?"

"She's going to be okay, Lizzy." Over her daughter's shoulder, Eleanor gave me a forbidding look. Did she actually think I was about to contradict her? *Actually, Lizzy, Bella's in a coma and she might have extensive brain damage.*

"Is she really?" Lizzy pushed away from her mother, her heartbreak turning angry and accusing. "Are you just saying that?" she demanded. "Do you really *know*?"

"Lizzy—"

"Don't lie to me!" Lizzy shrilled. "Tell me what's going on!"

This felt like too personal a conversation to be a part of, and I was also aching with exhaustion after having been up for most of the night, wondering what was happening with Bella. Freya needed a change of clothes, as well, and we could both use a hot shower.

"I think I'm going to go," I murmured into the fraught silence. "But text me, Eleanor, if you need anything... *anything* at all..."

Eleanor, still staring at her daughter, nodded tersely, a hardness in her face that worried me. At that moment, we didn't entirely feel like friends.

I fetched Freya from the den, liberated her from the iPad, and then we slipped quietly from the house. I breathed a watery sigh of relief as we headed toward my car, parked in the street; as much as I wanted to be there for Eleanor, I needed to get back to my own house, my own life.

.   .   .

Freya didn't speak as I started driving home, and I glanced at her, worried, because she'd been so *silent* since Bella's accident. I'd barely got a word out of her the whole time, not that I'd tried all that hard. But I knew I should try then, because we were alone, and Freya had had a lot to process. We both had.

"Sweetheart?" I asked gently. "Are you okay?"

She gave a little twitch of her shoulders and turned to the window. I decided to leave it. Freya had never been the most talkative child; she was nearly three before she said anything recognizable, and even after that, she'd always been content to stand silently and watch. The sidelines were where Freya had always liked to exist, even as I sought, in some subtle way, to drag her into the limelight. Some people just didn't want it. It was a lesson I kept having to learn, over and over again, in relation to my daughter.

Back at the house, Freya disappeared into her room, and I halfheartedly emptied the dishwasher, folded laundry, my mind on Bella. It felt like a lifetime since I'd been back in this house, worrying about mundane things—whether we had enough milk, if Freya's gym stuff was clean, whether I'd meet the sales targets this month.

At dinnertime, my phone buzzed with a text, and I saw it was Matt, asking how the party went. In the three months since our separation, he had continued to be involved, all things considered; I was constantly lurching between bitterness and gratitude. Right then, I felt only gratitude, and I swiped to call him, because I knew I desperately needed to talk to someone who was involved, but not too involved, in this wretched situation.

"Nat?" He answered after the first ring. "How was it? Intense as usual?" The wryness in his tone made my heart ache, because yes, it had been intense, but not in the usual Eleanor way. *If only...*

"You could say that," I managed, trying to sound level and failing.

"What?" He'd clocked my tone instantly. "What happened?"

"Oh, Matt..." My voice wobbled all over the place then, as the events of the last eighteen hours finally slammed into me.

Bella... sweet little Bella.

"It was... Something has..." I gulped, unable to go on.

"Natalie." Matt sounded genuinely alarmed. "Is Freya okay?"

"Ye-es..." A sob escaped me. "I'm sorry. It's just..."

"Do you want me to come over?"

It was an hour from Danbury to Wetherby, but at that moment I knew there was nothing I wanted more. "Could you?" I whispered, feeling pathetic, because since Matt left, I've tried not to ask him for anything, and maybe even not before. Independence has always been important to me... maybe too important.

"Yes, of course," he replied firmly, and an hour later, he was there, his dark hair ruffled by the evening breeze, his cheeks flushed with cold. I half-fell into his arms as soon as I opened the door; I couldn't help it. His arms closed around me, and it felt so *good* to be held. I don't think we'd so much as touched in the three months since he had decided "we weren't working anymore," without explaining what that meant, even as I recognized the truth of it. The only snuggles I'd received had been from Freya, and right then, sexist as it might have sounded, I needed a strong man's arms around me.

"Nat..." Matt's voice was muffled against my shoulder. "What happened?"

With a shuddery breath, I eased away from him and went into the kitchen; he followed and didn't comment when I opened a bottle of red and poured us both large glasses.

"Bella fell into the pond at the party," I told him. "Eleanor thinks she was pushed by one of the other children. And... she's in a coma and might have brain damage."

It felt surreal to say it all as plainly as that, and yet there was something vindicating about Matt's gaping mouth of shock. "What..."

I took a large swallow of wine. "I know."

"What exactly happened?" he asked, and I shrugged, tears coming to my eyes as I guzzled my wine.

"I don't know, I didn't see it. No one did. Eleanor was inside, doing the cake, and I was out there watching all the other kids, but Bella just *disappeared*..." My voice wavered. This wasn't, I knew, *strictly* true, but if I kept saying it, it felt like it could become reality. I was almost starting to believe it myself.

"And why do you think she was pushed?"

I explained about Kieran—his behavior issues, how he'd been standing right there, looking down at her. It felt so easy, so *right*, to blame Kieran, and yet Matt wasn't buying it, at least not entirely.

"But no one saw anything? Did he—Kieran—say anything about what happened?"

"His mom took him home pretty much straight away. Eleanor was screaming at them to get out..." Matt winced at my words. "He's a tricky kid," I said, in Eleanor's defense.

"What about Freya?" he asked. "Surely, she saw something? She's usually glued to Bella's side. Have you asked her?"

I frowned into my glass. "I tried a little, but... she's been so quiet... I didn't want to push anything. But now Eleanor says the police are going to get involved..."

"Nat, you need to ask Freya before the police do. We need to be prepared, and so does she." Matt had that anxious, faintly censorious tone that I recalled so well from our marriage—when I came home late from work, when Freya didn't have clean clothes for school, when dinner was another frozen meal. Somehow, it always felt like my fault, which infuriated me, because this was *not* the 1950s, and I was not Eleanor.

He never actually *said* as much, it was true, but I felt it all the same. I wasn't being the kind of wife and mother his had been—clothes always ironed, a casserole bubbling in the oven, ready at the door just like Eleanor, with a glass of wine and a smile. Matt's mother managed this and a part-time job as a librarian, but the truth is, my mother was a doormat, my father a serial cheater. They're still married, retired down in Florida, my mother quietly miserable, my father enjoying the best of life. I was never going to be that kind of woman, just *taking* it all the time, and if Matt married me thinking I was, well, more fool him.

"Okay," I told Matt, because I knew he was right. "Let's talk to Freya together."

Of course, that was easier said than done. Freya hurtled out of the playroom when she heard Matt's voice, thrilled Daddy was here; he caught her up in his arms and threw her in the air while she chortled with glee, seeming far more animated than she had in *weeks*, never mind since Bella's party.

But as soon as we sat her down and talked seriously to her, her expression turned closed, mutinous, and she wouldn't meet our eyes.

"I don't know," she kept saying, shaking her head, her legs kicking the rungs of her chair. "I don't know, I didn't see anything." And then, quite suddenly it changed. "I don't want to get anyone in trouble!" Freya burst out suddenly, before she clammed right up again.

Matt and I both stilled, exchanging telling glances.

"Who, honey?" he asked. "Who don't you want to get in trouble?"

"Kieran?" I suggested, and Matt gave me a quelling look, which I returned. I knew I was putting ideas in her head, but surely, they'd already been there, at least a little?

But Freya wouldn't say another word. She simply shook her head, her mouth buttoned up tight, her eyes dark and furious. Matt and I stared at each other helplessly, and after a few more minutes of trying, we finally gave up and let her scurry off. I poured us both more wine.

"Who do you think she means?" I asked, while Matt sighed and raked a hand through his hair.

"Does it even matter? I mean, whatever happened, it was obviously an accident. We're talking about seven- and eight-year-old kids here."

"Yes..." I must not have sounded convinced because Matt frowned at me.

"What?" he asked. "Do you disagree?"

"I don't disagree that they're *kids*," I replied, "Obviously. But if the police are going to get involved... we don't really live in a world of accidents anymore, do we, Matt? I mean, every-body always wants someone to blame. Someone who they can point the finger at, someone who can be guilty while they can be exonerated."

I must have sounded particularly heartfelt, maybe even vicious, because Matt gave me an appraising look as he took a sip of his wine.

"Are you talking about Eleanor?" he asked bluntly. "You think she—and Brian—are looking for someone to blame?" He sounded a little bit like he thought that might be the case, too; I'd always known there was no love lost between him and Brian, yet I found I couldn't answer, at least not truthfully.

But I'd actually been talking about myself. *I* needed someone to blame...

Because otherwise I'd blame myself.

Matt left a little while later, with a quick hug that I tried not to savor but did anyway, and then the rest of the evening was spent getting Freya ready for bed—bath with plenty of bubbles, pajamas, stories. The smell of her strawberry shampoo in her damp hair was enough to undo me. I longed for things to be normal, to be the way they'd been, even if I was honest enough to admit I'd been more or less dissatisfied with that state of affairs. Now I had a different perspective. Freya had a bossy best friend. *So what?* Eleanor could be a bit annoying? *Big deal.* I'd take it all back right now, in an instant. On top of everything else, I felt guilty for being so petty, about so many little things.

Cuddled up together in her bed, I read Freya one of her favorite books, enjoying the feel of my daughter nestled into me, her still-damp hair tickling my cheek as she helped turn the pages. I ached to hold this moment, to keep it. But like every other, it ended. It had to.

And so I kissed her goodnight, turned off the light, and then drifted downstairs, lonelier than ever. I wanted Matt. I wanted us as we were, or even just as we'd been that night. Even though we'd separated, it had felt like we'd been a team. Sort of, anyway, but in any case, I knew I wanted something other than this—a dark house, another glass of wine, an emptiness at the center of myself. I was getting far too used to all three.

By Monday morning, when I am getting Freya ready for school, things have settled down to a tense, new normal. Eleanor has been going back and forth from the hospital with Brian, although there will be no change in Bella's condition until she's brought out of the coma, in a few days, or maybe weeks.

Last night, when Eleanor had returned to the hospital, I'd checked on Lizzy and brought a frozen lasagna I'd bought at Stop & Shop because I knew I wasn't a good enough cook for it be homemade. She'd been subdued but not tearful, and I'd done my best to be cheerful and optimistic, although, in truth, I felt exhausted and close to despair.

Now, as I hunt for Freya's sneakers, my entire body aches. I need to put in a full day's work, but I feel like crawling back into bed and pulling the duvet over my head. I don't have the emotional space or strength to think—and worry—about Bella, about Freya, about Kieran, even. What is *he* thinking and feeling right now? And what about Joanna? The stricken, horrified look on her face when Eleanor screeched at her, *just get out...*

By the time we get to the schoolyard, my stomach is churning with anxiety. I haven't even dared to open the class parents' chat since Saturday evening, although I could see from the amount of messages—numbering over a *hundred*—that it was blowing up big time. Freya and I are late, so I half-hope we won't see many people; Mrs. Bryson has a strict policy of parents not hanging around once the school day has started.

Unfortunately, she seems to have made an exception for today, or maybe parents are just flagrantly disregarding it, because there are still a dozen parents lingering by the third-grade door when Freya and I arrive, nearly five minutes late.

At the door to her classroom, Freya suddenly turns to face me, a look of something almost like panic on her face. She throws her arms around me, her face pressed into my stomach, and I feel a shudder go through her body.

"I don't want to go."

"*Freya...*" I hold her helplessly. She *has* to go to school today; I can absolutely not call in sick, not now. Personal days are not possible at the end of the month, right as everyone is scrambling to make their sales targets, and today is the thirtieth. "We'll go for ice cream after school," I tell her cajolingly. She normally does the after-school club on a Monday, but I can take time off to pick her up, have a quick ice cream, and then log another hour and a half at my desk. "Okay? Two scoops, even."

Freya blinks at me, solemn and unimpressed by my offer. For a second, I almost relent, and tell her she can go home with me. We'll have a pajama day, movies and popcorn and snuggles in my big double bed. I want to be that kind of mother, but I'm not, and without a word, Freya turns around and walks silently through the classroom door as my heart breaks, just a little. I watch her head inside before I turn around, determined to get to my desk before nine.

"*Natalie*." Nails dig into my arm as I look into the avid expression of one of the mothers in her class—Jennifer Evans, mom to twins Riley and Cooper. "Oh my goodness, we have been *talking* about what *happened*." Nearly every other word is said in breathless emphasis; I can picture the italics. "Do you know how Bella *is*? Someone said she's in a *coma*."

"Yes, medically induced," I reply woodenly. As discreetly as I can, I remove my arm from her talon-like grasp. "It's a way for the brain to heal. Until she wakes up from it, they won't really be able to assess any possible damage." Saying it out loud makes it all the more real, and I feel a desperate, clawing need to get away from this woman.

"I cannot *believe* something like *this* happened at our *school*." Her face darkens, perfectly threaded eyebrows drawn together in the semblance of a scowl, except her forehead has no furrows thanks to an aggressive regimen of Botox. "We were just saying that the school needs to take a harder line on *you-know-who*." She's dropped her voice to a whisper for no good reason, because Joanna, I imagine, is long gone, if she even showed up today, and everyone around us is listening with bat-like ears.

"I don't know if that's really the solution," I protest, a bit feebly. "Whatever happened, it was obviously an accident."

Jennifer grabs my arm again. "What *did* happen, Natalie?" she demands, her voice rising almost petulantly. "*You* were *there*. You must have seen *something*."

She waits expectantly as once again I extract my arm. "I'm sorry, I'm late for work," I mumble, and I hurry away without looking back, even though I'm afraid my response will set tongues wagging all the more.

Because the truth is, I *don't* know what happened, and there's a reason why I didn't see anything...

Which is why I'm afraid this really is all my fault.

FOURTEEN

ELEANOR

The next few days pass in a blur of sleepless nights and days spent sitting next to Bella in an uncomfortable hospital chair, with Brian and I passing like the proverbial ships, dazed and exhausted, as well as unspeaking, save for the terse exchange of salient information. *We need milk and toilet paper. Lizzy has to be picked up from soccer practice. The car needs gas. No change in Bella.*

In between, there are moments of something almost resembling normality, surreal in their mundaneness. I make Lizzy a packed lunch because there is nothing she likes in the school cafeteria on a Tuesday. I ask her how she's doing, only to have her run upstairs in tears. Natalie texts me to ask how I am, and I don't reply.

I don't reply to anyone, about anything. I simply can't, because every text feels like nosiness rather than concern, judgment rather than sympathy. I don't know how much of that is just me, and how much is real; it's become impossible to tell.

As the days blur by, I feel as if I am existing in isolation, which is both ironic and sad, considering what a close community Wetherby is meant to be. And I am—or was—right at the bustling, beating heart of it. Certainly not now, though, and maybe not ever. When tragedy strikes like a streak of lightning through the center of your life, obliterating everything in its searing path, it makes you wonder if any of those things you brandished so proudly were real. My marriage? My friendships? My so-called perfect life?

I have a lot of time to think about these things, as I sit next to Bella, the only sound in her hospital room the persistent beep of all the different monitors she's hooked up to. I stroke her hair, away from the bandage, with a single fingertip, and touch her cool, slightly clammy cheek, and wonder what is going on in her brain.

I may have a lot of time to think during these empty hours, but my mind just spins and spins in pointless circles. I do not come to a single conclusion, at least not one that I'm willing to accept.

And then there are the questions. Is Brian having an affair? Who is this Tina, whose day with my husband meant so much to her? And why does Brian seem as if he blames *me* for Bella's injury? He hasn't said as much, but I feel it, in the coolness of his gaze, the way he lapses into silences that feel tense, laden. Or is it just that I blame myself? And then I think of who else there might be to blame—where was Natalie when Kieran was luring Bella to the pond and then pushing her in? And why did Kieran push her in, in the first place?

In my mind, I've turned Kieran into a little monster, some kind of seven-year-old sadist. It's not fair or reasonable, I know, but in its own twisted way, it provides a sort of comfort, or at least a relief. *If not for Kieran...* I can hang a lot on that thought. I can exonerate all sorts of people, including myself.

And yet... where *was* Natalie? That's the question that is nagging me like a splinter in my thumb that I keep picking at but can't get out. I'd *told* her to get everyone ready for the cake, which obviously meant Bella herself, standing by the table, the radiant birthday girl ready to blow out her candles. How on earth was she able, or willing, in the *very* few minutes I was in the kitchen—because I've decided it could have been no more than three or four, *tops*—to go all the way down to the pond, presumably with Kieran, and then have him push her in? *And* be lying there unconscious for at least a minute—that's what they think now, anyway—with no one noticing? Without Natalie noticing?

Where was she?

Brian has certainly asked those questions, and he is resolved to get the police involved. I was reluctant at first; we live in a small town, and the currents ripple out forever. Do we really want to create those kinds of waves? But then I looked down at Bella lying so still and lifeless in her hospital bed, her skinny little body barely making a bump under the white sheet, and I thought, *yes, yes, we do.* It was an easier prospect to consider after I'd demonized Kieran in my mind; I pictured him luring Bella away, maybe promising he'd show her something special. I saw his face, exultant in cruelty, as he deliberately pushed her into the water. Imagining such a scene made my stomach churn, but there was something strangely satisfying about it, too.

Why I preferred that scenario to an innocent accident was, unfortunately, all too easy to understand—it offered absolution. The fact that I was in the kitchen, more than a little drunk, didn't matter then.

Did it?

Sitting next to my daughter's bed on Wednesday evening, the hospital yawning quiet and dark all around me as the first stars come out in the night sky, I wonder if it is the tragedies in life that expose us for what we really are, in all our selfishness and fear. Did I really want a seven-year-old boy, *maybe* innocent, to take the fall for this?

Brian clearly did. "You hear about these kids," he told me seriously later that night, like he was some sort of expert.

"They're little criminals, from the get-go. Maybe it's the parents, maybe it's just how they're born—"

"*Brian.*" I shook my head, exasperated by his doggedness, even though I'd been having the same sort of thoughts. "Kieran is just a normal, if excitable, little boy." Somehow, when Brian said it out loud like that, I felt myself become more reasonable.

And yet we—by agreement—still called the police that night and asked them to open a formal investigation.

"It's standard procedure," Brian assured Lizzy when she came downstairs for a banana and overheard us talking.

"The police?" Her wild, wide-eyed gaze swung between us. "You're calling the *police?*"

"Anytime something like this happens," Brian said, sounding like he'd watched too many episodes of *CSI*, "even if it is an accident, the police need to make sure they have all the facts. Just in case."

"Just in case of *what?*" Lizzy demanded, her voice turning shrill. "Dad, it really was an accident. Everyone knows that."

"Were you there?" Brian shot back, keeping his tone reasonable, if only just. "Did you see something, Lizzy?"

"No." She turned away, disgusted now as well as emotional. "Why are you even asking me that?"

"Because," Brian replied, "I want to know what happened to my daughter."

Lizzy turned to look at him over her shoulder, her expression close to a glare, except her eyes were full of tears. "I'm your daughter, too," she said, and Brian blew out an exasperated breath.

"Lizzy, I love you, but right now this is not about you—"

"Trust me," she fired back at him, "I know that."

And then she ran upstairs, the familiar sound of her feet thudding on the steps becoming the soundtrack to our home life.

Brian turned to me with an expression of mingled mystification and defensiveness. "I know she's upset, but can't she see the bigger picture here?"

"What *is* the bigger picture, Brian?" I asked. I was standing half-stooped over the kitchen island, feeling like an old woman. My eyeballs itched with tiredness and my insides felt leaden, weighed down by grief and worry. It was Lizzy's birthday in two days and I couldn't even begin to think about celebrating it.

"Knowing what happened to Bella," Brian replied as if it were a no-brainer. "How did she get by the pond? Why did no one see? What did Kieran do?"

They were all the same questions I'd been asking myself all week, but I didn't particularly like Brian asking them—or the pointed way he looked at me as he did.

"Answering those questions won't make Bella better," I said quietly.

Brian didn't reply for a long moment, and the silence felt heavy, oppressive. I'd been wiping the counter, but after a full minute of nothing but his breathing, I forced myself to look up and meet his stonily assessing gaze.

"Brian..."

"Don't you want to know?" he asked quietly. "Or is there a reason why you might not?"

For a second, I could only look at him, my breath caught in my chest, hurting my lungs. "What..." I had to lick my lips, start again. "What exactly are you saying, Brian?"

He shook his head, shrugging his words aside as if they hadn't just been daggers poised to thrust straight into my heart. "I don't know. I don't know. I just..." He blew out a breath. "I want to know."

I accepted his hasty backtracking because I didn't want to deal with the alternative. I'd kept this family safe and happy for *fifteen years*. I'd failed once, I knew that, and Brian clearly did too, but did it invalidate everything I'd done before? Everything I'd been?

If Bella had brain damage, then yes, I feared it did.

The police come at eight o'clock the next morning. We kept Lizzy back from school, which made her furious. She stormed around the kitchen during breakfast, slamming the refrigerator door or her cereal bowl onto the counter, fuming as she poured cornflakes or milk.

I've been sitting at the table, drinking my coffee even though my stomach already felt as if it were filled with acid. Brian had been right. I didn't want to know what had happened. I liked the cartoon-villain version I'd settled on in my mind instead.

I don't know either of the plain clothes officers who come to the door, which surprises me because I genuinely thought I knew almost everyone in this town. But the Latina woman who appears, with her smooth, blank face and carefully styled waves of dark hair, and the red-headed, fortyish man who accompanies her, all somber geniality, are strangers to me, and that makes me not trust them, even though the police are surely the people whom I should, by the very nature of their profession, trust.

We sit in the living room, on the expensive sofas of cream velvet that we hardly ever use because I'm always worried they'll get stained. I offer coffee and then wonder if I shouldn't have when both of them politely refuse.

"So." The woman gives us a perfunctory, professional smile. "I'm Daniela Martinez, and this is my partner, Rory Scott." The man nods at us in greeting. "I'm so sorry to hear what happened to your daughter Bella. Why don't you take us through the events of the day?"

This delicately worded suggestion is met with what feels like a brick wall of silence that we have all just slammed into. No one speaks.

After quite a few seconds of this, Daniela raises her

eyebrows. "I know this might be hard," she continues in the same careful voice, "but it's important for us to develop a picture of what happened before Bella was injured." She turns to me, and I try not to shrink back. "Eleanor, why don't you take me through the day, as far as you can remember?"

"Um, all right." My voice sounds thin. "When do you want me to start?"

She gives a little shrug. "Why not at the beginning? Tell me about this party."

The *party*? Why do I feel like I am the one not just being questioned, but *suspected*, all of a sudden? I feel the blood rush to my face, and I do my best to will it back.

"Well... I'm not sure how relevant some of this is, but... my friend Natalie and I were getting ready for the birthday party from about noon..." I trail off, unsure how much detail to go into. How can this possibly matter?

"And what was Bella doing at this time?"

"She was upstairs with her best friend, Natalie's daughter, Freya."

"Did she seem excited? Happy in herself?"

"What?" These are not the questions I expected. "Yes, I mean, it was her birthday."

Daniela smiles. "Just trying to get a full picture."

"Okay..." I swallow. Tell myself to stop feeling like I'm being interrogated. Of course I want to know what happened. I want these police officers to get to the bottom of this. "Well, we set up the food and games and so on, and then Bella and Freya came down when the first guests started to arrive."

"And how did she seem then?"

I stare at her blankly. I realize I can't remember, and that might have something to do with the fact that I'd guzzled a strong gin and tonic minutes earlier. I feel my face heat again. "I was a little distracted by everything going on," I tell the two officers, "but she seemed fine. Happy, I mean." *Didn't she?* I am starting to doubt myself, for no good reason.

Bella wasn't *worried* about anything, was she? I cast my mind back to that frenetic afternoon, and I can't recall interacting with Bella at all. I must have hugged her, kissed the top of her head, wished her a happy birthday. I *must* have... I just don't remember.

"All right," Daniela resumes after a pause when I realize I've simply been staring into space. "And once the guests arrived... were any children seeming anxious? Unhappy?"

"Honestly? I'm not sure." My voice rises a bit stridently. "I had twenty-eight children in my backyard. I wasn't keeping tabs on all their moods. We were just trying to keep them all occupied."

"We? You and Natalie?"

"Yes, and Lizzy after a while." I glance at my daughter, who has her arms wrapped around herself, her gaze distant and unfocused.

Daniela raises her eyebrows again in a way I am starting not to like. "So, besides you, Natalie, and Lizzy, were there any other adults present?"

Her tone is so innocuous, I know it must hide judgment. Two adults for twenty-eight children. Is that even *legal*?

"Umm..." I have to swallow because my throat is so dry. "No."

Daniela's eyebrows inch up a little higher. "That must have been kind of tough to manage."

"Well, not really. We had games on the lawn, and I'd hired an entertainer to do balloon shapes..." I trail off, trying to catch Brian's eye to give him a pointed glance. Why is he letting her interrogate me like this? This has nothing to do with Kieran pushing Bella into the pond.

But Brian isn't meeting my eye, and then I notice the set of his lips, something almost like a smirk, except it's too resentful for that. I see the tamped-down fury in his eyes and, with a jolt like an electrical shock, I realize what this is. This isn't about finding out what Kieran did or didn't do. This is about punishing me because I failed. Because I didn't keep the plates spinning, the balls in the air. Everything fell down with a mighty crash, and it's all my fault.

And Brian, my wonderful husband who was out with someone called *Tina*, wants me to know it.

FIFTEEN

JOANNA

The week of Kieran not being at school ends up, against all my expectations, being a poignantly sweet time. A time out of time, which maybe is the reset we all needed. It started, strangely enough, with Kieran's tears.

Tim and I had both stared at him for a second, gaping, because I don't think either of us could remember the last time Kieran had cried, like any other overwrought little boy. We'd seen him enthusiastic about baseball or spaghetti and meatballs for dinner, avidly intent while playing on the iPad or reading one of his fact books, or most often, blank-faced, his expression an unsettling mix of indifference and boredom. But noisy, gasping sobs that tore through his chest? It was, in its own strange way, heartening.

"Kieran." I unbuckled my seat belt so I could lean over to take him into my arms, but he, in typical Kieran fashion, twisted away. I didn't let it deter me. "Sweetheart, please talk to us. Can you tell us what happened?"

But Kieran's moment of vulnerability had passed, like a cloud or a shadow, and he wiped his grimy face, shook his head, and then turned his face to the window, a sign I knew well and one that meant we would not get another word out of him.

Back at home, Tim and I had another whispered conference, huddled together on the sofa.

"This is good news, right?" Tim said. "Kieran didn't do it."

"Kieran *said* he didn't do it," I corrected, and Tim scowled.

"Jo, come *on*. You believe him, don't you? I mean, he *never* cries like that."

"I know." I was silent, apprehensive but also hopeful, because like Tim I'd been moved by our son's tears. And yet... something still didn't feel right. "There's something he's still not telling us, though. I'm sure of it."

He shrugged, the movement dismissive. "Maybe he knows who did it, and he doesn't want to rat them out."

"Bella's in a *coma*, Tim—"

"Yes, and we're talking about seven- and eight-year-olds messing around, causing accidents." He shrugged again, his eyebrows lifting. "Who cares who did it? Whoever it was, they didn't mean to. It's not like the culprit is going to be prosecuted."

I hesitated, because I didn't want to cause Tim any more anxiety, and yet I knew it had to be said. "This morning, at drop-off, one of the other mothers said the Daltons were calling the police."

"*What?*" Tim's eyebrows drew together as he leaned forward, his hands pressed between his knees. "The police?"

"I don't know if it's true or not, but, Tim, we have to be prepared."

"For *what?*"

"That there might be some... some kind of investigation." Just the words were enough to cause a visceral shudder to go through me. "They'll probably want to question Kieran, and maybe even me, at the very least."

Tim closed his eyes and breathed in and out slowly, a technique his therapist had taught him to ease anxiety. Many evenings in the last year, I'd come home from a long day at work to find Tim cross-legged on the sofa, practicing his breathing— no dinner made, Kieran having spent several hours on screens, the laundry still wet in the washer. I knew, in theory at least, that someone suffering from anxiety and depression had a genuine illness. I knew and accepted that, and I sympathized, especially at the beginning, when Tim had clearly been unwell —not sleeping, his eyes red-rimmed, his face pale, his body gaunt. Yet somehow it had all started to feel different a few months on, when he was able to spend hours working out at the gym, as well as watching sports and surfing the internet, all in the name of mental well-being.

I did my best to banish those thoughts as I waited for Tim to finish his breathing exercise. He opened his eyes, and I could tell his calm had been restored. "Then," he said, in the tone of a great pronouncement, "we'll take that as it comes."

"Okay." I suddenly felt too tired to argue about it with him, and in any case, I didn't even want to think about the police. And, as it turned out, Tim was right, and it was wise to take it as it came, because we ended up having four days of freedom that were incredibly sweet. I took the time off work, citing personal issues, which I never did, but I felt reckless and desperate enough to need to.

We decided to become tourists, avoiding everyone and exploring this corner of Connecticut that we'd never really been to before, visiting the Railroad Museum, as well as the Museum of Minerals and Mining Science, Salisbury's General Store and O'Hara's Landing Marina, where we rented a canoe and paddled on the placid waters of the Twin Lakes.

We *never* did this kind of stuff; pre-breakdown, we'd both been too busy, and post it, Tim hadn't been willing to do anything. And, it had to be said, I wasn't confident managing

Kieran on my own on a big day out. But somehow, during this week out of time, we all pulled together—and it was fun.

Kieran was fascinated with the minerals and the trains and spent hours poring over a set of semi-precious gemstones we bought him from the museum's store. He loved canoeing as well, gliding through the water, his face screwed up in concentration as he did his best to paddle.

Yes, there were blips; he was, after all, only seven. There was one of his enraged episodes when he couldn't make some stupid arcade game work outside the general store. He slammed his hands down so hard on the machine that the whole thing rattled, and the store manager came out and told us, quite severely, that it was an antique. When we had to return the canoe because our fixed rental time was over, Kieran was furious and slapped his paddle in the lake, spraying all three of us with surprisingly frigid water.

But those were only blips. When I looked back on those days, it was as if the hours were soaked in sunlight, when everything felt possible, *blissful*, and we didn't have to think about Bella, or Wetherby Elementary, or anyone or anything, but the three of us, cocooned in our little bubble of isolation. Then, the fact that we had no friends in this town felt like a blessing rather than a curse. No one missed us.

I could keep myself from worrying—too much—about what all the other parents were saying about us. When we didn't see anyone, it was so much easier to forget, at least for a little while, that our lives had been completely upended—or worse.

It was only in the middle of the night, when I woke up with a gasp, my heart racing and my eyes straining in the dark, that I realized I couldn't forget at all—not Kieran's potential guilt, not the whispers of all the other parents, and certainly not an innocent little girl lying in a coma.

In any case, it didn't last.

On Friday, the police come. They turn up unannounced at

our door at eight o'clock in the morning, which is already unnerving. Tim and Kieran are both still in their pajamas, and the only reason I am dressed is because I have to go back to work. I put down my coffee cup as the doorbell rings, my stomach hollowing out because no one has rung our doorbell since we moved here, save for the Amazon delivery guy, and it's surely too early for that.

As I walk toward the front door, I see that there are not one, but two people, standing on the doorstep.

"Tim." My voice is hushed, tense. "Tim, get dressed."

"What..." He falls silent as he sees the two silhouettes.

I think already we both know who it is, and yet as I open the door and Daniela Martinez introduces herself and her partner, I still feel winded with shock.

"Come in," I tell them, all careful politeness, as I step aside so they can enter. I cast a quick eye around the living room, noticing the dirty coffee cups on the side table, the newspapers on the floor, Kieran's dirty clothes from last night in a heap at the bottom of the stairs. I'm usually diligent about housework— before the breakdown, Tim and I split all the household chores fifty-fifty—but these last few days, I've let things slip. Now I think how slovenly it looks. How suspect.

"We're here with regards to Bella Dalton," Daniela states without preamble as they take seats in the living room.

I sweep newspapers aside and quickly take the coffee cups to the kitchen before taking a seat. Tim has hightailed it upstairs to get dressed, and Kieran is in the den.

"Yes, of course," I say, amazed at how calm I sound. "How is she?"

"I'm afraid I can't answer that question," Daniela replies with a small, apologetic smile. "HIPAA compliance, you know."

I, of all people, know about the Health Insurance Portability and Accountability Act, which prohibits anyone from revealing a person's medical information. As an actuary who works in health insurance, I am intimately acquainted with it. Now I just nod in acceptance, tuck my hands in my lap, and wait for Daniela Martinez to ask me something.

"We're just trying to get all the information we can about the day of the party," she explains, her tone conversational but with a hint of hardness underneath. "To build up a picture of what happened, and how."

"Of course." Another nod, and even a small smile, although inside I feel cold and trembly. If they start asking Kieran questions, I have no idea what he'll say, or, more alarmingly, how he'll come across. He can seem so *cold* sometimes. I don't think that kind of attitude in a seven-year-old will impress the police, but it's just how he is. How I was, as a child, too—self-contained, seemingly unemotional. I understand it in myself, but it's still unnerving to see in your own offspring.

"I understand from some other parents that Kieran has had some difficulties adjusting to his new school?" Daniela asks, her tone matter-of-fact rather than sympathetic, and I stiffen.

Where did she get that information?

"I wouldn't say that," I tell her, and now my tone sounds cool, even though I'm trying to stay friendly.

"No?" She makes a face that is a parody of surprise, before she glances down at the notepad she's taken out and rested on her lap. "Wetherby Elementary's principal, Helen Bryson, told me she's had to call you into school five times in the first month of school in regard to Kieran's behavior."

I resist the urge to close my eyes. "I'm sorry, but I'm failing to see what this has to do with Bella's accident at the party?"

"When you arrived at the party, where was Kieran?" Daniela asks. Her voice has turned hard; clearly, the gloves are off.

"He was standing by the pond, near Bella." I have no inten-

tion of lying about anything. I have nothing to hide. I don't think
Kieran does, either. *Or at least, not much.*

"Eleanor Dalton believes Kieran pushed Bella into the
pond."

Daniela speaks calmly, matter-of-factly, and it feels like a
slap in the face, a punch to the gut. It sounds like she believes
Eleanor, before she's even spoken to me—or Kieran. Is this how
everyone thinks? I know it's what Eleanor more or less said on
the day of the party, and it's what the mothers standing in the
schoolyard hissed at me on Monday... but to hear it from the
police...

Still, I manage to hold my nerve, as well as Daniela's gaze.
Her partner, Rory, hasn't said a word; the expression on his face
is open and affable, his large hands loosely clasped together. If
he's playing the good cop, I think resentfully, he could try a little
harder. "Did she *see* him push her into the pond?" I ask, my
voice level.

"No." Daniela admits this without any embarrassment or
apology for how hard she's coming across. "She did say when
she came upon the scene, Bella was face down in the water, and
Kieran was standing over her."

"I know that. At least, I believe it," I amend because I don't
actually *know* very much at all. "I arrived basically at that
time—"

"And what did you see?"

"Eleanor was running toward Bella, and Kieran was
standing nearby." I feel proud of myself for getting through all
this without a tremor, but I am wondering when I should
mention that Kieran has said he didn't do it... and that I believe
him. But will they believe me?

"Is Kieran here, Mrs. Walters?" Daniela asks.

I tense. "Yes—"

"We'd like to ask him a few questions."

"He's *seven*." My voice comes out sharp.

I glance up the stairs, wishing Tim would hurry up and come downstairs. I need some support, some strength, because these questions are starting to take it out of me; I feel my composure beginning to fray.

"Yes, and we'll certainly take that into consideration," Daniela replies calmly. "We're trained in questioning children, and it's important to remember that we're just trying to establish the facts here."

"It *sounds*," I tell her, knowing I sound far too frosty but unable to keep myself from it, "like you've taken Eleanor Dalton's word about what happened and are trying to incriminate my son."

I know immediately that I've said the wrong thing, because Daniela's expression freezes, and then her eyes turn flinty. "I assure you," she states in a decidedly cool voice, "that we are just attempting to find out the facts. The *truth*." She pauses to let that sink in for a moment before continuing. "By law, we are allowed to interview your son, as long as a guardian or parent is present."

I feel my hands curl into fists, and I force them flat on my lap.

"You know," I tell her, and now my voice trembles, "we moved to Wetherby because after life in New York, we wanted to live in a small, welcoming, accepting community. But since we got here, it's been the polar opposite. *No one's* been friendly."

I think of Rachel and feel a flash of guilt for writing her off, but it's not like she was actually my friend or anything. It was all just a possibility, one that feels remote now.

"I know Kieran's had some difficulties at school," I continue, my voice starting to wobble, "but what seven-year-old boy hasn't?" I sniff, tellingly, as I cling to my composure. "But since this party," I tell the two officers, and now my voice hardens, "it feels like the entire class—or, really, all the *parents*—want to make him some kind of... of bad seed. The scapegoat for whatever happened." I think of the women's angry faces in the schoolyard—eyes narrowed to slits, mouths pursed up like prunes, manicured fingers pointing. On some level, I think, they were *relishing* it. "He's just a little boy, you know?" I end on something between a whisper and a whimper. "Like any other little boy."

I stare down at my lap, blinking back sudden, unwanted tears.

To my surprise, when I force myself to look up, I see that Daniela's expression has softened in a way that seems genuine.

"I understand that, Mrs. Walters," she says gently. "And I'm sorry you've had such a hard time. We really do just want to ask him a few questions."

Fortunately, Tim chooses that moment to come briskly down the stairs. He's freshly shaven, his blond hair brushed back, and he's wearing a pressed button-down shirt and khakis, the kind of clothes I haven't seen him in in months. I feel a wave of relief crash over me like a tsunami; right now, this is the Tim I remember, the husband I fell in love with—smart, focused, relaxed and confident.

"Officers?" He holds out a hand for them to shake in turn. "I'm Tim Walters, Joanna's husband and Kieran's dad. How can we help you?"

I want to both weep and laugh at the performance he's putting on—confident without being arrogant, assertive without being annoying.

He joins me on the sofa, offering a brisk smile of inquiry as he puts his arm around me. I resist the urge to burrow my head into his shoulder.

Daniela doesn't miss a beat. "We were just talking about

events of the day of the party, leading up to Bella's injuries," she says smoothly. "I don't believe you were present?"

Ouch. I try not to flinch while Tim speaks just as easily as Daniela. "No, Joanna picked him up from the party, but, of course, we talked about what happened, went through it all together. What is it exactly that you want to know?" He raises his eyebrows, alert and poised.

"We were hoping to talk to Kieran," Daniela tells him mildly. "Since he might be the only one who really knows what happened."

"Of course," Tim replies. "Jo can go get him from the other room." The slightest of pauses. "He spoke to us already, you should know, and told us that he didn't push her. He was pretty upset about it, actually. Burst into tears."

"Oh?" Daniela's tone gives nothing away. "Did he tell you how she happened to come by her injuries?"

"No," Tim admits without a flicker. "He refused to say anything. I suppose he might not have seen who might have done it, or maybe—here's an idea—Bella fell in without being pushed at all?" He cocks his head, his narrowed eyes turning shrewd. "It would be a tragedy upon the one that's already happened, don't you think, to see a crime where none was committed?"

I am jolted, because I realize since this whole thing began, I have not thought for one second that Bella just fell in. Why on earth not? Why was I so quick to jump to conclusions? Why was *everybody*—about my son? Eleanor certainly did, and the other mothers were all too eager to follow suit. I suppose I was too panicked and shell-shocked to question the narrative, but is there any reason—any reason at *all*—not to think that Bella might have been balancing on a rock all by herself, and just fell in?

It really was an accident, in the truest sense of the word. The idea is so startlingly simple, I almost feel like laughing.

There's an answer here, an answer that satisfies the conundrum, that means nobody at fault.

Doesn't it?

Daniela, however, looks unimpressed by Tim's suggestion. "Why don't you go get Kieran?" she asks, and wordlessly I rise from the sofa to find my son.

SIXTEEN

NATALIE

Eleanor gives me some warning, at least. On Friday morning, less than a week after the party, she texts me with the short and seemingly terse message: *The police want to speak to you.* As I stare down at those seven alarming words, my stomach hollows out, the sip of coffee I just took sloshing around queasily.

I knew there had been murmurs and whispers about the police opening an investigation. Parents had talked about it in hushed voices in the schoolyard, some seeming horrified, others almost seeming to relish the drama. Nothing this *exciting* had happened in Wetherby in years, I supposed; certainly nothing like this happened when I was a kid at this school.

But the police? For an *accident*? Some people were saying an investigation was standard procedure; others mentioned Brian and how he was "out for blood." I told myself they were just stoking the fire, piling on the drama, but the whole thing made me nervous. I didn't want to talk to the police.

As I stare down at that terse text from Eleanor at eight o'clock on Friday morning, I realize she hasn't contacted me in days. I scroll back to see her last message—Tuesday, in response to mine, saying there has been no news about Bella. I've sent her at least a text a day, just checking in, trying to be a good friend, but Eleanor has blanked me. I didn't really notice, with so much else going on, and in any case, I know she has much bigger things to worry about than texting me a reply. And yet... I feel the silence now, like an ominous, physical thing. Not a good sign.

I tell myself there's no reason to be nervous. I've asked Freya a few times about what happened, if she saw anything, but she's refused to talk, getting upset if I mention it, and so for the last few days we've subsided into a silent sort of truce. We spent an hour making a glittery get well card for Bella, which I keep meaning to drop by Eleanor's, but I haven't yet. Maybe she's not the only one who has gone silent; I have, too.

The doorbell rings, and my stomach clenches. The police here, *already*? It's barely past eight, and I'm meant to drive Freya to school in just a few minutes. This is not a good time.

Freya looks up from the kitchen table where she has been silently ploughing through her bowl of Cheerios. "Who's at the door?"

"I don't know, honey." I try to smile, but my lips tremble, and my heart has started thudding way too hard.

I go to open the door, and even though they're in plain clothes, I can tell by their serious faces and squared-off stances that they must be the police, and, sure enough, they are. The woman introduces herself as Daniela Martinez, shows her badge and asks if they can come in for a "couple of questions." Her partner, who gives me a silent nod, is Rory Scott. He has reddish hair and an affable manner that doesn't fool me.

"Yes, of course," I say as graciously as possible, "but I need to drive my daughter to school in a few minutes."

Daniela Martinez's gaze immediately tracks to Freya, who has come to stand in the doorway of the kitchen, one skinny leg wrapped around the other as she sucks the end of her braid.

"We'd like to talk to Freya, too," she states, more of a directive than a question. "But we shouldn't take up too much of your time."

I glance between Freya, whose eyes are wide and dark behind her glasses, to the two police officers filling my doorway. "Okay," I say slowly, and usher them into my house. What else can I do?

I lead them into the living room, with its L-shaped sectional sofa and one big squashy armchair by the fireplace that Matt and Freya used to curl up in for stories. He was always such a great bedtime story reader; it's something I know Freya really misses. He'd put on funny voices, and read with such emotional flair, while I usually descend into a monotone whether I mean to or not. Looking at that armchair makes me miss Matt, and no more so than in this moment, with the police in my house and Freya looking terrified.

"Um, please sit," I say, gesturing to the sofa. I perch on the edge of the armchair and beckon to Freya; she comes slowly, dragging her feet, and I put my arm around her, pull her in close before giving Daniela a perfunctory smile. "How can I help?"

She has, in TV show fashion, flipped open a little spiral-bound notebook and consulted whatever she's scribbled there. "It's my impression," she begins, raising her head to look at me, "that you were the only adult in attendance in the backyard at the time when Bella Dalton sustained her injuries?"

I swallow and nod. "Yes, that's correct." Unconsciously, I have matched her formal tone.

"Where were you specifically in the yard at the time of the accident?"

"Um, I was by the patio, I think." I'm worried I sound like I don't actually know what I'm talking about, which, of course, I don't. "Eleanor had asked me to gather all the children together there so she could bring out the cake."

"And was Bella on the patio with you, at that time?"

Obviously not, I think, and have to bite my lip before I trust myself to speak in the same matter-of-fact voice.

"Well, she *was*, I mean... I'd asked her to come, you know, to... to be there when Eleanor brought the cake out." I am sounding flustered, which I hate, but I don't know how to stop. "And I remember seeing her standing by the table, but... at some point, I suppose when I was dealing with the other children, she must have slipped away."

"You didn't notice her leave?" Her voice is toneless.

"No."

"And when Eleanor brought the cake out, she mentioned that she couldn't see you anywhere? Were you on the patio then?"

I fight a flush. "I suppose I must have been."

Daniela raises her eyebrows. "You *suppose*?"

"Well..." I swallow. I am coming dangerously close to lying, to the *police*, which is not a smart thing to do. I should just admit it, I realize. If I don't, it will look far worse for me. And yet a few nights ago, after a glass of wine, I did a panicked Google search and saw that I could potentially be sued for negligent supervision of a child.

The law states, according to the website I frantically scrolled through, that failure to protect a child from emotional or physical harm from another child counts as negligent supervision. The case against me would hinge on whether I had duty of care, since I'm not Bella's guardian or parent, a fact which first brought relief and then alarm when I read that a duty of care is considered to exist if the adult in question believed themselves to be in charge at the time of the incident. Whether it was right for me to be or not, I know that's what Eleanor expected, what I believed.

And yet the injustice of it burns. Eleanor spent almost the whole party—for her own *daughter*—hiding out in the kitchen, maybe even sneaking another gin and tonic. Why was I put in charge? Why did I allow myself to be?

The answer, I know, is because I have *always* let Eleanor call the shots in our friendship, from the first day we met and she took me under her wing, declaring that since Freya and Bella got along, so should we. It is, I recognize, the same dynamic that exists between our daughters.

I can analyze why for as long as I want, and come up with any number of unpalatable truths, but it doesn't change the simple fact that I knew I was in charge, and I failed in my duty of care.

"Mrs. West?" Daniela prompts, and I realize I have been simply staring into space for some time, probably looking fairly wretched. "Were you on the patio or not?"

"Mommy was over by the bush, on her phone," Freya whispers into the taut silence, and it feels as if the very air suddenly pulses with an electrical charge—a jolt of sudden comprehension that comes onto the officers' faces that makes me feel faint.

"On her phone," Daniela repeats, her tone dangerously neutral. She turns to me and waits.

"I did take a call very briefly." I have to squeeze the words out through a too-tight throat. "While Eleanor was putting the candles on the cake. The children were all sitting, waiting for her to come out..." I can't keep a pleading note from entering my voice. Isn't that understandable? They were all quiet, expectant. No one was acting out. The call was important, the client I'd been waiting for all afternoon. I had missed two calls already. What was I supposed to do?

"Where was this bush, where you took this call?" Daniela asks.

"Not that far away," I reply quickly. Too quickly.

"It was the big one with prickles," Freya interjects.

"The holly bush on the far side of the patio," I confirm.

Of course Freya is choosing *now* *to* speak up. She's been virtually mute for four days, but when the police turn up, she sings like a canary? I almost want to laugh, except I know this is absolutely no laughing matter. Could I go to *jail* for this? According to the website I looked up, negligent supervision could potentially count as child endangerment, which is classed as a felony and carries a maximum jail sentence of ten *years*.

I can't believe I might go to jail for taking a phone call.

But surely that is the absolute worst-case scenario... Eleanor wouldn't *prosecute*, would she? I think of the other mothers whispering about how Brian is out for blood, and my stomach clenches. She might not, but he certainly could. Is that why she's gone silent on me?

"It's right by the patio," I explain more forcefully. "I could keep an eye on all the children while I spoke on the phone." Not that I'd been looking all that closely; I'd been desperately trying to salvage a sale I could tell I was losing, because I'd been distracted by Bella's stupid party.

Again, the injustice of it all burns like acid in my stomach, crawling up my throat.

"So," Daniela resumes after a moment, "while you were on the telephone, did you see either Bella Dalton or Kieran Walters leave the patio?" Her eyes seem to bore into mine as I swallow dryly.

"No, I didn't."

"But they must have, correct?"

I feel like I'm on a witness stand. "Yes, they must have," I agree, an edge entering my voice. "Clearly. I did my best to keep my eye on all the children, but I had an important work call that I had to take, and they were all sitting down, waiting for their cake. It didn't feel like an inopportune moment, and Eleanor was about to come out."

"When did you realize Bella was missing?"

"I heard Eleanor scream, and then I came running."

"Had you finished your call?"

"I was just wrapping it up, but I ended it, of course, when I heard her scream."

Daniela writes something in her notebook, and I am itching to know what it is. "Do you know how long you were on the phone, Mrs. West?" she asks as she looks up. "It could be an important way of determining the exact window of time when Bella might have sustained her injuries."

I am trying not to see the direct correlation she seems to be making—that me being on my phone led to Bella's accident. "Not long," I assure her. "A few minutes at most...?"

Her gaze, boring into mine, feels relentless. "I imagine it's logged on your phone," she remarks pleasantly. "Why don't you check?"

There's nothing I can do but rise from my chair and go fetch my phone from the kitchen. My hand is slick with sweat as I swipe for the call's log. As I glance down at the number, my stomach swoops, and I am hardly able to believe it.

Six minutes. Six whole minutes—and twenty-four seconds —that I was on the phone, and Eleanor was inside the house. It's no time at all, and yet it's an absolute age. It's long enough for Bella and Kieran to go down to the pond, and for Kieran to push her in.

I feel a pressure in my temples as tears gather behind my lids. This is not going to look good. This is not going to look good at *all*.

Silently, I return to my chair. Daniela raises her eyebrows.

"Six minutes," I inform her tonelessly. "And twenty-four seconds. You can check yourself if you want." I hold my phone out like a challenge, but she shakes her head.

"That won't be necessary at this point."

At *this* point? At what point will it be? I feel as if my life, my whole future, is disintegrating before my eyes. I want to scream, weep, rail, sob. *This can't be happening.* And yet it is.

"All right," I say after a second's pause, and I return my phone to my lap. I put my arm around Freya and draw her close, anchoring her to my side. What will happen to her if I go to jail? Matt will take her, presumably. Will he move back to Wetherby? How will Freya hold her head up in this insular place, with her mother in prison? How will she possibly *thrive*?

I'm starting to hyperventilate with panic. Am I really going to be blamed for Bella falling into the pond? *Prosecuted*? And what if Kieran really did push her? The thought galvanizes me.

"Have you questioned the Walters family?" I ask, a little sharply. "Kieran's parents? Because Eleanor believes—I think *everyone* believes—that he was the one who pushed her into the pond."

"We talked to them yesterday," Daniela replies. Her tone gives absolutely nothing away.

"I'm just saying," I persist, afraid I'm digging a hole for myself but needing to say—to do—*something*, "that he's had some behavioral issues that the school has documented—"

"All the more reason, wouldn't you say, to have kept a close eye on him?" Daniela returns evenly.

Something in me snaps. "It wasn't *my* child's birthday party," I reply tightly. "I came to help out a friend, that was all. And Eleanor spent almost the whole afternoon in the kitchen and left *me* in charge."

Daniela's eyes narrow. "Why was that, do you think?"

No matter what danger I'm in right now, I can't make myself admit that Eleanor had been drinking. Besides, I'd have to admit that I'd been drinking, too, and that is a whole other variable I don't need to bring into the equation right now.

"I don't know," I tell Daniela, flinging up my hands, "but it wasn't what I was expecting—or wanting, frankly. I certainly thought she'd be more involved with the kids." Even saying that much makes me feel guilty, like I'm turning Eleanor in. "I'm just saying..." I swallow. "It's not illegal to take a phone call."

"No one has said it was," Daniela replies. I feel like my little protest has not helped my case at all. Her gaze moves to Freya. "May we ask you a few questions, Freya?"

Freya stares at her, wide-eyed and wordless. She doesn't answer.

"What kind of questions?" I ask, drawing her a little closer to me. "I really don't think Freya saw anything. Kieran and Bella were off by themselves. The pond isn't even visible from the patio." Belatedly, I wonder if this further incriminates me, but I am past caring. The need to protect my daughter is fierce.

"Were you friends with Bella?" Daniela asks, gentling her tone in a way that feels fake.

Slowly Freya nods.

"And what about Kieran?"

Freya makes no reply, but this doesn't seem to deter Daniela.

"Did you see them leave the patio?"

Again, Freya makes no reply. She simply stares at Daniela, her face expressionless, her dark braids framing her pale cheeks. She presses more deeply into me, her cheekbone grinding into my shoulder, hard enough to hurt.

I glance at the other officer, Rory Scott, who has not spoken this whole time. He is sitting in a relaxed pose, his hands clasped loosely in his lap, but his gaze is narrowed and alert. I wonder what his purpose is. Is he quietly assessing our body language, discerning if and when we're lying?

"Freya?" Daniela prompts. "Did you see them leave the patio?"

Freya turns her head away from the officers, into my shoulder. Her refusal to speak isn't all that unusual, considering her selective mutism, but I don't feel like explaining that to these officers. Still, I'm worried she thinks Freya's stubborn silence means she's hiding something.

"I don't think Freya saw anything," I state firmly, even

though I know instinctively I should probably stay as silent as Freya on this one. "I'm pretty sure she was on the patio the whole time."

Daniela raises her eyebrows. "How could you know that, Mrs. West, if you were on the phone?"

"I was keeping an eye out," I retort, unable to keep from sounding defensive.

"But by your *own* admission, you didn't see either Bella or Kieran leave the patio." She turns back to Freya. "Freya? Were Bella and Kieran arguing about something?"

Talk about a leading question. I force myself to stay silent and after an agonizing few seconds, Freya finally mumbles something that we all strain to hear.

"Freya?" Daniela asks, gentling her tone once more. "Can you say that again, please, honey?"

Freya pushes harder into my shoulder, her face screwed up, her eyes scrunched up. "Bella was being mean," she says, each word coming out in a suffocated little gasp. "To... to Kieran."

I stare at her in stupefaction. *Bella* was being mean? Bella is never mean. She's spoiled, maybe, and a bit self-centered, in a sweetly childish way, but *mean*? And, I realize, Freya never says a word against Bella, just as I don't against Eleanor. It's what has driven me crazy about their friendship... as well as mine and Eleanor's. There are far too many uncomfortable parallels between the two.

"How was she being mean?" Daniela asks. There's an eagerness in her voice she can't hide. "Can you tell me?"

Freya shakes her head, her eyes still closed, her braids flying. I know Daniela won't get another word out of my daughter.

"Freya," she insists, sounding a little impatient now as she leans forward, "how was Bella being mean to Kieran? Did he get angry with her—"

"I think that's enough," I say firmly. "Maybe you need to ask

Kieran or his parents about that. It's clear that my daughter was just a bystander to this whole sorry affair."

Daniela yanks her gaze from Freya to me, and I see a hardness in her expression that alarms me. After a second's silence, she flips her little notebook closed and rises from her seat on the sofa. Her partner follows suit, so they are looming above us.

"We'll be back if we have any further questions," she states tonelessly, and I just about hold onto my composure as I nod.

They nod back, a farewell, and then, thankfully, they are gone. As the door clicks closed behind them, I sag back in the chair, hugging Freya to me.

"Freya, sweetheart..." I don't even know where to begin. In any case, I don't get a chance. With a violent jerk, Freya twists out of my arms and bolts upstairs to her bedroom; the slam of the door practically makes the whole house rock on its foundations.

I close my eyes. I want to call Matt, but he'll already be at work, and I know there's nothing he can do. I just wish I had another adult in the room right now, but I don't, and so, wearily, I head upstairs.

I tap gently on Freya's bedroom door and then open it to see her lying curled up on her bed, her arms wrapped around her knees, which are tucked up to her chest. She blinks up at me as I come into the room, and for a second her little face with its dark eyes and pointed chin is screwed up in fury, or even hatred. I take an instinctive step back.

"I don't care!" she cries wildly. "I don't *care*! Bella deserved it."

I stop where I am and stare at her. "Freya..." I begin warily. "Deserved what?"

Her expression hardens into defiance, her face blotchy with both tears and anger. "She did," she insists. "She deserved to be pushed."

My heart flutters in my chest like a trapped bird. "You mean

Kieran..." I begin, but I already know. I feel it, like a dark, pulsing thing right there in the room with us, malevolent and overwhelming.

"*I* pushed Bella," Freya states defiantly, although her voice trembles and she has to blink back tears. "But she pushed me first."

SEVENTEEN

ELEANOR

It has been nine days since Bella fell. Nine days since I've seen my baby girl's beautiful golden-green eyes open, filled with excitement, joy or love. The doctors have been cautious, refusing to give me any promises or warnings. *We just have to wait and see* is something I am sick and tired of hearing. And meantime, I trudge through the days, weary and despairing, my mind full of thoughts I can't bear.

After that awful, awkward interview with the police, I tried to talk to Brian, but I couldn't find the words, or maybe just the courage. I was so sure that he was trying to punish me somehow. The way he let the police go at me; he didn't do the same when they turned to Lizzy, asking her where she'd been, what she'd seen.

"I didn't really see anything..." Lizzy began, her voice wobbling as her lips trembled and she had to blink back tears.

"Try to remember..."

"I *really* didn't see anything," Lizzy protested. "I was up on the patio..."

"I think my daughter's getting too upset for this," Brian had said in that authoritative way he has. "She's said she didn't see

anything, she was up on the patio, organizing the children."
Even that sounded faintly accusatory; I should have been *organizing the children*.

Daniela Martinez, however, took him at his word, or acted
as if she did. "Thank you," she said simply as she rose from her
seat. "We'll let you know if we have any further questions."

As soon as the police had gone, Lizzy disappeared up to her
room. Brian had seen the police officers out, and he followed me
back to the kitchen, where I was putting coffee cups in the dishwasher, trying to maintain some semblance of normality in our
lives.

"One of us should go to the hospital," he stated, like it was
something I didn't already know, or might disagree with.

"I was planning to, after I drive Lizzy to school," I replied, a
little stiffly.

Brian raised his eyebrows at my tone. This wasn't how Brian
and I related—these tense silences, these notes of accusation or
anger, so much unspoken, unknown. In the midst of my endless
worry about Bella, a little, needling voice kept burrowing into
my brain. *Tina. Who the hell is Tina?*

"Brian..." I spoke with import, and Brian stilled, his
eyebrows still raised. The trouble was, I didn't know what I was
brave enough to say. Ask him about Tina, or whether he blamed
me for Bella's accident, never mind who actually pushed her?
Did I want to know the answer to either of those questions? I
knew I would need to, one day anyway, but I wasn't sure I had
the strength just then. And so I shook my head, and scooped my
car keys from the little pottery dish we bought on vacation in
the Keys. "It doesn't matter," I told him without meeting his eye.
"I'm going to go get Lizzy."

Upstairs, Lizzy was in front of her mirror, determinedly
putting on mascara, her gaze focused on her reflection. We'd
never allowed her to wear makeup, and certainly not at school,
and yet any gentle rebuke I might have made died before I

could even think of what to say. I couldn't think of anything less important right now.

"Lizzy." I spoke quietly, but she tensed as if I'd shouted. "I'm sorry about the police. I know it's upsetting, to talk to them. We're just trying to get to the bottom of what happened..."

"*Why?*" Lizzy burst out before she grabbed her denim jacket and shrugged into it. "It's not like it changes anything. Who cares if it was Kieran or some other kid who pushed her? Or maybe she just *fell*? I mean... whatever... it was just an accident." She tucked her chin low as she grabbed her backpack and slung it over one shoulder.

"Lizzy..." I stared at her helplessly, unsure why she was being so aggressive. Was it just fear, or did she know something? Could she have seen something that she hadn't told us? The thought filled me with both dread and hope. If I could figure out what happened, I thought I'd feel better about it all, but it wouldn't change Bella's situation, and I wasn't sure I could handle having my other child involved in this whole situation.

"It's just procedure," I told her, a feeble reassurance. "The police have to investigate anything that seems..." I couldn't quite finish that sentence.

"It's not, though, Mom, is it?" Lizzy snapped at me. "It's *Dad*, because he's got to go after anyone who hurt his precious *Bella-bee*."

I flinched at the use of our nickname for Bella, and the savage way Lizzy practically sneered it. I knew she was upset and scared, but she sounded... *vindictive*. And for a second, I felt as if I was catching a glimpse of something I had never seen before, something I hadn't realized was even there. It was like a curtain had been torn away, and then, with one blink, it dropped back into place and Lizzy flicked her hair as she stomped out of the room.

What was going on with my daughter?

I gave a little shake of my head, relieved to step away from whatever I'd just seen. Maybe I'd been imagining it. We'd just had the police in the house, after all; we were all afraid and on edge. I had enough to be dealing with, without getting into all of Lizzy's issues, as well.

Neither Lizzy nor I spoke as I drove her to the high school on the edge of town, a sprawling mass of low brick buildings under a bright blue sky. As I pulled into the school's drive, I tried for an upbeat tone.

"It's your birthday tomorrow."

A twitch of her shoulders. "I don't care about that."

"We could go out to dinner—"

She gave me an incredulous look. "Are you even serious?"

"Lizzy..." I stared at her helplessly, having no idea how to comfort her, or even just reach her. Should I ask her if she saw anything? I was afraid I didn't have the emotional energy for that conversation, for either her furious denial or tearful confession.

She glanced at me, half out of the car, already impatient, wanting only to walk away.

"I love you," I said, and it felt like both the truest and most useless thing I'd ever said.

That was several days ago, and there has been no change. Bella is lying next to me, still barely breathing, her skin pale and slightly clammy, which apparently is common with people in comas.

In all those days, I've done little but sit by this bed, or go home and try to eat, sleep. We didn't celebrate Lizzy's birthday, although I left her a card and some presents, including a pair of designer jeans she'd wanted, on the kitchen table. They disappeared without comment.

Brian and I continue to exchange information about Bella, as well as the bare necessities to maintain a semblance of normal life—for Lizzy's sake, even though she isn't really talking to either Brian or me. Until Bella wakes up, we continue to exist in this stasis—not talking about anything real, not changing our attitudes, not addressing our fears. It's like we're all in a coma, not just Bella.

My Bella. I come into her room, the beep of the machine that connects her to life a strangely soothing sound. My purse slides off my shoulder as I drop into the vinyl chair next to her bed. I press my hand to her cheek, searching for a sense of warmth, of life. I close my eyes and imagine I can feel her stir, smile. Her eyes will open, she'll blink sleepily.

Mommy?

It's torture, to dream this way, and yet I have to, because sometimes that hope, fragile as it is, is the only thing that keeps me going.

"Eleanor?"

The sound of a voice has me startling. I know it's not Bella, she wouldn't call me Eleanor for a start, but it still jolts through me, as if it is, or at least it could be.

I open my eyes, drawing my hand away from Bella's cheek.

Natalie is standing in the doorway.

For a second, we simply stare at each other. I haven't seen or even spoken to her since Tuesday, nearly a week ago now, when she dropped off a store-bought lasagna for our dinner. I'm not sure why we've been avoiding each other, although maybe *I've* just been avoiding *her*. Is it really just because she wasn't one hundred percent on the ball when Bella slipped away? Can I even blame her for that?

It was *my* daughter's party. I shouldn't have been hiding in the kitchen. I shouldn't have landed my best friend with all the responsibility. These thoughts flit through my mind without ever landing; I simply sit and stare at Natalie in something of a daze.

"Eleanor..." Her gaze moves, inexorably, to Bella. For a

second, she looks transfixed by the sight, the sheer awfulness of it, and it stirs me into something like rage.

"Have you just come here to gawk?" I ask coldly.

Natalie jerks her gaze back to me, flinching visibly. "*Gawk?* Eleanor, I..."

"I'm sorry." I speak in a rush, knowing I was out of line but not wanting to have to get into it. "I didn't mean... Anyway." I shake my head. "Were you just coming to say hi?" I don't mean to sound snide, but I think I might, and I can't make myself care.

"No... I mean yes." She sounds unsure of herself in a way I'm not used to. Natalie has always been queen of the dry, even acerbic, humor. Sometimes it has made me feel a little... not *dumb*, but close to it. Not that I've ever verbalized that to Natalie, or even to myself, at least until this moment. "I wanted to see how Bella was, of course," she continues, taking a step into the room. "And you, too. I feel like I haven't seen you for ages. Not that... I mean, I understand why, of course..."

"It's all right, Natalie." I've half-risen from my chair and I now slump back into it. "I know what you mean."

She inches a little bit more into the room, clutching her purse. "How are you? I mean... how are you holding up? Has there been any news?"

We both, instinctively, glance toward Bella, flat and motionless in her hospital bed.

"No," I say after a moment, and I sound cold again. "No news."

"The police spoke to me on Friday." Natalie speaks in a careful tone, like she's trying not to imbue these words with any particular significance.

"Oh?" I'm not sure what she wants me to say.

"Eleanor..." Natalie hesitates, and then says in a rush, "Look, I told them—well, actually, to be perfectly honest, Freya told them—that when Bella and Kieran went down to the pond, I was actually on my phone."

She says this like a confession, and I suppose it is, and yet it leaves me flat and, I realize, completely unsurprised. "Work," I say after a moment. "That client or customer or whatever." I don't need her shamefaced nod to know it's true, and I realize it doesn't really matter. At least, it might matter, and maybe if Natalie hadn't been on the phone, she would have kept Kieran and Bella from sneaking off, but I know there's absolutely no point in thinking that way. I also know there's something else that needs to be said. "I shouldn't have left you out there on your own," I say woodenly. "I know that. I knew that, then. I'm sorry."

"Oh, Eleanor." To my surprise, Natalie's eyes fill with tears. I'm not sure I've ever seen her cry; even when Matt left, she was dry-eyed, stony-faced. *I'm* the emoter in our friendship. "You don't..." she begins, swiping at her eyes before starting again, "I know something was going on with you..."

I shake my head. I can't talk about Brian, not now. "It doesn't matter. I still shouldn't have."

"Well..." She lets out a shuddery breath. "There's something else I have to tell you." Her tone makes everything in me freeze. What could she possibly have to tell me? What could she possibly *know*?

And do I want to hear it?

"It was Freya," Natalie says in a low voice. She's staring at the floor.

I stare at her, trying to figure out what she could possibly mean.

"*Freya...?*"

"Freya pushed Bella," Natalie whispers. She lifts her gaze from the floor and her expression is agonized. I can only stare.

"Freya," I say again, and it still doesn't compute. In what world, in what parallel, skewed, alien universe, would Freya push my Bella? "I don't understand." I really don't. Bella is Freya's best friend. She loves Freya... and Freya loves her. They never fight; I have never seen so much as a single cross word between them.

"After the police came," Natalie continues stiltedly, "Freya ran upstairs. I went after her, and she told me... she told me she'd pushed Bella."

I shake my head slowly. I am too dazed to be angry or even upset. I simply cannot get my head around the notion. "Why..." I have to stop, start again. "Why on earth would Freya push Bella?"

"She... she says Bella pushed her first."

I jerk back then, in affront as much as shock. Natalie sounded more apologetic than accusing, and yet my dazed confusion is quickly coalescing into fury all the same. It's so much *easier* to feel angry. And if Natalie is somehow implying that this is my daughter's fault... that she's lying lifeless between us because of something *she* did...

"I don't believe you," I say flatly.

Natalie is still fighting tears. "I'm not saying it's what happened," she tells me, her voice choking. "But it is what Freya said."

"Why would Bella push her?"

"I... I don't know. I can't get anything else out of her. You know how quiet she goes sometimes—"

"Oh, yes, I know." Freya has always been a little bit quirky. It has unsettled me sometimes, how silent and watchful she can be, just *looking* at you with those big, dark eyes. I admit, at the beginning, I would have preferred Bella's best friend to be more... well-adjusted. Normal, even. Not that Freya isn't, but she's just not the kind of little girl I would have chosen for my daughter's best friend. But Bella did choose her, and I accepted that; I welcomed Freya into our home and lives more times than I can count... and *this is* the thanks I get? This kind of accusation? "This is not Bella's fault, Natalie," I tell her, my voice low and lethal. "Please do not try to act like it is."

"I'm not." Natalie has the gall to look hurt. "Eleanor, I'm just trying to explain—"

"What? That you believe *my* daughter pushed *yours*? Bella wouldn't harm a fly—"

"She wasn't," Natalie says quietly, "perfect. Bella was like any other little girl, Eleanor—"

I stiffen, my whole body twanging with fury. "*Was?*"

"I'm sorry," Natalie says quickly, her face coloring. She looks mortified by the slip. "I didn't mean that. I'm just trying to say, if Bella pushed Freya, it was a completely normal thing for a little kid to do. Maybe they argued. If they pushed each other, it doesn't have to be something sinister. They're children, Eleanor. It was just an accident. We can let it go."

"That's very convenient for you, considering you were on your *phone* when you were supposed to be in charge of twenty-eight children." The words are out of my mouth before I can stop them.

Natalie's expression hardens. "And for *you*, hiding in the kitchen at your own daughter's party, sipping a gin and tonic," she returns evenly. "Or two."

I flush and have to look away.

We are both silent for a few moments, the only sound our agitated breathing. I can't believe we're arguing like this. We never argue... just as Freya and Bella never argued. But maybe it's not really a friendship if you aren't able to disagree, thrash it out. Another aspect of my life that is falling apart. That wasn't real in the first place.

"Bella and Freya were whispering together right before I went in to get the cake," I remark after a moment. My voice is toneless. "Maybe they were arguing then."

"I didn't see that," Natalie admits. "And that wasn't when I was on my phone, by the way."

"I know." I push a hand through my hair, feeling exhausted all of a sudden. None of this really matters. None of it changes

Bella's situation now. And yet I find I want to know the truth. I want to understand what went so wrong. "Bella called Kieran over," I recall slowly. "She was smiling. I couldn't see Freya's face." And minutes, maybe seconds later, they were down by the pond, and my daughter was lying face down in the water, unconscious and bleeding from her head.

"I think," Natalie says slowly, "we need to talk to Joanna. If you can brave the school pickup, we can meet her there and then maybe go somewhere private."

The way she is talking, it sounds like she's considering kidnapping the poor woman. But if Kieran didn't push Bella... The realization ripples through me, with all its repercussions. Kieran might be blameless, and I've gotten this whole thing completely wrong.

What else might I be missing?

EIGHTEEN

JOANNA

By Monday morning, when Kieran is finally back at school, I am feeling stronger, more certain. I think we all are. Since the police interview, Tim has been more of himself. It's been such a *relief*, to remember the man who had always been so confident, so relaxed, and to find he's back again, or at least the promising shadow of him.

As for Kieran... he handled himself well with the police, all things considered.

I could tell immediately from the way Daniela Martinez spoke to him that she'd thought he'd done it. *Can you tell me what happened at the pond, Kieran? Were you angry?*

He'd stared at her in that cool, disinterested way he has, completely in control of himself. "I didn't push her," he stated flatly. "I wasn't the one who did it."

Daniela frowned thoughtfully as she cocked her head, a parody of someone willing to listen. "Who did, then?"

But Kieran pressed his lips together and refused to say a single thing more.

Still, it was enough for both me and Tim. Kieran is unflinchingly honest, except when he lies. But his lies tend to be over small, silly things—like whether he brushed his teeth, or who ate the Oreos, or who tracked mud all over the floor. And even then, he isn't lying to deny what he did; it usually comes out anyway, with a laugh and a shrug, which always makes me wonder why he lied in the first place. Was it just to see how we'd react? Because often he doesn't seem to care whether he gets into trouble or not, and so I believed him when he told the police, just as I believed him in the car. I know that he didn't push Bella.

But I don't understand why he won't say who did, because it's clear from what Kieran isn't saying that it wasn't an accident. *Someone* pushed Bella… but who?

Still, my son's innocence, and my husband's return to himself, at least a little bit, is enough to put steel in my spine for the inevitable walk of shame through the schoolyard. I hold my head up high, my hand on Kieran's shoulder, as I steer him through the wooden gates. There are clusters of parents dotted around the playground, some whispering in that hushed way from last week, others chatting more normally.

"*Joanna.*"

I stiffen at the sound of my name, only to relax a little bit when I see who is addressing me—Rachel, mother of Toby, who reached out to me the day of the party, at the café. "Hi, Rachel."

She grasps my arm in a gesture of solidarity, her eyebrows drawn together in concern. "How are you holding up?" she asks in a low voice.

"I'm okay." Gently, I squeeze Kieran's shoulder. "We're okay." I figure she knows about the suspension, so I add, "We actually had a really nice week away from all this."

"I just want you to know, I didn't sign it," she tells me. "I never would."

I have no idea what she's talking about, and she must see that in the blankness of my expression, because she immediately looks like she is regretting saying anything.

"Sorry... have you not heard?"

"No, I don't think so." I bend toward Kieran's ear. "Hey, why don't you go play, bud?" I suggest quietly.

He takes off toward a big rubber tire kids like to scramble over, and I watch him go, praying he'll behave himself. Whatever is going on in my son's psyche, surely he knows now is not the time to act out. When I see him climb onto the tire as docilely as any other child, I turn back to Rachel.

"Sign what?" I ask bluntly.

She shakes her head. "I shouldn't have said anything..."

I am too tightly strung to deal with her prevarications. "Rachel," I snap, "just tell me."

"There's... there's a petition going around the class, to have Kieran expelled."

I blink, absorbing this, letting it filter through me. "A *petition*? Started by whom?"

"I'm not sure. I think Jennifer Evans, Cooper and Riley's mom? The twins?"

Vaguely I recall a pair of blond, blue-eyed twins, both of them small and quiet and generally well-behaved. I don't know who their mother is, and considering I've never once interacted with her, as far as I know, I am stunned that she would do something like this without even talking to me. It's so mean-spirited, so utterly vindictive, that it takes my breath away.

How can my family possibly stay in this community, after this?

"Kieran *didn't* actually push Bella," I tell Rachel. "I'm one hundred percent sure of that."

"Oh..." She regards me uncertainly, and I can tell by the conflicting emotions chasing across her face that she wants to believe me, but she doesn't. She, like every other parent at Wetherby Elementary, like *I* did, assumed that Kieran was guilty.

Tim's accusation that I believed the worst of my son cut

deep. For once, I am not going to do that. No, now I am going to stand by him and what he said he didn't do.

"I don't know who did," I tell Rachel, "and Kieran is refusing to talk about it. But I believe my son, and he has served his suspension for misbehaving at school. He can't be expelled for something he didn't do." And then I turn away from her because I'm afraid I might start to cry or shout, and I don't want to do, either.

"Joanna..." she calls after me, sounding abject, but I keep walking and she doesn't call again.

Kieran is sitting by himself on the tire, and I have the urge, deep and visceral, to gather my son in my arms, and protect him from every single person here.

I know Kieran is different. I understand he can be difficult. I suspect there is some diagnosis for him, if we dare find it. But I love him, and I want what's best for him, and I will protect and care for him with every breath in my body. This knowledge anchors me. I brush the hair away from his eyes and he ducks away from my hand, just as the bells rings for the children to go inside.

"Okay, bud." I reach for him again, but he scrambles away, off the tire, and toward the school door. I watch him go, feeling as if my heart is being carried away from my body; I am an empty shell, and yet I am determined. I will *not* fail my son.

Parents are lingering in the schoolyard, and I catch a few people shooting me curious glances, which I ignore. I fix a small, cool smile to my lips, and with my head still held high, I walk out of the yard.

Rachel catches me at the gate, looking anxious.

"Joanna, I'm so sorry. Maybe I shouldn't have said anything..."

"It's fine." I am surprised by how calm I sound, how calm I *feel*. I am on my son's side, and the maternal harpies of

Wetherby Elementary will not dissuade or undo me. "Better to know what I'm dealing with."

"It's not everyone," Rachel says in a rush. "Jennifer Evans has a real axe to grind, I think..."

I shake my head, bemused. "As far as I know, I've never even met her."

Rachel sighs unhappily. "She's just one of those people, you know? She didn't invite Toby to her twins' sleepover last year. Said there was only room for twelve in their rec room, but guess how many boys were in the class?"

"Thirteen?" I guess with a small, wry smile.

"Fourteen," Rachel admits with a rueful smile in return. "My son Drew didn't get invited, either. He was diagnosed as being on the spectrum at the start of second grade."

I shake my head again, amazed at how petty and cruel someone can be, even as I reluctantly, sort of understand it. Including kids with challenging behaviors can be *hard*. But that doesn't mean you shouldn't do it.

"I'm sorry," I tell her. "That's really unfair."

"Well." She brightens, both hesitant and hopeful. "Look, do you want to have a coffee at the café in town—"

"I'm sorry, I have to get to work." I touch her arm, like an apology. "But another time, okay?" I realize I mean it. Rachel is genuinely kind, and I need a friend.

She nods, and there is almost a spring in my step as I head back to my car, until I remember Bella. It might be a load off my mind that Kieran didn't push her, but she's still an eight-year-old girl who is currently in a coma. How can I forget that for a moment?

My heart sinks, and my steps falter. It feels as if this—whatever *this* encompasses—will never be over.

. . .

I spend the next six hours working but also tense, half-expecting a censorious call from Mrs. Bryson. *I'm afraid we've had some trouble with Kieran.* Fortunately, there's nothing—at least nothing to warrant a call—and my heart is lighter as I head back to school. Tim, somewhat incredibly, spent the afternoon looking at jobs online, something he has not stirred himself to do since he walked out of his office six months ago, without a word of warning, leaving three clients waiting for designs he never finished. The fact that he'd so much as looked at his LinkedIn profile was enough to make my heart lift in hope. Somehow, improbably considering how difficult the last few weeks have been, it feels as if we are turning a corner.

Now, in the drizzly grayness of an early October afternoon, wet leaves papering the schoolyard, in muted shades of red and yellow, I stand apart from the usual clusters of parents as I wait for Kieran, and so I'm by myself when I am approached by, of all people, Eleanor and Natalie. They march up to me, not arm in arm but feeling like it, clearly a united front and I am instantly tense, bristling.

"Joanna?" Natalie speaks first; Eleanor isn't quite looking me in the eye. Does she still blame Kieran, I wonder, or is she feeling guilty for shrieking at me the way she did?

I jerk my head in the semblance of a nod without offering any greeting in return. I have no idea what they want.

"How are you?" Natalie asks, her voice gentling a little. She looks tired and tense, as does Eleanor, but I am not ready to warm to them just yet. "How is Kieran?"

I stare at her, having no idea how to respond. Does she really think this is the right moment for a chat?

"We're all right," I tell her before I face Eleanor directly. "How is Bella?"

She startles at the question; she clearly wasn't expecting me to ask it. Now that I'm looking at her properly, I can see just how tired she looks. Her skin has a papery fragility to it, and there are dark shadows under her eyes. Her clothes, while expensive, look thrown on and careless, rather than in the effortlessly relaxed way she dressed before. There is, I notice, a coffee stain on her shirt.

"There's been no change," she answers, her tone both cautious and stiff. "But they're hoping to... to wake her up from the coma soon. Maybe even in the next day or two."

"That's good news," I reply. At least I hope it is.

Eleanor nods jerkily, her gaze skittering away from mine, when Natalie says abruptly, "Joanna, we know Kieran didn't push Bella."

Now I'm the one startling in surprise; that is, I realize, just about the last thing I expected them to say.

"I'm... glad," I venture.

"But we think he *might* have seen what happened," Natalie continues. "And we... know some things, too, that we should tell you." She sounds unhappy about this, which makes me wonder what on earth they know. "We were wondering if we could all talk to him, together..." She trails off as I stay silent. As glad as I am that these two women have accepted Kieran is innocent, I'm not sure I want them interrogating my child.

The bell rings, and the doors to the classrooms start to open, children tumbling out in a flurry of backpacks and lunchboxes, coats trailing the ground even though it's drizzling. Parents straighten or spring to attention, arms outstretched to receive their offspring. I see Eleanor's gaze move to the door of the third-grade classroom, and her expression wobbles as she blinks rapidly. Bella, of course, won't be coming through those doors, and my heart aches for her.

My son is coming through now—the knees of his jeans splattered with mud, his hair is mussed, and there is a streak of dirt on his cheek. He looks full of vitality and life, and my heart swells with love for him.

That rush of love, as well as a swell of sympathy for Eleanor, is enough to have me turning to both of them. "I can see it might be... useful... to talk," I tell them carefully. "But not here."

"We could go to a café?" Natalie suggests, but I shake my head. I can't deal with Kieran in a public space, not when he's being asked questions that might make him shut down—or blow up.

"Let's go to my house," I say, although I'm not entirely thrilled at the idea of inviting these women into my private space.

Still, it's the most comfortable place for Kieran, and the truth is, I want to get some answers—and find out the truth— just as much as they do.

Eleanor and Natalie, along with Freya, follow me in my car back home; as we crawl down Main Street through the rain, I start to have some serious second thoughts. What am I doing, inviting these women into my home? Agreeing to let them question my son? And yet they seemed so grateful when I suggested it... I was surprised by the look of naked relief on both their faces. I could see they want to know what happened as much as I do, if not more.

"Kieran," I tell him as we pull into the driveway, "Freya's and Bella's moms are coming over for a little while, along with Freya. They were hoping to ask you a few questions about what happened. They know you didn't push Bella," I assure him quickly. "But they think maybe you saw something. Maybe you could help them out? They just want to find out the truth. Nobody's going to be in trouble."

"Whenever grownups say that, they don't mean it," Kieran remarks in a bored voice, but then he perks up. "Freya's coming too?"

The little spark of interest in his voice heartens me. "Yes, she is. Maybe you could... play together." As far as I know,

Kieran doesn't really *play* with anyone all that much, but to my surprise, he gives a brief nod.

Eleanor and Natalie have pulled up behind my car, and they seem both curious and apprehensive as they follow me to the front door, Freya holding Natalie's hand.

"What a pretty spot," Natalie remarks, a bit inanely, as she glances around at the trees looming darkly up all around us. "I've lived in Wetherby pretty much all my life and I don't think I've ever been out this way."

Probably because there's nothing much out here, besides a few lone houses among the trees.

Silently, I open the door and usher them in. As they step into the living room, I try to see my house from their eyes. It's nothing on Eleanor's sprawling palace, and I have no idea what kind of house Natalie lives in. Everything about this house hints at impermanence, as it's so clearly a rental—the magnolia walls, the brown wall to wall carpet, the cheap fixtures and fittings in the adjoining kitchen. Our furniture takes up space without really inhabiting the rooms or making them individual. We haven't put up any pictures, because there's a policy about no nails in the walls, and so everything seems a bit... blank.

As I close the front door, Tim comes in from the kitchen, dressed in sweats and an old, faded T-shirt. I tense because I didn't think about him being here, or these two women getting this insight into my life. He falters in his step as he takes in Eleanor and Natalie looming in the doorway; Freya, to my surprise, has already slipped away to join Kieran in the den.

"Hello," Tim offers uncertainly, and then glances at me for introductions.

Eleanor and Natalie, I can tell, are surprised by his presence. Since he's never come to school besides that one unfortunate visit with Mrs. Bryson, maybe they thought he didn't exist.

"This is my husband, Tim," I tell them stiffly. "Tim, this is

Eleanor, Bella's mother, and Natalie, Freya's mom. They wanted to ask Kieran some questions."

Tim's attitude immediately becomes about twenty degrees cooler. "Oh?" He glances at me in query, clearly surprised that I have gone along with this, that I have brought them here.

"They know Kieran didn't push Bella," I tell him quietly.

Tim tries to mask his surprise, but his stance relaxes a little. "Oh, well..." He glances at Eleanor. "I'm sorry about Bella. Has there been any...?"

"News? No."

A silence descends upon us all, tense and expectant. I don't know whether to offer coffee, or tell them to sit down, or if we should just all stand here and have it out.

"So," Natalie asks hesitantly, "can we all... talk to Kieran?"

Kieran. Of course.

I glance at the door of the den, now closed, and take a deep breath. "I'll go get him. What about Freya...?"

Natalie looks around, seeming surprised; I don't think she noticed her daughter slip away. "Um... I guess she should be here, too," she says.

In the den, Kieran is sprawled on the sofa with the iPad, and Freya is perched on the edge, watching him. He turns to tell her something, and then catches sight of me, his open expression turning guarded.

"You guys look like you're having fun," I remark, and they both stare at me silently. I try again. "Kieran... remember I told you Freya's and Bella's moms wanted to ask you some questions?" His eyes narrow. "They know you didn't push Bella," I tell him again, like a promise, and he and Freya look at each other, still not speaking. A sudden thought occurs to me—if Kieran didn't push Bella, did *Freya*? Is he *protecting* her? "They just want to know what happened," I say, directing this remark to both children. "No one is going to get into trouble."

Freya just blinks at me and Kieran's face closes up. I have a feeling Eleanor and Natalie are not going to get any of the answers they want.

"Kieran." I perch on the edge of the sofa and rest one hand on his knee. He looks at it, but doesn't shrug it off, which feels like progress. Freya simply watches us. "Do you know anything, bud?" I ask softly. "Because if you do, you should say. You wouldn't get into trouble, I promise."

He glances away, shifting where he's sprawled so my hand falls away.

The silence stretches on, punctuated by the ticking of the clock on my desk. One minute, two. Kieran goes back to his game, and Freya peers over his shoulder. After another full minute, I rise from the sofa and go back out to the living room, where Tim, Eleanor, and Natalie are all perched on the edge of the sofa and chairs, looking incredibly awkward.

"Jo...?" Tim half-rises from his seat.

"I'm sorry, but I don't think Kieran is up for answering your questions. And Freya doesn't seem to be either, frankly."

Natalie looks unsurprised, but Eleanor's face both falls and hardens. "Couldn't we at least try?" she asks after a moment, struggling to moderate her tone.

"You could, but I don't think you'd get anywhere," I reply evenly. "Trust me, when Kieran decides he's not going to speak, you will not get a word out of him."

Natalie manages a faint smile. "Freya is the same," she says, and we share an unexpected look of solidarity. After all this, could Kieran and Freya become *friends*?

Eleanor, however, is looking like she's on the brink of either a breakdown or an outburst. Her fists are clenched but her voice wobbles as she speaks.

"Please, can we just *try*?" she begs. "I just want to know what happened. I... I need to know..." Her voice breaks and she draws a shuddery breath. "Freya says Bella pushed her first." *First*? So I'm right, and Freya is the one who pushed Bella? This is what they said they knew. Why didn't they tell me earlier? "And I can't... I can't..." she stammers, "I just can't *believe*..."

Natalie gives her a sudden, sharp look. "What can't you believe, exactly?" she asks, her voice hardening.

With a jolt of understanding, I realize that this little episode isn't about Natalie and Eleanor presenting a united front against me. Bella and Freya versus Kieran. It's far more fractured than I ever suspected.

"I can't understand why Bella would do something like that!" Eleanor bursts out as she wipes her eyes. "She wouldn't! She just... *wouldn't*."

"Bella was being *mean*." Kieran's voice, flat and hard, has every single one of us stilling.

Slowly we all turn to him, standing in the doorway of the den, Freya lurking behind him like a shadow.

"She was teasing both of us," he continues in the same hard voice, his face screwed up with anger. "She was saying that we didn't have dads." He glances at Tim, both in accusation and appeal. "We *do*..." he says, more uncertainly this time.

Now he sounds like a lost little boy. My lost little boy.

NINETEEN

NATALIE

For what feels like an age but is probably only a second or two, no one speaks. Then, Joanna says, faintly, "*Kieran...*"

He whirls around, back into the room he emerged from, Freya following. Kieran slams the door behind them so the sound reverberates through us all. We stay where we are, all of us frozen in silence and shock.

She was saying we don't have dads, but we do.

Why on earth would Bella be saying something like that... about *Freya*? She knows it's not true.

I glance at Eleanor and see her face is ashen, and in an instant, I know exactly why—or at least *how*—Bella came to be saying something like that.

Because she heard it from her mother.

Finally, Eleanor tries. "I..." She glances between Joanna and me without meeting either of our eyes. "I didn't realize..." she begins, before trailing off, abject, even terrified.

"Where did Bella hear that, Eleanor?" I ask. My voice is as hard as Kieran's was. "Where could she have *possibly* heard that Freya doesn't have a dad? Why would she think that when she knows that she does have one? Matt has taken Bella and Freya out for pizza, bowling, to the movies..."

"I didn't..." Eleanor begins, before her abject expression hardens. "Maybe Matt isn't as great a dad as you think he is," she bursts out, and I reel back.

"What?" My voice comes out in a shocked whisper. "Why would you say that?"

She hesitates, looking torn as she shoots a glance at Joanna, who is watching us, white-faced. Then she says in a low voice, "Look, Natalie, I didn't want to tell you this but... I was down in Danbury Hospital over the summer, for my blood work, because they couldn't do it up here."

I know Eleanor has to get her blood tested every three months for an underactive thyroid, something she doesn't really like talking about, but what on earth does that have to do with *Matt*?

"I saw him there," she tells me, like a confession.

I am still drawing an alarming blank. "You saw him at the hospital?"

"Yes, with a woman. A pregnant woman. They were clearly together... he accompanied her in to the doctor's."

A pregnant woman? I blink slowly, trying to absorb the implications. Is Eleanor saying Matt has a... a mistress? And a *baby*?

"Did..." I am struggling to put words together. "Did you confront him?"

Eleanor shakes her head. "No. They were called by the nurse before he even saw me. And then I was called in, and when I came out, they were gone." She glances again at Joanna, who hasn't spoken a word.

I have no idea what to do with this information, and I know I can't process it now, not on top of everything with Bella and Freya that we're dealing with, and Kieran, too.

I look again at Joanna. Why did Eleanor have to say all this in front of her?

"So because of this... *sighting*, you told Brian Freya didn't have a dad?" I infer in something like a sneer. "And you didn't feel you needed to talk to me about any of it? Thanks a lot, Eleanor. I thought you were my friend."

As much as I want to be angry with her, I know it's Matt who has really hurt me. Is he really a *cheater*? A cheater with a secret family?

It's so absurd, it almost makes me want to laugh, and yet the unpalatable facts Eleanor revealed, unfortunately, speak for themselves. Now I understand why he wouldn't tell me why he was leaving, but I can't believe he made it sound as if it was my fault. That is almost as hard to forgive as the adultery, the *baby*, and yet I'm not currently of a mind to forgive anything... or anyone, including Eleanor. Why would she gossip about Matt and me to her children?

"I'm sorry..." she begins wretchedly, but I'm not ready for her apologies.

"Did you really say that?" I demand, needing her to admit it. "Did you tell Bella that Freya didn't have a dad? Because I don't know where else she might have heard that kind of thing."

"And what about Kieran?" Joanna interjects, her voice rising. "Why on earth would you say that about him... about us? You don't *know* us." Her voice hardens as color floods back into her cheeks. "You haven't even *tried* to know us. How dare you say such things?"

"I didn't..." Eleanor begins, a sentiment which once again trails away to nothing.

I glance at Tim, who is pale-faced, glancing between us all, his forehead furrowed as he slowly connects the dots. Eleanor said that Kieran didn't have a dad, and he's right here in the room.

"I didn't say it quite like that," Eleanor amends in something close to a whimper. "Honestly. And I had no idea Bella was listening, of course. It was just some idle talk..."

And right then, I can picture the scene so vividly I might as well have been there. Eleanor and Brian in their massive kitchen; Eleanor reaching for the bottle of white from the fridge, rolling her eyes a little while Brian frowns, rocking back on his heels as they both discuss how other families aren't like theirs... *working mothers and deadbeat dads, really, what is the world coming to?*

Something very much like that.

"So this is what you and Brian talk about during your precious quiet time," I spit.

Eleanor lets out a small, hurt sound. "Natalie..."

"Isn't it?"

"Please..."

"I think," Joanna announces in a loud, firm voice, "I'd like you both to leave."

Admittedly, it *is* a little awkward to have us trashing the remains of our friendship in the house of someone who is essentially a stranger, but I don't even want to discuss it anymore. I'm too furious, but also too devastated. There have been too many terrible surprises today to come to terms with. And what might be the hardest thing to believe is that after all the finger-pointing and blaming, Eleanor herself might be the guiltiest one of all.

If she hadn't said those things...

"I'm sorry," I tell Joanna, meaning it, and she gives me a short nod in return.

Eleanor turns to her, hands flung out in appeal. "Please... I didn't mean... I don't even remember what I said, just something about never seeing... Tim... around..." She can't quite look at him.

Joanna gives another brief nod and then looks pointedly at the door.

. . .

No one speaks as we climb in the car to drive Eleanor back to Wetherby. It's not until we're on the lonely country road leading back to town that Eleanor finally says something.

"Natalie, I don't know why Bella would say that." She glances back at Freya, who is staring out the window. "If she even did—"

I let out a harsh laugh. "Are you suggesting that Kieran is lying?"

"No, no, it's just..." She emits a harried sigh. "Look, Brian and I might have said—I don't even know what! I had no idea Bella was overhearing any of it. And it wasn't like that," she insists, caught between frustration and apology. "I wasn't *literally* saying that Freya or Kieran didn't have a dad—" She glances back again at Freya, worriedly, but the damage has so clearly already been done.

"But that was obviously the gist," I state quietly. "Wasn't it?"

"*No.*" Eleanor presses the heels of her hands to her eyes. "No, it wasn't. Not... not like that. It wasn't... it wasn't meant to be *anything*. Just stupid chatter, like I said." She takes a quick breath. "My daughter is the one in a coma," she tells me in a pained voice. "Freya and Kieran are *fine*. Please, please don't make this my fault—"

"I'm not, Eleanor," I reply, gentling my voice because I can see how much she is struggling, "but you, you and Brian, were the ones who were trying to make it somebody else's fault." I feel I have to remind her, even though my anger has fizzled right out at the mention of Bella. How can we be getting angry about *anything*, when she might be fighting for her life? And yet why was Eleanor—and presumably Brian—so quick, so eager, to make someone guilty? When, really, I realize heavily, we were all guilty. I was on my phone, Eleanor in the kitchen, the gossip about our fathers, Matt having left, and Tim not there...

Every one of us had a part to play in this tragedy.

Except, I realize with a pang of guilt, maybe Joanna... and Kieran.

"Why do you think we've never seen Tim before?" I ask Eleanor, and for a second, we're like we once were—two friends, or maybe just a commander-in-chief and her deputy. I'm not sure I know the difference anymore—or if there ever was one—when it came to Eleanor and me.

She shakes her head slowly as she drops her hands from her eyes. "I have no idea. It didn't seem like he has a job, at least not one outside the home?"

"I know. Something's a little off there, I think."

We glance at each other, and then look away, conscious once more of Freya in the car. The last thing we need is to stoke any more gossip about anyone, yet, in that moment, I realize how easily it can happen. How innocent it can seem. It's just like Eleanor said—stupid chatter. And I know I don't feel angry about anything, just unbearably sad... for all of us.

"I'm sorry," Eleanor says quietly. "Truly."

I nod, and we don't speak for the rest of the journey back into Wetherby.

Freya remains silent after I've dropped Eleanor off, and yet I know I need answers from her. I'm not about to try to get them on my own, though.

Later, back at home, when she's upstairs in her room and I am defrosting some hamburgers in the microwave, feeling both anxious and purposeful, I call Matt.

"We... we need to talk."

He is instantly alert; I've already told him that Freya admitted to pushing Bella, but that Bella pushed her first, but I didn't know why. Now I do. "About Freya?"

I think of what Eleanor told me earlier. "Yes, mostly. Can you come over? It's important."

"I'll be there in an hour."

Is that the response of a man with another woman and a baby? I wonder as the microwave dings and I take the burgers out, drop them into a frying pan. If Eleanor saw him months ago, is the baby born already? Surely—*surely*—he would have told me about it? If he has a new family, wouldn't he have had to, for Freya's sake? She might have a baby half-sister or brother... it feels impossible.

Freya and I eat dinner in silence and then I run her a bath, sit on the edge of the tub while she slowly soaps herself. We have a ritual where I wash her hair for her; she loves when I rub her head as I lather the shampoo, and I enjoy the sight of her smile, the way she tilts her head back into my hands. Sometimes loving Freya feels complicated because she's so quiet, so wary, so much of the time. But right now, as the water runs clear and I teasingly pile her wet hair on top of her head, it feels wonderfully easy.

By the time Matt comes over, an hour and a half later, Freya is in her pajamas, curled up on the sofa with a storybook. Her whole face lights up when she sees her dad walk through the door.

"Daddy!"

"Hey, Frey-frey." He drops a kiss on top of her head as he sits next to her, pulling her in for a quick hug. "How are you doing?"

She doesn't answer, just thrusts the storybook at him.

He gives me a questioning glance, and I nod. We won't be able to talk until Freya's in bed, anyway.

Four stories later, she finally is, and Matt and I are alone in the living room. I glance around the room, all the memories it contains—the vase of rose crystal that my aunt gave me. The watercolor of Bar Harbor that we picked out on our honeymoon. There is a framed photo over the mantel of the three of us on vacation in Cape Cod. It's a perfect shot—the golden sunlight glancing off the beach, the waves behind us. Freya is six, has lost a front tooth, and has a sun-freckled face full of joy. Matt looks relaxed and proud, his arm slung around our shoulders, his dark hair ruffled by the wind. I am on the other side of Freya, looking off into the distance, my hair blowing into my face. Matt used to tease it was my thoughtful pose, and I've always liked the artistry of it, but now as I look at it, it just makes me think that maybe I wasn't fully present in that moment. As I recall, I was worried, once again, about sales targets, a new line manager. Matt had to keep asking me not to check my email.

"Natalie?" Matt asks now, quietly. "What's going on? Have you learned anything more about what happened?"

"Yes." I turn back to him, my thoughts tumbling over themselves. There's so much to say, but I don't know how to begin.

"Natalie," Matt says again, sounding worried.

I stare at his familiar face, his *beloved* face—the straight eyebrows, the slight kink in his nose from when he broke it wrestling in high school. The mole by his mouth. The broad set of his shoulders. Everything. I know *everything* about this man.

Except it seems that I don't.

"Matt, are you seeing someone?" I ask abruptly. "Are you... *with* someone?"

He blinks at me. His mouth works for a moment and then he says, a bit incredulously, "*What?*"

"Are you?" Now I sound hard.

He shakes his head slowly. "Natalie... where is this coming from?"

I hesitate and then admit baldly, "Eleanor told me today that she saw you at Danbury Hospital with a woman. A pregnant woman. She was getting her blood work done or something, and you were with her."

Once again Matt looks dazed with shock. He rakes a hand through his hair before dropping it to his side as he starts shaking his head in a slow, disbelieving back and forth. "Are you... *serious*?" he asks. "Are you saying what I think you're saying, that I was accompanying my... my girlfriend or something? That was back in the summer. Do you think I have a *baby*, and I didn't say anything?"

"You tell me," I reply tonelessly. "Because I don't know what to think."

He slumps against the sofa and lets out a groan, his fists pressed to his eyes. "No, Natalie," he says as he drops his hands and glares at me. "No, I don't have a baby. That woman wasn't my girlfriend or mistress or whatever. It was Molly, my work colleague. You remember I mentioned her? Her husband died in a car accident in April."

I feel my cheeks heat. "Oh..." I say, because I can't think of anything else. I remember him talking about Molly; he went to her husband's funeral. I didn't, because I'd never met her, and, well, I needed to work.

"Is that why you asked me here?" he asks. "To ask about that?"

"Well... partly," I admit. I feel ashamed, but also annoyed and relieved. It's a strange mix of emotions. "It really threw me for a loop, when Eleanor told me. She assumed—"

"Of course she did." Matt shakes his head again.

"What is that supposed to mean?" I ask, more curious than accusing.

He shrugs. "They're not my favorite people. They never have been."

Somehow, I am not surprised. I knew Matt was never overwhelmed with affection for either Eleanor or Brian. But then, I realize rather suddenly, neither was I. Strange, how I didn't realize it until this moment. I think I was so grateful to be included in her orbit, to feel important and popular in the world of young mothers.

I lean my head back against the sofa and close my eyes. A feeling of fatigue seeps through me—physical tiredness, but also an emotional exhaustion about everything: my marriage, my motherhood, my friendships, my job. It all feels like such a sorry, weary mess right now.

"I'm sorry I thought that of you, that you might have been with someone else. I didn't really, at least not entirely..." I trail off as Matt gazes at me, his head cocked to one side, a thoughtful look on his face. "But Matt..." I say. *Have* to say. "Why did you leave? You never would tell me. You said if I didn't know there was no point, but... I'd still like to know. I'd like to understand, at least, even if—"

"Natalie, I didn't tell you when you asked me because I was fed up with trying to tell *you*." He sounds tired rather than angry.

"What..."

"I felt like I was *always* telling you. You were always working—"

"You work too, you know," I retort a little sharply.

"I know," Matt agrees. "But I leave it behind when I come home. You never did."

I shift guiltily in my seat then because I know that is true.

"It wasn't just that, though," he continues on a sigh. "I mean... yes, that was a large part of it, but... you didn't seem happy. With me. You were tense all the time. I felt like you resented my presence—"

I straighten in indignation. "What—"

"Admit it," he says quietly. "Come on. I'm being honest, and you can be, too. I felt like I couldn't open the fridge without you snapping at me to be a little quieter, or not to take the last of the orange juice, or do anything. I started to think you'd rather I wasn't there, and then I thought maybe I didn't want to be there. I thought..." He stops, lapsing into silence as he shakes his head while I do my best to sift through the painful memories.

I know he has a point, even if I don't want to acknowledge it. I did act resentful. I *felt* resentful because I was working so hard even when I didn't want to be, and yet I couldn't *not* work, because if I stopped, then I'd become my mother, dependent on a man who might not need me. And what's the best way not to be needed? Not to need anyone yourself.

This neat bit of psychoanalysis isn't instantaneous; it's been hovering in my subconscious for years. Matt even knows some of it, at least the bits I've been able to tell him—my father's affairs, my mother's refusal to leave him. Whether he's made the correlation to my own behavior... Well, I suppose it would be hard not to.

"You thought what?" I ask after a long moment of contemplative silence.

Matt looks startled, and then he sighs. "I thought if I'd left, maybe you'd start to miss me."

I let out a sharp laugh of disbelief. "So, what, were you waiting for me to ask you back?"

He shrugs, smiling crookedly. "Sort of."

My heart feels as if it is tumbling in my chest. I stare at him, my mouth agape, my mind whirling. "Matt... You could have said..." *Three months* I've been living in misery, thinking my husband just gave up on me. But now he's telling me I more or less gave up on *him*?

"I just did," he replies with that same crooked smile. "But it had to come from you first, Nat. I wanted—I *needed*—you to want it. To want *me* back."

I'm not sure how to answer. There's a pressure building in my chest, and I can't tell whether it is hope or hurt. Why didn't we have this conversation before?

I can already hear Matt's reply—*because you wouldn't have been willing to*. And maybe that's true; I was cynical long before Matt left me, I acknowledge. Witnessing my parents' dysfunctional marriage, my mother's utter abjectness, hidden by an overbright smile and a little mascara and blusher... I didn't want to be like that. I just didn't know how else to be.

We are both silent for a long moment as the shadows grow deeper around us. I should turn on one of the lamps, but I don't move. A montage of memories slides through my mind like shards of broken glass sparkling in the sunlight—each one beautiful yet jagged. Slamming the fridge door, just to show my irritation. Matt tickling Freya's tummy as she shrieks with laughter. My mother, discreetly wiping her eyes when my father came back smelling of someone else *again*, not wanting him to see she was sad.

"Anyway," Matt finally says, and I can't tell if it sounds like a beginning or an ending. "That's all... to be processed, I guess. Was there something else you wanted to talk about? About this thing with the party—and Freya?"

More memories—Matt and I slow-dancing at our wedding, my head on his shoulder, his fingers splayed across my lower back. Buying this house, both of us so proud as we took the keys. Taking Freya to her first day of kindergarten together, hand in hand, grinning at each other over her head, knowing we'd both turn teary when she ran off, into the classroom. For the first time since it happened, Bella's accident isn't foremost in my mind. I am thinking of my husband, my family, the life we once had together... and maybe we could have again.

"Nat?" Matt prompts, his forehead furrowing.

I reach over and turn on a lamp, let the warm light spill over me. "We can talk about that later," I tell him.

TWENTY

ELEANOR

I feel broken, like a handful of jagged shards of glass, as I walk inside my big, beautiful, empty house after Natalie drops me off. Brian is at work; Lizzy is out with friends... and Bella, my dear little Bella-bee, is lying in the hospital in Hartford, still in a coma.

And there's really very little doubt now that it is all my fault.

I'm not sure I can bear to live with that knowledge, like a cancer eating me from the inside out. *My fault. All my fault.*

If I hadn't stupidly, pointlessly gossiped about Matt and Tim, implied they were absentee fathers, and *why*—? Was I being smug, sanctimonious, or just bored? I can't even remember. I can vaguely recall the moment with Brian—his pursed lips, my soothing answer. My attempt to backtrack, but yes, that vicious little dart of pleasure we all get—at least I think we do—at pointing out someone else's flaws and feeling better about our own.

I hate myself right now. I don't think I could hate myself more.

I drop the key on the hall table and look around the elegant rooms, homely but decorated with style, the perfect blend of coziness and sophistication, as if I've never seen them before. I wish I hadn't. Right now, I hate this house and all it represents, because none of it is true. My close and loving family? My tight and trustworthy marriage? *Myself*, the undisputed queen of Wetherby Elementary, chair of the PTA, mother extraordinaire everyone secretly—or not-so-secretly—envies?

None of it was real. And this house, a temple to all those lofty yet shallow ideals, is built on mirages and lies.

I start to climb the stairs, thinking I only want to curl up on my bed and sleep forever, when I glimpse the photograph on the wall by the first step—Bella as a baby, her gummy smile lighting up the world, with Lizzy standing behind her, looking just as beautiful, but serious-eyed, the responsible big sister. Without even realizing what I am going to do, I rip the picture from the wall and hurl it to the floor.

The sound of splintering glass is both heartbreaking and satisfying, and I do it again with the second picture—this one of Bella at a year old, taking her first tottering steps, Lizzy holding the fingertips of her right hand. *Smash.*

I go up the stairs step by step, taking each photograph and throwing it onto the floor, which is now littered with splintered shards of glass. *Crash.* Bella, at three, with Lizzy ten years old, both of them in matching corduroy overalls. *Crash.* At four and eleven, in white party dresses for New Year's. *Crash.* On and on it goes, until I'm nearly at the top of the stairs, the last picture, of the four of us last year, in my hands. Why did I never notice how smug I looked, with my artfully messy bun, my beaming smile, the way I tilt my head as if I'm surveying the whole world, complacent mistress of it all?

I am raising my hand over my head to hurl this last photograph when a voice, a traumatized scream, stops me.

"Mom! *Mom, stop!* What are you *doing?*"

Lizzy is standing by the front door, surrounded by a sea of

broken glass, a mixture of terror and disbelief on her pale, shocked face, her backpack sliding off her shoulder. As I stare back at her, I slowly lower my arm. I look around at the mess I've made, the bent frames and shattered glass, the photographed faces of my children staring blankly up at me, and I feel nothing. Then, as I come back to myself, I realize just how out of control and *insane* I've been acting. And yet I can't regret it.

"I was..." I can't even begin to explain what I was doing, or why. "I'll clean it up," I say instead, and my voice is flat, dead.

"*Mom.*" Lizzy picks her way through the glass, until she's at the bottom of the stairs, gazing up at me, wide-eyed, one hand on the newel post. "What's going on? Why are you... *destroying* everything?" Her voice hitches. "Is it... is it Bella? Has... has she..."

"No, it's not Bella. She's fine. I mean, she's... the same." *It's me,* I think, but I can't make myself say the words.

Suddenly, I realize how shocking, how *frightening* it must be for Lizzy, or any child, to stumble upon something like this. Parents, and mothers in particular, need to keep the home a safe, sacred place. That's what Brian would say...

Brian.

I have to clean all this up before he comes home. The thought fills me with panic that borders on fear. If he sees this, he'll freak out. And he'll know I haven't kept a single plate spinning all this time.

"I'm sorry, Lizzy," I tell her helplessly. "I'm sorry... I don't know... I shouldn't have..." My voice chokes, and I can't go on.

To my surprise, Lizzy comes up and hugs me. I can't remember the last time she has.

"It's okay, Mom," she says gently, as if she's talking to a child. "It's okay."

I hug her back, so grateful for her compassion, even if we both know it isn't okay at all.

"I love you," I tell her, my voice thick, and as she pulls back, I see her eyes fill with tears. She looks upset by my words, which alarms me. "Lizzy..."

"I'll clean this up," she tells me, her voice clogging on the words. "Maybe you should go rest."

"No, no, I'll do it." The thought of Lizzy sweeping up the broken glass, trying to fix the bent frames, makes me want to weep. I can't let her do that.

"I don't mind, Mom." Her voice comes out more strident now as she turns away from me. "Let me do it."

"Lizzy..." I stop as she turns, her sleeve falling back from her wrist. There are three reddened lines on the inside of her elbow. Cuts. They're cuts, and they're far too straight and systematic to be from an accident.

Her gaze tracks mine and she pulls her sleeve down. "What?" she asks defensively, almost like a dare.

I can't ask her if she's harming herself now, not when I've just been throwing family pictures down the stairs. Heaven help us, but how did we get to this awful, awful place?

I close my eyes, and Lizzy's voice softens. "Go upstairs, Mom," she says. "It'll be okay."

And, to both my shame and relief, I obey. I let my daughter clean up the awful, pathetic mess I made, and I head toward my bedroom, thinking only to sink onto the bed and close my eyes against the world for a few minutes. In front of Bella's bedroom, I stop. The door is very slightly ajar, and I push it open with my fingertips.

I haven't been in here since Bella's party. I haven't been able to bear seeing it—her pink and white bed piled with novelty pillows, the gauzy curtains at the window. The collection of stuffed animals, all panda bears, that crowd the top of her dresser. She has a thing about pandas, has since she was tiny. Every year she gets a new one for her birthday, sometimes for Christmas, too.

I tiptoe into the room cautiously, my gaze moving slowly around the room. What am I doing? It can only hurt me more. I walk over to the bed and perch on the edge. I know if I rest my head on the pillow, I'll smell Bella's scent—bubblegum shampoo and the smell that is uniquely *her*, a sweetness I'd recognize anywhere, anyhow.

As I look around the room, I realize I am looking for clues. Something that will explain why my beautiful, kind, caring daughter—and yes, I know she wasn't perfect, but she was *close* —would tease her best friend and a boy she'd wanted to be kind to about their fathers. No matter what I said, why would Bella pick up on it? Why would she dangle that information in front of them, taunt them with it, if Kieran is to be believed, and I know there is no reason not to believe him, especially if it's true that Bella pushed Freya first.

It still doesn't make sense.

Of course, I know it could just be a childish spat, one that happens every day, in every classroom, everywhere. They blow up and then are forgotten in a matter of minutes. This one just happened to have tragic consequences, with Bella hitting her head and falling face down in the water.

And yet... something about it still feels off. Wrong. This just isn't the way Bella operates. The way she *is*. Unless I've been deluded about Bella the way I was deluded about Brian. *About my whole life...*

A soft whimper escapes me, and I lie down on Bella's bed, tucking my knees up to my chest like a child. Misery swamps me, so my chest hurts and my whole body feels heavy. All I want is for Bella to open her eyes, smile sleepily at me and say *Hi, Mommy...*

I want it so much it's a physical pain, an endless ache that reverberates through me, too painful to bear. Every single second, every breath I drag into my lungs, feels like too much.

I don't know how long I lie there, simply existing, moment

to moment; distantly I hear the sound of Lizzy cleaning up the photos, the broken glass. Outside, clouds slide across the sky, obscuring the sun, and the day darkens into evening, the wind rattling the dying leaves in the maple trees, a skeletal sound. I should go back to the hospital, be with Bella, or maybe just go downstairs and be with Lizzy. I think of those cuts on her arm. We've neglected her since Bella's injury, I know we have. I need to be more present for her, a better mother all around...

When I open my eyes again, the room is nearly dark, and my body is stiff. I must have been up here for hours. Brian will be home soon. I think of our "quiet time," which feels like a relic from a bygone age. We haven't indulged in it since Bella's accident, and maybe that's all it ever was—a stupid, smug indulgence. A waste of time.

"Eleanor?"

I raise my head, blinking in the gloom and see that Brian is standing in the doorway of Bella's room. In the twilit darkness, I can't read the expression on his face, but I can imagine what it is. Surprised disapproval, even affront. I am not behaving the way I am meant to behave. I am not being the mother he expects and needs me to be, so unlike his own.

I know this, and yet I don't move.

"Eleanor..." His voice is confused, troubled. "What's going on? Why are you in here?"

"I just wanted to feel close to Bella." I lower my head back down, onto her pillow, breathe the soapy sweet smell of her in and close my eyes.

"Oh, hon." Brian comes and sits down on the edge of the bed, resting one hand on my hip. "I'm sorry." His voice is soft, full of sadness, and so far from what I realize I was expecting— some kind of advice that I'd take like a scolding. *If you want to be close to Bella, maybe you should go to the hospital and sit with her. How long has she been on her own?*

How much of Brian's disapproval, I wonder, is from him, and how much is in my own head, born from my own childhood?

"Has it been a bad day?" he asks gently, before sighing. "I mean, every day is a bad day at the moment, I know that..."

"Freya pushed Bella."

"*What?*"

"But Bella pushed her first. Natalie told me this morning. We went to see Joanna, Kieran's mother, and it all came out. Bella was teasing Freya and Kieran about not having fathers. She must have overheard us talking about it—do you remember?"

I glance back at him, squinting in the dark; he is shaking his head slowly. "I mean..." He pauses. "I guess so, yes? I remember we said something about it, but... Bella *teasing* Freya? I find that hard to believe."

"I know. I'm trying to make it make sense, but I can't. I know she wasn't an absolute angel, but..."

"She was pretty close. *Is* pretty close." He sighs and rubs a hand wearily over his face. "Any news from the doctors?"

"They're hoping to wake her up soon, take her off the anesthetic drugs. Maybe tomorrow or Wednesday. It'll be a slow process, though. They said it could take days before they know... anything." I swallow, close my eyes again before I force them open.

I have so many things to tell Brian, so many questions to ask, that I don't know where to begin. Has he even noticed that all the pictures on the stairs are gone? What has Lizzy done with all the mess? The fact that he hasn't mentioned it makes me think he hasn't. And if he hasn't noticed, what's the point?

What's the point of *any* of this, if we end up where we are now?

"Should we get takeout tonight?" Brian suggests. "I can grab a pizza in town. Keep it easy."

I haven't thought about dinner. I haven't gone grocery shopping in a week; I have no idea how much food is in the fridge.

"That would be good," I say. "Maybe we could spend some time with Lizzy. She's been on her own so much lately." I need to tell him about the cuts on her arm. I need to ask him about Tina.

Brian squeezes my hip and then rises from the bed. "That sounds like a good idea. Maybe take a break from the hospital if there's no change? I can go in tomorrow if you like. Take the morning off work. We both can if they're going to start taking Bella off the drugs."

"Okay."

Brian pauses in the doorway of Bella's bedroom, his body haloed by the light from the hall. "Eleanor..." he says, and I tense. I have no idea what he's going to say next, and I'm not sure I want to hear it. "I love you."

Oh.

"I love you, too," I whisper.

He nods and smiles briefly; I glimpse the gleam of his teeth in the darkness before he heads downstairs, past the bare walls he still doesn't notice.

I stay there, lying on Bella's bed, for another few minutes, knowing I should move but still unable to. Eventually, I hear the front door open and close, the sound of Brian starting up his car to go get the pizza. I force myself to sit up; my head spins and my hair is in a tangle I have to push out of my face. I take a few deep breaths and then I head downstairs to find Lizzy.

She is in the family room, curled up in one corner of the sofa, simply staring into space in the dark.

"Hey." My voice sounds croaky.

I switch on the lights, and she doesn't move. I come into the family room and sit on the edge of the sofa opposite her.

"I'm so sorry about earlier, Lizzy. I don't know what I was thinking, throwing all those pictures. I think I was just having some kind of moment..." It's a feeble excuse, but it's the only one I have.

She gives a little shake of her head. "It's okay." Her voice is barely audible, and she is staring straight ahead, refusing to look at me. Once again, I feel a scalding rush of guilt. How could I have subjected her to that sort of scene?

"It isn't okay," I tell her. "I shouldn't have done that." I pause. "Thank you for cleaning everything up. What... what did you do with it all?"

She glances at me, her hair sliding in front of her face. "I put the frames and glass in a trash bag out in the garage. And I put the photos in that box you have."

I nod slowly. I have a big box I decoupaged years ago, to keep all our family photos in, before I put them into albums. I picture the wrinkled, ruined photos from the wall on top of all the others, and something in me twists, breaks. It never should have been this way. My life, all the choices I made, all the effort I put in, should have protected me from this. Protected us all. It was, I think numbly, meant to be foolproof, but then, of course, nothing is.

I turn back to Lizzy. I need to talk to her about what I saw, and yet I don't know how to begin. "Lizzy..." I hesitate and she tenses before turning to look at me.

"What?"

"I saw the cuts on your arm," I tell her gently. There's no other way to say it but bluntly. "You're harming yourself." I don't let myself make it a question.

Lizzy turns away from me and doesn't reply.

"Is it because of Bella?"

She hunches her shoulders. "Everybody does it, Mom. It's not really a big deal."

"It's a big deal to *me*."

She shrugs. "It doesn't matter."

"Lizzy, it *does* matter." I can't bear the thought that she thinks it might not. "*You* matter," I add, feeling my way through the words. "To me. To your dad—"

"Do I?" she flings back at me wearily, before turning away again, as if she doesn't care about my answer.

"*Lizzy.*" I try not to sound aggrieved, hurt. This isn't about me, not now. "Yes, you do. I know that since... the party, things have been hard, and we haven't spent as much time with you as we should have—"

"It's not that." Lizzy draws her knees up to her chest, hugging them to her as she rests her chin on top. "I mean, I understand that. Bella's in a *coma*." Her voice catches, breaks. "I meant before. But it doesn't matter now, anyway."

I pause to sift through her words, what they might mean. "Before...? What about before? And why doesn't it matter now?"

But I've lost her; she's rising from the sofa, tossing her hair as she moves through the family room, away from me. I stretch out one hand toward her, but she evades, moving steadily through to the kitchen, and then the hall.

"Lizzy!" I call. "Please, let's talk."

No answer.

"Dad's bringing pizza," I add, a bit desperately.

"I'm not hungry." Her voice floats from the stairs, and then I hear the decisive click of her bedroom door, which somehow feels more final and worrying than if she'd slammed it in a temper.

After a minute or two, I rouse myself to get plates, glasses. I set the table on autopilot, and it isn't until I'm folding the last napkin that I realize I've set it for four, not three. For a second, I have the urge to hurl the fourth plate to the ground, but I've broken enough of our possessions today, surely. I put it back in the cupboard, close the door firmly, and take a steadying breath.

I can get through this. I *can*, if I just try hard enough.

The front door opens, and I brace myself for Brian's sing-out: "Honey, I'm home," but it doesn't come.

He walks into the kitchen silently, holding a pizza box in his hands, looking dejected. Far more downcast than I've ever seen him before, which makes me realize just how strong he'd always been for us. For me.

For a few seconds, we simply stare at each other across the expanse of the empty kitchen. Then, as if my voice is coming from somewhere outside of myself, I hear myself asking, "Brian... who is Tina?"

TWENTY-ONE

JOANNA

When Eleanor, Natalie, and Freya walk out of my house, it feels like a storm blew out with them, leaving an almost eerie stillness behind. For a second, in that unsettling quiet, neither Tim nor I speak. I glance toward the door of the den.

"I should talk to Kieran," I say. I don't move.

"Yes..." Tim's voice sounds distant, even faint, and then he gives himself a little shake, and speaks more firmly. "But let's talk to him together."

I glance at him uncertainly; I have no idea what he thinks about anything Eleanor or Natalie—or Kieran, for that matter—have said. *Bella said we don't have dads, but we do.* That had to have been an uncomfortable, even painful, thing to hear. But before we have that conversation, we need to talk to our son.

I head over to the den, tap once on the door, and then open it. Kieran is sprawled on the sofa just as he was before, playing on the iPad with an almost ferocious level of concentration, as if his life depends on it. As I perch on the edge of the sofa, I realize I have no idea what to say to him.

Thankfully, Tim does.

"Hey, buddy." His voice is gentle, full of love, and it makes my eyes sting. It reminds me of who Tim was, who we were as a family, before all this. Before Tim's breakdown, before Bella's accident. Because that's what it was, I know, no matter what she said or who pushed her. An accident. A terrible, tragic accident whose repercussions continue to ripple out.

Tim sits in the desk chair, scooting it next to the sofa so he can rumple Kieran's hair, briefly enough that our son doesn't have time to shrug his hand away. "I'm glad you said what you did, before," Tim continues. "I know it can be hard to tell grownups that kind of thing."

Kieran looks briefly up from the iPad and then down again, without saying a word.

"You're not in trouble," Tim tells him. "I want you to know that."

Kieran looks up again. "I know I'm not," he says. "I didn't do anything wrong." He speaks matter-of-factly, which should be reassuring, but for some reason it isn't, not quite, and I don't understand why.

He's back at the iPad, as good as if we've left the room.

"So, just to be clear, Kieran," I say, "Bella was teasing you and Freya about... about your dads, and then Bella pushed Freya, and she pushed her back? That's what happened?"

The look he gives me is completely clear, without a flicker of guilt or deception, and yet again, for a reason I can't quite fathom, it makes me feel uneasy. Some maternal instinct is telling me there is still more to this story. "Yeah."

"Where did Freya go, after Bella fell?"

Kieran shrugs. "She ran away."

"But *you* didn't," I point out.

His gaze doesn't waver from mine, but he doesn't say a word.

"Jo," Tim interjects, his voice sharpening. "I think we get the picture of what happened. Kieran doesn't need to tell us any more."

He smiles at Kieran, but he's already gone back to the iPad, and we—and no doubt Bella and Freya, as well—are forgotten.

After a second or two, we both leave Kieran to his screen time, and head back out to the living room.

"What was that all about?" Tim asks me, and then continues before I can answer, "I think it's pretty clear what happened at the party, and that Kieran didn't do anything, no matter what people might have thought. He's completely innocent, Jo. We should be relieved."

I shrug, knowing I can't explain my unease in any way that is specific or tangible. "I just wanted to make sure."

"Of what?"

"What exactly happened. It still feels…" I pause, uncomfortably. "Off."

Tim shakes his head, not quite condemning of me, but almost. "It's tragic, is what it is. Tragic most of all for Bella, of course, but for everyone involved. The second something happened, it was all about pointing fingers and assigning blame. But maybe no one was to blame. It just happened. No one needs to feel guilty." He gives me a pointed look. "But I think we've had enough of scouring through the details, don't you? It would be better to put this whole episode behind us. Move on, as a family."

"That's going to be hard to do, with Bella still in a coma," I reply quietly. "And…" I hesitate before admitting, "at pickup today I heard that there's a… petition circulating to have Kieran expelled."

"*What!*" Tim's jaw goes slack before his eyes flash with anger. "That's ridiculous."

I nod slowly. "It might be, but it's still happening."

He scowls, shaking his head. "Some people…"

"I know."

We are silent then, absorbing the implications. There might be no real cause to expel Kieran from the school now, but we will still have to deal with the tide of ill will toward us and our son.

Tim must be thinking the same thing because he wonders aloud, his voice low, "Should we take him out of school? Permanently, I mean? Find somewhere else?"

The thought fills me with equal parts dread and relief. Start over... *again*? Where no one knows us? *And yet*, I acknowledge, *no one really knows us here*.

"I don't know, Tim," I admit. "I don't know what we should do."

We signed a year-long lease on this house, so we're tied into that, at least. And, I realize, I don't want to feel like we're running away. I still like Wetherby, even if I'm not sure about a few of the third-grade parents. I slump onto the sofa, exhausted by it all. It feels like there are no easy answers.

"It might just be one or two people," I venture. "Another parent told me about the petition, but I have no idea how many signatures there were, or whether it was just something people talked about..." I think of Rachel's anxious words, *I didn't sign*. Somehow, that made it sound like most parents might have.

Tim joins me on the sofa, leaning back against the cushions as he stares up at the ceiling. "Do you think we made a mistake, moving here?" he asks.

I ponder this for a moment and come up empty. "I don't know."

Tim is silent again, still staring at the ceiling. "I didn't realize," he says after a moment, "that that's what people were saying. That Kieran didn't have a dad."

I tense, before making my tone as neutral as possible. "I didn't, either."

He turns to look at me, and the expression on his face is utterly bleak. "Is that what *you* think?"

"I know Kieran has a dad, Tim," I reply gently.

But he is not to be deterred.

"You know what I mean."

I do, because for the last six months, yes, it *has* felt like Kieran doesn't have a dad in some ways, and also like I didn't have a husband. I don't want to hurt Tim by admitting all that, but maybe it needs to be said. Maybe he needs to know. And he did ask, after all.

I take a deep breath. "Well..." I begin, and Tim lets out a tired laugh that ends on a far sadder sound. Not quite a sob, but something close to it.

"Have I been that bad?" he asks.

I think of the days of managing Kieran alone, while Tim napped, or, when he was feeling better, went to the gym or for a walk. I think of the nights he went to bed early, while I caught up on work, hunched over my keyboard, my eyes gritty with fatigue. There is nothing quite so lonely as the sterile glow of a halogen lamp late at night when you're working alone. But can I explain all that? Do I want to tell him now?

I'm not sure I do, and so I shrug helplessly, because the truth is, I don't know how to answer. There have been times— many times—in the last six months that I have wanted to *scream* at Tim. I've longed to take him by the shoulders and shake him and demand to know if he realizes what he is doing to me, to Kieran, to our family. But I haven't, because I've known he's struggling, and I haven't wanted to make it worse. But now that he's asking me point blank? I realize I don't want to hurt him by admitting to it all.

"Jo," he says, more of a plea than a question. "Have I?"

"It's been hard," I admit with careful reluctance. "And I know it's been hard for you, too."

"But for *you*?" he presses, and I almost can't believe he's asking, that he finally wants to know.

"Yes," I say quietly. "It's been hard for me."

We are both silent as Tim nods slowly in acceptance, staring into the distance, his hands clasped loosely in his lap. "I'm sorry," he says after a moment. "I should have..." He trails off, and I wonder how he meant to finish that sentence. How I want him to.

Because, I am realizing, this is the first time I've actually *told* Tim it's been hard. I might have showed it a thousand tiny ways, from small, pointed sighs to the unnecessarily firm closing of a cupboard door, but I never said. I never told him I was struggling too, that I needed help, that we were in this together. And maybe I should have. Maybe that is on me as much as him, or maybe even more.

"I realize I've probably seemed self-indulgent," Tim says after a moment, stating it like a fact. "Especially when I know you've been working so hard. I'm not sure if I can explain how I felt at the beginning..." He stops, and I wait. He's never actually explained why he left his very good, very well-paid job at a large graphic design firm. How he simply walked out one afternoon, without any notice at all, and never went back. The only explanation he ever gave me was simply "I couldn't do it anymore."

It was, at times, a little hard to accept.

"I'm not sure I can explain it," he continues after a moment, "because I'm not sure I even know what happened. We were constantly getting squeezed at work, try to do more with less, and the pressure to come up with ideas that were fresh and original and challenging..." He gives a gusty sigh. "It's so tough out there, Jo. I felt like everyone was starting to look at me like this middle-aged no-hoper who was borderline irrelevant." He lets out a huff of tired laughter. "Which sounds like a whine fest, and maybe it is, but I just... couldn't do it anymore. I don't mean I didn't want to do it, although I didn't, but I *couldn't*. It felt as physically impossible as if my arms were tied to the chair." He turns to look at me, a pleading look in his blue eyes. "I know that sounds lame—"

"It's not lame," I say quietly. I mean it.

"Walking out felt like such a relief," he confesses in a low voice. "I know it looked like failure, and everyone in the office was talking about how I'd just *snapped*, but it felt... it felt like the first time in a long while that I was actually taking control of my life. Can you understand that?"

"I think so," I reply cautiously. I wish he'd told me this before, but maybe he tried. Maybe I wasn't able to listen, because I was so overwhelmed by what had happened, how quickly everything seemed to have derailed.

"Anyway." He slumps back against the sofa. "It felt like a relief at first, in the moment, but then after... I just felt like a failure. And seeing you go to work every day, bringing home the bacon, juggling our family and your job, and basically doing everything... well, it paralyzed me. And I found myself doing less and less. And I *know* how that sounds, how it must have felt for you. And I don't blame you for being angry."

"I wasn't angry," I protest, and Tim gives me a look that reminds me so much of who he used to be—wry, humorous.

"Jo," he says, smiling a little, "you were angry."

So those little sighs and careful slams of cupboard doors *were* noticed, I suppose, and probably made him feel even worse. We really should have had this conversation long before now, I think, and yet I understand why we weren't able to.

"I was frustrated," I admit. "But I wanted to be supportive. I still do..."

"And I want to step up," Tim replies. "When Kieran said that... that Bella thought he didn't have a *dad*—maybe that was the wakeup call I needed." He rubs his hand over his face. "I hated hearing it, but yeah, maybe I needed to."

"I should have told you how I was feeling earlier," I tell him. "I just thought you needed time, but... it started feeling like a lot of time."

"I know. I'm sorry."

"Tim, you don't need to be sorry." I turn to him, laying my hand on his arm. "No sorrier than I am, anyway. We both contributed to this—whatever this even is. The important thing is, we can still make a fresh start. I know we haven't had the greatest beginning in Wetherby, but we can still move forward. I want to. I want to try."

He lays his hand on top of mine, squeezing my fingers gently. "So do I."

Later, lying in bed, I can't sleep. I should feel some modicum of peace as well as hope after Tim's and my conversation, and I *do*, but a sense of unease is still leaving me staring at the ceiling at 2 a.m. *What am I worried about?*

I know the atmosphere at school is not going to be easy. It's going to be hard to hold my head up high and get past the ingrained prejudices and assumptions that people have made, but I still think we can do it. That fills me with as much determination as dread, and I know it's not what is keeping me from sleeping right now.

No, it's something else. *It's Kieran.*

The fact that he didn't push Bella isn't enough for me, I realize. Yes, it makes him innocent, *technically*, but the image I can't get out of my head, the one that keeps flashing through my mind as if in neon lights, is of Kieran standing over Bella while she lay face down in the water. He didn't move to help her. He didn't bend down to see if she was okay. He just stood there, *staring*.

I know it's a lot of responsibility to put on a seven-year-old, to rescue someone in trouble. I understand that he might have been frozen in fear, paralyzed by indecision or shock. I recognize that, really, it was probably only a few seconds that he stood there, immobile, while Bella was basically drowning.

And yet I keep coming back to it, because when I came into the yard, when I saw Eleanor run to Bella and crouch over her, I looked at my son's face. And the expression there wasn't fear or shock or even indecision. It was a cool, impassive kind of curiosity.

Quietly, I slide out of bed, push my feet into my slippers and head downstairs. In the den, I turn on the desk light and open my laptop. I'm not sure what I'm looking for, only that I need to at least try to find some answers. We've dipped our toes into the pool of potential diagnoses, but we've never gone farther. Never wanted to.

Now I do. I need to, for Kieran's sake as much as my own, as Tim's. There was something *off* about the expression on his face, his part in the whole sorry situation. And I need to know why.

I open the internet browser and hesitate, my fingers hovering over the keyboard. I don't know what to type, what rabbit hole to disappear down first. Just the thought of it has my heart rate skittering with both anticipation and terror. Do I really want to do this?

Yes.

After a few moments' consideration, I type *indifference to other children potential diagnosis*.

The results that come up are all about disruptive behavior disorder, ADHD, autism. All the usual suspects, and the symptoms aren't quite right; it's more about a lack of awareness than what I think Kieran feels... which is, I realize, a lack of care.

I go back to the search bar and type *uncaring about other children potential diagnosis*. I press return, and then I hold my breath.

And when the first search result comes up and I start to scroll through the symptoms, I realize, with a judder and thud that feels like the emotional equivalent to falling down a flight of stairs, I might have found a diagnosis.

TWENTY-TWO

NATALIE

Is it wrong, to feel hopeful when Bella is still in a coma, when Eleanor cannot possibly know yet what the damage to her daughter will be? It *feels* wrong, and yet I can't help it, because hope is persistent, stubborn even, and when Matt suggests he stay the night after our heart-to-heart, after I've told him everything that I know happened at the party, I agree. He offers to stay in the guest bedroom, and I tell him that he doesn't need to.

We spend the night lying in each other's arms, remembering how we used to be. It feels both funny and wonderful, to listen to Matt breathe, to remember the funny little snort he makes when he's asleep. It used to drive me crazy; now I revel in it. In him. In being able to lay my head on his chest as his arms tighten instinctively around me, even in sleep. I've missed this —*us*—so much.

When Freya comes downstairs the next morning, tousle-haired and still in her pajamas, and sees Matt and I sitting at the kitchen table, sipping coffee, she is incredulous, her face wreathed in sudden joy.

"*Daddy?*" Her voice is filled with wonder.

Matt's response tugs at me, because instead of his easy smile, he almost looks near tears. He hugs her hello, his gaze meeting mine over Freya's head, and I know exactly what he's thinking—*how could I have stayed away for so long?*

Eleanor's gossipy conjecture about his colleague Molly might have had no basis in truth, but maybe her musing that Freya more or less didn't have a dad *did*. Because Matt was mostly gone for over three months, and that is a long time for a little girl... as well as for a wife.

"How come you're here?" Freya asks as she clambers onto her chair, and I pour her some Cheerios.

"Mom and I stayed up talking last night, so I decided to sleep here," Matt replies, keeping his tone light. "Is that okay?"

Freya's gaze is fierce. "*Yes!*"

This time, Matt doesn't glance at me; he takes a sip of coffee, his eyes lowered, and I know Freya's response has humbled and moved him.

It feels normal yet strange to be a family of three again, at the breakfast table, chatting inconsequentially, spooning up our cereal. In the back of my mind is the present and pressing knowledge that I need to talk to Eleanor. She hasn't been in touch since I dropped her off at her house yesterday afternoon when we left things so miserably tense. Bella is meant to come off her medications today or tomorrow, and—please God—hopefully begin to wake up. I should phone or at least text Eleanor to support her, try to make things as right on my side as I can. Because, at the end of the day, no matter what Bella said or did first, it was still Freya's push that landed Bella where she is now.

A weary sigh escapes me at the thought, and Matt gives me a troubled, questioning look.

I force a smile. "Time to get our skates on, sweetie," I tell Freya.

She looks untroubled, so clearly happy that her dad is here, that I wonder if, at seven years old, Freya can even understand what happened to Bella. I don't want to explain it any more to her, but I worry for the future. For Bella, but also for Freya. If Bella's brain damage is serious, what will that mean for Freya as she matures and realizes her part in the whole sorry tale? It's not something that will ever have an ending, I realize. Maybe not for any of us.

"What if we took the day off?" Matt suggests suddenly, and I look at him in surprise while Freya's whole face brightens.

"Can we?" she asks eagerly.

"I don't know," Matt replies with a smile. He glances at me, his eyebrows raised. "Can we?"

I hesitate. We *can*, but I have already taken time off work and my line manager will be breathing down my neck more than ever. And yet... what is more precious than this? I frittered away my family once already. I don't want to do it again.

"Yes," I tell them both. "We can."

It's a beautiful fall day, the sky clear and blue, the leaves turning scarlet and gold. It's nearing the end of the apple-picking season, and so we head to a nearby farm for the classic experience—a ride on a tractor out to the orchard, a burlap sack full of apples, and then hot apple cider and cinnamon, sugar-dusted doughnuts outside the farm shop afterward.

"I want to try again," Matt announces with no preamble once Freya runs off to the playground and I am licking the sugar from my fingers. "With us, I mean," he clarifies with a small, crooked smile.

I smile back. "I know you meant us."

"Well, I'm trying to be a little better about communicating these days," he tells me. "I left it too long, before."

I gaze off in the distance, the sky bright and blue above us, the sun warm on my face, although there is an autumnal chill in the air. *Try again with us.* Yes, I want that too; I want Matt to try, and I know *I* want to try, as well, because I didn't, before. Not nearly as much as I should have. I see that now; I feel it.

"Natalie?" Matt prompts, and I turn back to him with a smile.

"Yes," I say firmly. "I want to try again, too."

The rest of the day passed in a golden haze. At least, it feels that way in retrospect, everything rose-hued and perfect. Freya catches both our hands and walks between us, back to the car, with Matt lugging a sack of apples across his back like Santa Claus. We go to the diner on Main Street for lunch, ordering hamburgers and milkshakes.

Every so often, I take out my phone, check for a text from Eleanor, but there's nothing. I tell myself I'll message her when I'm back home, when I have a moment to myself. I don't want anything—not even that—to spoil this time, our family made whole again.

And soon enough I have that moment, when Matt heads back to Danbury to get some of his things, and Freya is tucked up in bed. I pour myself a glass of wine and curl up in the big armchair in the living room, gazing unseeingly at the dark night, the yard bathed by the light of a sliver of moon. It really feels like fall now, and I consider lighting a fire, but decide I'll wait until Matt returns. I sip my wine and think of what on earth I can say to Eleanor.

In the end, I decide not to leave it to a text. I call her, but the phone just rings and rings before switching over to voicemail. In some ways, it's a relief, but in another way, I wish I could talk to her. Can we salvage our friendship? How much friendship, really, is there to save? We've been self-declared best friends for five years now, but right now I feel almost as if I could walk away from it all without a qualm, maybe even with relief... To not have to exist in Eleanor's shadow all the time. To not be her deputy and gofer. To not be in thrall to her life, because my rueful teasing of her over-the-top style as both mother and wife has, I know, its root in envy, or maybe just guilt, because I'm not like that. I'll never be like that.

I chose that, as the opposite to my mother, but I'm not sure it really was the opposite, or at least not a healthy, positive one. Not needing anyone or deriding domesticity aren't exactly the foundations of a happy and stable family life.

And as for Eleanor... do I still want to be her friend? The question, I realize, doesn't even matter, because I know I need to be her friend now. Really, I'm the only one she has.

I still haven't heard from Eleanor by the next morning, when Freya is getting ready for school, and Matt has already left for work. He's slotted back into our lives so neatly and easily, it's almost like he never left. *Almost...* but not quite.

We bump into each other in the bathroom; and in the kitchen, I forget and make only enough coffee for one. I apologize, profusely, and Matt laughs softly and kisses the top of my head.

"Nat, it's okay," he says, and I believe him.

I am smiling as I drive Freya to school, parking down the street and walking along the sun-dappled sidewalk, both of us scuffing our feet through drifts of leaves. At the door to her classroom, I give her an extra hug and kiss, just because. She tilts her head up to me to give me one of her rare, full-beam smiles, and then runs off. I am watching her go when someone taps me, decisively, on the shoulder.

I turn to see Jennifer Evans brandishing a piece of paper

and giving me a beady-eyed stare. "*Natalie*," she gushes, although there is a steeliness to her voice that makes me tense. "I am *so* glad I caught you. Have you had any news about Bella?"

"No, not anything in particular," I reply, because I am not about to tell this woman anything personal about Eleanor or Bella or, frankly, anyone.

"Really? I was hoping maybe there was *something*." Jennifer flicks her perfectly highlighted blond hair behind one bony shoulder.

She's the kind of woman who always wears expensive exercise gear and carries a trendy water bottle everywhere. She's also judgmental, a terrible gossip, and resents Eleanor for being the queen bee of the class mothers when she so clearly covets that role. Sometimes the playground dynamics feel more brutal for the parents than they do for our children.

"I don't think you've signed this," Jennifer says, and waves the piece of paper in her hand.

I glance at it, nonplussed. "What is it?"

She widens her eyes theatrically. "The *petition*."

Unease crawls along my spine. "For what?"

Am I imagining the look of spiteful glee in her eyes? I don't think so. "To have Kieran expelled," she states, as if it's that obvious.

"What?" I stare at her blankly before I withdraw my hand from the paper I'd been about to take. "Who started that?"

A flicker of displeasure crosses her features. "I did."

I am truly appalled. I know Kieran wasn't anyone's favorite kid before the party, but to have him *expelled*? Can parents even do that?

"But Jennifer..." I shake my head slowly. "Why?"

"*Why*?" she repeats incredulously. "Why? Because he's a menace, Natalie. You know it as well as I do! How could you not? He *pushed* Bella in cold blood—"

In cold blood? What does she think this is, an episode of *CSI*?

"Jennifer, it was an accident," I say sharply. "They're *children*. Even... even if Kieran did push Bella, he didn't mean to hurt her. And in fact I know that—"

"Just like he didn't mean to hurt her when he pulled out her chair?" she cuts across me before I can explain that I know Kieran didn't push her. Not that I want to get into all that. "Or when he punched my Cooper?"

That's what this is about, I realize. Kieran must have decked her precious little Cooper. She has twins who are small and a bit frail-looking, thanks to being six weeks premature.

"You can't petition to have a child expelled," I argue. "That's not for the parents to decide."

"For the safety and well-being of our children—" Jennifer begins piously, and my temper boils over.

"For heaven's sake, Jennifer," I snap, "Kieran is not that much of a menace. He's an active little boy who is adjusting to a new school. Give him a break."

Jennifer jerks back like I've struck her. "Really, Natalie?" she demands. "You can say that when your daughter's best friend is in a *coma*, and you know that boy was the one who pushed her?"

I press my lips together. I cannot *not* say something, I realize, even if the last thing I want is for Freya to be the subject of one of Jennifer's pernicious petitions. "He didn't push her," I state quietly. I am ashamed of my own reluctance to state the truth.

Jennifer's finely threaded eyebrows arc upward. "Oh? Did you see something?" she asks, a slight sneer in her voice. Does she think I'm *lying*?

"I know he didn't," I affirm. "So why don't you just leave it, Jennifer?"

Of course that's not enough to satisfy her. "Do you know who pushed her, then?" she demands.

"Maybe no one did!" I explode, causing several heads near us to turn as parents goggle. "Maybe she fell."

Jennifer cocks her head. "I heard Kieran was just standing over her and *staring*."

I recall seeing that very thing, but, in truth, the whole afternoon has become a blur. "He was probably in shock," I dismiss. "Give it a rest, why don't you? Isn't there enough to be dealing with?"

Jennifer looks like she wants to keep arguing, but then she shrugs and waves the sheet of paper. "So, you won't sign the petition?"

"No, I will not," I practically spit.

Jennifer huffs and moves off, and I stand there for a moment, amazed at how quickly my mood of hopefulness and gratitude has morphed into a boiling rage—and fear.

If Jennifer Evans finds out it was actually Freya...

Without meeting anyone's eye, I turn on my heel and head for the door to the reception area. Parents are generally *not* welcome at the start of the school day, when teachers and staff are all rushing around, but I am heedless of that rule as I march up to the reception desk, where Mrs. Taylor, a stern-looking woman in her fifties with a helmet of dyed brown hair, wire-rimmed glasses, and thin lips outlined in deep red, eyes me beadily.

"Yes?" Her voice radiates disapproval.

"I need to speak to Mrs. Bryson."

"Mrs. Bryson?" Mrs. Taylor's lips go even thinner. "I'm afraid that's not possible right now. You can make an appointment—"

"It's a matter of some urgency." I keep her stare. I'm going to be late to my desk, but I don't even care. This is more important. "*Considerable* urgency, in regard to the situation with Bella

Dalton in third grade." I pause meaningfully for the barest of seconds. "Could you get her, please?"

Mrs. Taylor holds my gaze for another second, and I can tell she wants to refuse me just because, but finally she gives a brief nod and walks out of the office.

My shoulders sag as I release a long, slow breath. What exactly am I doing here? I'm not really sure, and yet it feels right.

A few minutes later, Mrs. Bryson welcomes me into her office. She is standing in front of her desk, wearing a navy twinset and gray slacks, her hands clasped in front of her like a nun, although to be fair, the expression on her face is mingled sympathy and caution. She must know how involved my child is in what happened with Bella.

"Mrs. West..." she begins, but I cut her off.

"Are you aware there's a petition circulating among parents to have Kieran Walters expelled?" In my nervousness and outrage, my voice comes out too harsh.

Mrs. Bryson's expression instantly becomes guarded. "I am aware that something like that was going around, yes," she informs me carefully. "However, no such petition has been approved by the school."

I stare at her incredulously. "But surely that's not allowed?"

She draws herself up. "I appreciate it might be upsetting to the parties involved, but I'm afraid this school is not responsible for how parents choose to—"

"But it's happening on school grounds!" I cut across her. "And I think circulating such a petition would count as bullying and harassment. Frankly, I'm surprised that you haven't issued a statement that you will not tolerate such aggressive and unpleasant behavior among our close-knit community of learners."

I can tell I've annoyed her with the slightly mocking edge to my voice, but really? Is all that close-knit crap just for the privileged few?

If it's not for everyone, I think resolutely, *it's not for anyone.*

"Again, I appreciate that this must be upsetting for those involved," Mrs. Bryson says in that same careful voice. "And I can assure you, the school is dealing with the situation." Her voice is firm, final. "As it happens, we are in the process of drafting a response, and with particular concern for what happened to Bella Dalton—"

"Kieran Walters did not push Bella Dalton," I tell her flatly. "And even if he did, that should have no bearing on how he is treated by this school, since the incident happened *out* of school."

I can tell I've surprised Mrs. Bryson with this news. Her eyes flare and she presses her lips together. "I wasn't aware of the circumstances," she admits, "but—"

"It was an accident," I inform her. And then, because I know I can't keep it secret and maybe I shouldn't even want or try to, "Actually, it was *Freya* who pushed Bella. They were arguing, as children everywhere so often do. Bella pushed her first, and then Freya pushed back, and unfortunately—*very* unfortunately—Bella lost her footing and hit her head when she fell. That's *it.* A tragic accident, nothing more." I stop, realizing I am breathing hard, as Mrs. Bryson stares at me, speechless.

"Thank you for telling me," she says after a moment, and I can't tell anything from her tone. Does she feel any sympathy? Is she just protecting her territory? Suddenly, I don't care anymore. Why did I come out swinging for *Kieran*, of all kids? But then I remember how he and Freya were on the sofa, happily playing the iPad together, and I know why. At the end of the day, he's just a little boy. He's not a monster. He doesn't deserve to be vilified. And maybe, who knows, he might become Freya's friend.

"Thank you," I tell Mrs. Bryson shortly, and then I wheel

around and stalk out of her office. My heart is still racing as I head back to my car, amazed at what I just said and did. Will it make any difference? I hope so.

I've just slid into the driver's seat when my phone pings with a text. I glance down at it, half-expecting something from Matt, but it's not. It's from Eleanor.

Bella's awake.

TWENTY-THREE

ELEANOR

I have been sitting by Bella's bed for three hours before her eyes open. They started bringing her slowly off her cocktail of medications on Tuesday night, monitoring her responses, warning me when I arrived this morning that the whole process takes a lot of time. The TV version of someone waking up from a coma and immediately asking where they are or what year it is, it turns out, is not at all realistic. Instead, it is hours of aching exhaustion and perilous hope, straining to see something new— a flicker of an eyelid, the twitch of a finger. Anything to reassure me that my baby girl, my Bella-bee, is still in there somewhere.

It has been an exhausting few days. First that confrontation with Natalie at the hospital, then with Joanna, and then my stupid destruction of our photographs, the cuts on Lizzy's arm I need to talk to her more about... and last of all, finding out about Tina.

Brian looked winded with shock when I asked him outright; I was amazed that I'd finally had the nerve to do it. But once I'd said the words, I felt only relief, because I knew he could not prevaricate his way out of this. Finally, for better or worse, I would know... even if I dreaded having that knowledge.

"Eleanor... what..." he had begun to bluster. "Why would you..." Apparently, he *was* going to try to prevaricate.

"I know you spent the day of the party with her," I told him in what I hoped was a matter-of-fact tone. "I know she texted you and said how much the day *meant* to her." I almost used claw-like air quotes but managed to keep myself from it. "I know you've been working late and that you changed the pass-words on your phone and laptop, so that means you must be hiding something from me. What is it, Brian?" I raised my chin a notch, forced myself to ask the question I was dreading knowing the answer to. "Are you having an affair?"

"An *affair*..." He practically choked on the word, his eyes bulging as his face flushed.

"It's a reasonable assumption to make, don't you think?" I replied levelly, half-amazed at how calm I sounded. Maybe I'd got out all the rage and despair when I'd destroyed all those photos, a whole trash bag of anger and grief in the garage, along with the splintered wood and broken glass. "Those are the classic signs, after all."

"Eleanor, I am *not* having an affair." He had sounded utterly certain, as well as more than a little affronted by the whole notion, which gave me a flicker of something almost like hope. "I would never do that. I love you."

"*Do you?*" I asked, the question, the raw honesty of it, along with the blatant cynicism, surprising him as well as me.

"What is that supposed to mean?" he demanded.

"Do you love me, or do you love who I've had to be for you?"

He shook his head slowly, his expression deepening into a frown. "I... I don't even know what that is supposed to mean."

"No, I don't imagine you do." And I didn't think I had the emotional energy to get into all of that just then. I wasn't sure if I knew how to explain it, and so I folded my arms and did my best to stare him down. "All right, then. Who is Tina?"

Brian took a deep breath, let it out slowly, which gave me time to brace myself. Did I want to hear this? Was I ready to?

"Tina," he said slowly, in the manner of someone making an announcement of grave import, "is my mother."

"What..." The word escaped me in a single breath. His *mother*? The possibility had not once crossed my mind. Brian hadn't been in touch with his mother for years, decades; I'd met her only once, an awkward, weepy occasion when we'd first got engaged. He'd done it for form's sake, and I remember feeling both disgusted and filled with pity; she'd been drunk, overly sentimental, knocking over her glass of red wine at one point during the meal, so a waiter had to come running. After that, Brian had cut off all ties. I was sad that the girls wouldn't have one grandmother, but I accepted that considering how Christina was, it was probably better that they didn't.

But to learn he's been in touch with her *now*? And he kept it a secret? I didn't even know where to begin with the questions and, in any case, I didn't have time to ask any because Lizzy drifted downstairs, looking tearful and quiet but at least *there*.

We ate pizza, the three of us at the table, no one saying anything much, but we were together. Afterward, Brian closeted himself in his study, saying he had to catch up on work, although I suspected it was just an excuse to keep from continuing our conversation. I didn't mind; I wasn't sure I was ready for a massive heart-to-heart about yet another thing right then. Still, the memory of what was spoken kept circling around in my head.

What had I meant, *do you love who I had to be*? The words had just slipped out, unthinkingly yet unsettlingly heartfelt, and I wasn't ready to examine them. Not when Bella was about to wake up, and now she *has*, or at least started to, although it isn't until after I've been sitting there for several hours that her eyelids actually flicker.

I lurch forward, everything in me aching, straining. "Bella...

Bella, honey, it's Mommy. Are you there? Can you hear me? Sweet girl..." The words bubble from my lips, and I have the desperate sense that I can somehow compel her to open her eyes by sheer force of will. But they don't open.

After a few minutes pass, I slump back against the seat, wondering if I'd imagined that tiny twitch.

When a nurse comes in, I mention it, hopefully, like she's going to tell me I can expect Bella to sit up any moment and start speaking. She smiles sympathetically and goes out again without saying a word in response. Despite my daughter lying right next to me, I feel very alone. Brian said he would come in after lunch, since things "wouldn't get going" until then, at the very earliest; he made it sound like a party we were attending.

I scan Bella's blank face, longing for something. *Anything.* Another twitch. A flicker.

Anything, anything, Bella, please...

Another half-hour passes, and I text Natalie, because I need something to do and she's the first person I think of contacting, even before my parents, who have been concerned from a distance—their usual MO. Not that I would have even wanted them to sweep in and take over. Their presence would have just made me even more anxious.

Natalie phoned me yesterday, which I appreciated, but with everything else going on, I haven't yet called or texted her back, and, in truth, I haven't known what to say. Now I text that Bella's waking up, as if typing it out somehow makes it true. As if Bella will sense what I've said and open her eyes.

And then, after another twenty minutes, she does. If I hadn't been looking at her, I would have missed it. I see a blaze of golden-green and then they close again, pale lashes fanning her paler cheeks, but it's enough to make me let out a sob of relief, of joy.

"Bella..."

She's coming back. She *is*. She really is.

I text both Brian and Lizzy, even though I know Lizzy's not supposed to check her phone during the school day. Undoubtedly, she will, and I want her to know.

Natalie has texted me back—a message I can't reply to, not yet: *That's wonderful, Eleanor!! Is she speaking? Thinking of you.* With several heart and prayer hands emojis.

No, I think in frustration, *she just opened her eyes, that's it. Can't that be enough?*

But I know I'm not really annoyed with Natalie; she wants Bella's recovery as much as I do—or almost. Nothing quite compares to a mother's fierce love, but I'm sure Natalie feels guilty that Freya pushed Bella, no matter what Bella might have done first.

The funny, or maybe the sad, thing is, now that I know it was Freya and not Kieran, I feel completely differently about it all. I might have been tempted to make Kieran into a monster, but I certainly don't want to do that with Freya. She's just a little girl, as well as Bella's best friend. Whatever happened was, I am finally willing to accept, a genuine accident, and no one's fault... not even mine.

The realization trickles through me, settles. I feel relief rather than resentment, a sense of peace on the horizon, rather than the dissatisfaction of something left unsettled. The police, I'm sure, will come to the same conclusion as I have; they've gone quiet since they visited on Thursday, but I'm not sure I even care anymore. I hope Brian doesn't, either. I just want to put it all behind me, well and truly, and focus on Bella getting better.

Open your eyes again for me, baby, please...

I lean forward. Hold my breath. Pray.

A tiny breath escapes her, a puff of air, a miniscule sound, but it is enough to lift my spirits, especially when her eyes flutter again. She really is coming back to us. In that moment, I can believe she will truly wake up, give me that wonderful, sleepy smile and whisper my name.

Hi, Mommy.

I can almost hear it.

I don't know how long I sit there, fists clenched, body straining, willing Bella to do what I'm so sure she can and will.

Please...

But nothing more happens. She slips back into sleep like a wave lapping over her, pulling her out to sea, away from me.

I slump back in my seat and close my eyes. I'm so very *tired*. Of everything... Bella being here, Lizzy being so unhappy, Brian being so secretive. His *mother*? And as for Natalie... a few perfunctory texts aside, are we even still friends?

My eyes are still closed when the door to Bella's room opens, and someone clears his throat. I lurch upright, a flush coming to my face when I see it's one of the neurological consultants. There is a whole team of them, and I keep forgetting their names. This one is on the younger side, mid-thirties, with a shock of brown hair and tortoiseshell glasses.

"Mrs. Dalton." He smiles at me with brisk sympathy. "I hear Bella is starting to wake up?"

"Yes... she opened her eyes once, but she's fallen back asleep now. You know, *really* asleep..." Coma level. I'm trying to sound matter-of-fact, but my voice wobbles.

"That's perfectly normal at this stage of the process," he assures me as he reaches for the clipboard at the end of the bed and scans it with a thoughtful frown. "We should be seeing more stirrings in the next few hours, but, as hard as it is, I'd advise keeping your expectations low for today. It takes a long time for someone to come out of a coma, and Bella's awareness, or lack of it, is not necessarily an indication of her functioning levels as we go forward."

Not necessarily. I'd prefer a little more certainty, more

assurance than that, but I know at this stage, I will simply have to take what I can get.

"Okay," I say, nodding.

He takes an ophthalmoscope, barely bigger than a pen, out of the pocket of his white lab coat and shines it in front of Bella's eyes one at a time, lifting each eyelid with a perfunctory professionalism that makes me tense. Then he taps on the beds of her fingernails before pressing his finger to the curve of her neck. The look on his face is detached, assessing. I am absolutely aching to know what his findings are, but, of course, he doesn't tell me.

He simply turns to me with another one of his brisk smiles. "All as expected at this stage. I'll come back again at the end of my round."

"But..." I'm not sure I even want to ask what I am so desperate to know. *Will she wake up? Will she know me? How much damage has her brain sustained?*

"Tomorrow," he tells me as if I've asked all that aloud, "we'll book her in for an MRI to get an accurate scan of the brain." His mouth curves up another notch, like he's twirled a dial. "Try not to worry."

Right. As if that helps. Still, I murmur my thanks as he leaves for his next patient.

The rest of the morning passes slowly. Bella stirs again but doesn't open her eyes. Her fingers twitch, and once she lets out a breathy sigh; it's almost as if I can hear her voice. At noon, I head to the cafeteria for a ready-made sandwich, tasteless and chilled from the refrigerated cabinet.

When I go back upstairs, Brian is in Bella's room. He turns as I come to the door.

"Brian... I only left for a minute," I say quickly. "To get some lunch, that's all."

"I figured you had," he replies with a frown. "Eleanor... of course I don't expect you to be here every second of the day."

"Don't you?" I reply before I can think better of it. I don't look at him as I take my usual seat next to Bella's bed. "Has she opened her eyes?"

"No, but there have been a few twitches and sighs and stuff. Eleanor..." He hesitates, sounding torn, sad. "We should talk."

I stare at my hands, neatly folded in my lap. "About what?"

"About us."

A heaviness settles inside me. We're meant to be the kind of couple that doesn't *need* to talk about us, but clearly, we do... for a whole host of reasons. And yet right now I absolutely do not possess the emotional energy for any of that.

"Bella could wake up at any moment, Brian," I state. "I don't think now is the right time for some kind of heart-to-heart."

"Fair enough," he replies after a moment. "But soon."

I nod, not trusting myself to speak. I have no idea what *talking about us* actually means.

Or what the result will be.

The rest of the afternoon passes slowly. Bella continues to twitch or sigh, and a couple of times she opens her eyes, only to close them again, sink back into sleep. Around four, when I should head back for Lizzy, her eyes open and finally stay open.

"Bella..." Her name explodes out of me, and I reach for her hand; her fingers curl, just a little bit, around mine.

"Hey, Bella-bee," Brian says, his voice as warm and full of affection as ever. "How's my little girl?"

She blinks slowly—once, twice, three times. We both hold our breath, waiting. Her fingers curl a little bit more around mine. I stroke her hand.

"Bella, sweetheart..." I'm afraid to ask her questions, but I so desperately want to know if she's actually *there*. "Bella, it's Mommy. And Daddy. We're here... and Lizzy... she's at home..." I trail off as Bella's eyes close once more, only to suddenly snap open.

Brian and I exchange a surprised, slightly panicky look. Bella's gaze moves slowly from Brian to me. Her fingers tighten on my hand, nails digging in.

"Bella, you don't need to be scared," I tell her gently. "You're in a hospital because you had a fall, but you're getting better, and you've got such nice nurses and doctors taking care of you. You're going to be okay, honey, I promise." I glance at Brian again. "We both do."

But it's been too much for Bella; her eyes close again, and her fingers slip out of mine. I long to hold her hand again, to feel her fingers tighten on mine.

I sit back, drained yet exhilarated from that brief interaction. "What do you think?" I ask Brian. "Did she seem..."

"She seemed like she knew what was going on, at least a little bit," he says. I can't help but think he sounds like he is trying to convince himself.

"Yeah, she did," I say, doing my best to feel hopeful. "She did..." I rub my eyes as a wave of exhaustion crashes over me. I've been sitting next to Bella's bed for over nine hours.

"El, you look exhausted," Brian tells me. "Why don't you head home, have a bath, a sleep? Check in on Lizzy, too. I can stay here for a while."

I realize what a good idea that sounds—not just for me, but for Lizzy. We've neglected her too much, and we need to have a serious conversation about those scars on her arm.

"Okay," I tell Brian. I rise from my chair slowly, and as I pass him, he puts his hand on my arm, pulls me into a sudden and surprising hug; it takes me a second to respond and put my arms around him. I realize we haven't touched much since

Bella's accident. I thought that was on him, but maybe it was on me.

"We're going to get through this," he tells me, his chin resting on top of my head. "And the four of us will be stronger than ever."

For a second, I let myself rest in his arms, squeezing my eyes shut as I will his words into truth.

"I love you," he says softly. "I feel like you're doubting it right now, but I do. I love you, Eleanor—*you*, and not whatever you think *I* need you to be."

My throat thickens. How much of the expectations I felt Brian put on me, I wonder, had I really put on myself? Wanting to be perfect. Needing to prove to my parents, my siblings, the whole world, that I was more than they'd ever thought I was? I don't know the answer to those questions, not yet, but it is revealing that I asked them. That the answers might not be what I once thought they were.

"I love you, too," I whisper, meaning it as I slip out of his arms.

The house is empty even though it's after five and Lizzy should be back. I text her to ask where she is, and then I find myself back up in Bella's room, even though I'm not sure it does me much good to be in there. I don't curl up on her bed this time, though; instead, I prowl around the room, running my hand along the top of her dresser, straightening her panda bears, glancing down at the papers on her little desk.

On top is a drawing she did in crayon, childishly drawn but carefully colored in, and I smile faintly as I pick it up. It's a drawing of our family—Brian is recognizable with his shock of blond hair and blue button-down shirt; I'm wearing a patchwork skirt, and my hair is a mess of corkscrew curls. Lizzy is there, next to Bella, both of them blond and smiling. But there are two other people in the picture, right behind Brian, a blond boy and a girl with two dark braids. Even in Bella's childish stick figures, I know who they are. Freya and Kieran.

What on earth are they doing in our family picture? When did Bella draw this? Obviously, before her accident, but how long before? And why did she include them, standing so close to Brian, like they are part of our family, connected to him?

A kaleidoscope of memories swirl through my mind, a confusing blur until the image settles and gathers shape. Bella telling Freya and Kieran they didn't have daddies. The way Bella smiled when she saw Kieran, her little face lighting up. This picture.

And *Lizzy*... the cuts on her arm. The accusation she made that she was our daughter, too. The way she skulked about the party, how upset she's seemed since, more than just for Bella. She was so panicked about the police coming...

She's been hiding something, I realize with a jolt. I had an inkling that she was earlier, but I'd suppressed it, because I knew I couldn't deal with anything more than I already was. And yet... I'd known all along that something was off about the whole scenario that had been reformulated—Bella a bully, taking them off somewhere and teasing her friends? Even knowing she is far from perfect, it didn't feel right.

And now I think I am starting to get a glimmer why.

From downstairs, I hear the front door open and close. Without thinking too much, acting on instinct, I head downstairs. I am at the curve of the stairs when Lizzy sees me. She is by the front door, phone in hand, a guilty and tense look on her face.

"Mom?"

"Bella's woken up," I tell her. "I think... I'm hopeful she's going to be okay."

"She is?" Lizzy sounds as surprised as she does relieved. "Did she... did she say anything?"

Suspicion hardens into knowledge, or something close to it. "Lizzy..." I hold up Bella's drawing. I have no idea how to articulate what I'm feeling, *fearing*, but in the end, I don't have to.

Lizzy sees the picture in my hand and her face drains of color. "Mom..." she whispers, and it sounds like an apology.

I open my mouth to speak but nothing comes out and, once again, it's Lizzy who says something. Her eyes fill with tears, and they spill over as she shakes her head.

"Bella," she whispers. "What happened... it's all my fault."

TWENTY-FOUR

JOANNA

As an actuary for a health insurance company, I, more than most people, know the dangers of Dr. Google. Self-diagnosis on the internet is a foolish and fear-inducing exercise and causes so much needless worry and panic. And yet, since finding a diagnosis for Kieran on the very internet I warn against, I can't help but feel as if all the pieces have slotted into place... and it's a picture that scares me with its unknowns.

I read the list of symptoms in the blue glow of my laptop screen, my gaze flicking down each one as a leaden feeling settled in my stomach. *Aggression, tantrums or losses of temper, lack of remorse, disregard for authority, indifference to others.* Check, check, check, check, check. There are other symptoms that Kieran doesn't have—cruelty to animals, bullying, stealing. Vandalism? Not *really*, but he does wreck things sometimes, for seemingly no reason. Once I came into his room to find he'd systematically smashed all his Lego pieces into smithereens. Pathological lying? I hesitated on that one, because sometimes he can be starkly, unsettlingly honest; other times he lies for seemingly no reason.

All together it was enough to make me think that we need to

see a specialist. Kieran needs a diagnosis—if not this one, then another, but this one, with all its implications, feels instinctively right.

The next morning, while Kieran is at school, I confront Tim.

"We need to talk about Kieran," I tell him, the words alone causing a shudder of fear to go through me. I am afraid of what the future might hold.

Tim, on the sofa with his laptop, looking at job opportunities, which is positive in itself, raises his eyebrows. "What about?" He sounds interested, unworried; things were good this morning, at breakfast, but also between us. He kissed me good morning and we hugged before I took Kieran to school. Tim even suggested he could pick him up this afternoon, the first time since we've moved that such a thing has even been considered. It felt like we were recovering some of our old normalcy, and now this.

"I think Kieran needs to see someone," I tell Tim. "For a proper diagnosis."

Tim frowns, one hand on his laptop like he's about to close it, but he doesn't, almost as if he doesn't want to give this conversation that level of time—or credence. "Jo," he says on a suppressed sigh, "we've talked about this."

"I know we have." I sit opposite him, my hands tucked between my knees. I feel as if I am shaking inside, but when I speak again, my voice is very calm. "Tim, I didn't tell you something about Bella's accident. Not about who pushed her or how, but when I came upon the whole scene..." I trail off as I recreate that unsettling image in my mind: Bella, lifeless, face down in the shallows of the pond, blood in her hair. Eleanor running toward her, her face an expression of agony and terror. And *Kieran*... Kieran standing just a few feet away, a look of curious, clinical detachment on his face, almost as if he were a scientist observing some kind of abstract phenomenon. It wasn't natural, that look. It wasn't *right*.

"What about it?" Tim asks, sounding a little impatient.

I realize I've been simply staring into space. "About Kieran, and how he was. When Bella was lying in the water, she'd clearly been injured... her face was *in* the water, Tim, and Kieran... he was just... standing there."

Tim gives a little, irritable shrug. "So?"

"*So?*" I repeat, wishing I didn't have to battle against him at every step. "Why didn't he do something? Help her? Get her out of the water, at least? Or shout to someone for help? Or... I don't know... *something*." Anything. Anything but stand there looking almost indifferent to a girl whose very lifeblood was ebbing away.

"He's *seven*, Jo," Tim says, as if I need reminding of our son's age. "Don't you think you might be putting a bit too much responsibility on him? He was probably completely shocked—"

"He didn't look shocked," I reply quietly.

Tim rolls his eyes, a determined gesture. "So, you're demanding a diagnosis because of an expression he *didn't* have on his face?"

When he puts it like that, it does sound a little bit ridiculous. Over-the-top and paranoid, and God knows, *I would like it to be*. But I know, on a gut level, right down to my bones, that we both need to stop hiding from the truth that keeps punching us in the face, day after day after day.

"It's not just that, and you know it," I say in a low voice. It hurts to talk this way, but I know it's time. It was probably time a while ago. How long, I don't want to think. "It's a whole raft of behaviors," I continue. "His sudden losses of temper. His willful destruction of things. The way he seems so indifferent, so *remorseless* sometimes, if he does something wrong or someone gets hurt..."

"You make him sound," Tim scoffs, "like some kind of psychopath."

"Not a *psycho*path," I reply with emphasis, and Tim's eyes widen. For the first time, he looks like he's taking me seriously.

"*Jo.*" My name is a reprimand. "What the hell is that supposed to mean?"

I take a deep breath. "I looked up some of Kieran's symptoms last night."

"What, on WebMD?" More scoffing, but I feel his fear underneath, a pulsing river of it, and it makes me ache, because I'm afraid, too, and yet we need to be united about this... for the sake of our son, whom we love.

"No, on a therapy site for children," I tell him as evenly as I can. "But on some others, too, for confirmation. The point is, on all the different sites, it was clear that a lot of Kieran's symptoms fit a certain diagnosis."

Tim stares at me for a long moment, with neither of us saying a word. It feels like the calm before the storm, the *before* moment we'll never get again. He doesn't want to ask, and I don't want to answer, but we both know there is only one place this conversation can go.

"Okay," he finally says, and now his voice is as level as mine. "What is this diagnosis?"

I take another breath; it feels like there is no going back now. "Conduct Disorder."

Tim raises his eyebrows as if it say, *that's it?*

I admit, it sounds innocuous, on par with the host of other diagnoses so many children these days seem to get—ADHD, ADD, PDD. But it's different. At least, it *feels* different, in this moment, but maybe it doesn't have to be.

"All right," he says. He settles back into the sofa, his eyebrows still lifted, and now it's as if he's saying *I'll humor you.* "What is Conduct Disorder?"

"Well... it's a diagnosis for children with the following

symptoms." I pause to ready myself. "Disengaged, withdrawal from relationships with parents or peers is one," I feel as if they're all seared on my mind. "Social isolation. Limited emotion other than impulsive anger. Little attachment to anyone. Unremorseful. Impervious to punishments or rewards..."

Tim opens his mouth like he wants to argue, but he doesn't say anything.

"There are other ones that Kieran doesn't have," I continue. "More disturbing ones, frankly, like hurting animals or stealing. But the ones I just mentioned are the main ones that would indicate a diagnosis."

Tim nods slowly, his arms folded, his jaw bunched. "And if he did have this disorder," he says after a moment. "What would it mean? Would he have to go on some medication that knocks him out or something?"

"No, there's no medication for Conduct Disorder." I pause. "And there's no cure. There are just therapies that could help mitigate some of his symptoms and help us to help him. Teach him how to have empathy, how not to lose his temper..."

"How to have *empathy*?" Tim repeats incredulously. "Jo, you're making him sound like some kind of monster."

"No, no, not a monster," I reply quickly. I do not ever want to think that way about my child. "Not at *all*, Tim. But... Conduct Disorder in children is the precursor to an adult diagnosis of Antisocial Personality Disorder... which is commonly known as sociopathy."

The words rest heavily between us, a burden I had to lay down, even as I tell myself it's just a word.

"Socio..." Tim shakes his head slowly. "Jo, are you saying he's a *sociopath*?"

"Children can't be diagnosed as sociopaths," I explain. I sound like an expert, when all I really have is an agonizing hour doing a deep dive on the internet, and an unsettling certainty that I'm right. "But the child version of it, yes. But that doesn't mean... It isn't necessarily what people think it is. Far more people are sociopaths than you or I would ever even realize. They can live normal lives." Even if they can't feel emotions, like remorse or empathy or *love*, the way most other people do.

Tim keeps shaking his head. He doesn't speak, and I know he's absorbing everything I've just said, everything we know about our son. I wait because he needs time. Even though I've had a sleepless night to accept it, it still feels like a shock every time I think about it, and yet I am determined to believe that there is still possibility and hope. I hold fast to the fact that I love my son exactly how he is. But it still feels like a lot to accept.

"How did you come up with this?" he finally asks, an accusing note entering his voice. "I mean, what, you typed in *unemotional, remorseless, unloving*? Is that how you think of Kieran?"

His words hit home, and make me wince. "Please don't make this about me," I beg him. "Although..." This part is even harder to say than everything that's gone before. "The truth is, some of the symptoms I... I recognize in myself."

Tim reels back. *"What?"*

I swallow dryly. "Just that... well, you know I've never been close to my family—"

"Jo, that hardly makes you eligible for this type of diagnosis," Tim protests. His face has softened in sympathy, and I know he's thinking that this fear of mine, irrational as he believes it to be, has influenced me when it comes to Kieran. But I know the opposite is true: it's Kieran's potential diagnosis that has made me re-evaluate myself. Made me consider why I'm so reserved, so distant, so physically unaffectionate, because it's true, I *am*. Maybe the seeds are there in many of us... and if we get Kieran the therapy he needs, the therapy we *all* need, we can prevent those seeds from taking root, from growing into something damaging.

What I do know is that we need to accept and love Kieran for who he is, and that means getting him the help he needs.

"The point is, we need to talk about Kieran," I say firmly. "And get him the help he deserves. Tim, if we can prevent Kieran from..." I trail off, and his expression hardens.

"From what?"

Fine, I think, *I'll say it.* "From his symptoms becoming more ingrained and, frankly, worse," I state bluntly. "That's what we're trying to avoid here. Kieran is our son and I love him very much. But I also recognize his limitations. And I want to help him deal with them, maybe even overcome them." My voice throbs with emotion. "Do you blame me for that?"

Tim drops his head into his hands, raking his fingers through his hair. A shudder goes through him. "No," he finally says quietly, his head still in his hands. "No, of course I don't."

I exhale quietly, a near-silent sigh of relief. "Then..."

"Make an appointment," Tim says. He lifts his head to look at me with so much grief and sorrow in his eyes that I ache. He had his head in the sand far more than I did about this, I know. "Is that what we do? With a therapist or specialist or...?"

"Yes, with a child psychiatrist." I've looked online and there is an esteemed one at the Connecticut Children's Medical Center—the same hospital where Bella is currently being treated. There is probably a waiting list a mile long, but with my connections in the industry I might be able to jump the line a little bit. That's not fair, I know, but I'm willing to use what I can to help my son. Isn't every mother?

"Okay." Tim nods, looking haggard, like he's aged in a matter of minutes.

I reach across the space between us and clasp his hand. "Tim, I'm sorry," I say.

His fingers close over mine as he gazes at me with a mingled look of sympathy and sorrow. "It's not your fault, Jo," he says, but I can't help but wonder if it is, at least a little bit.

That afternoon, I wait for Kieran in the playground—Tim ended up having a nap, which annoyed me less than it once would have—conscious of the knots of other mothers around me. A woman with a high blond ponytail, wearing expensive-looking exercise gear, keeps shooting me pointed looks, and then glancing away again to whisper furiously to her friends. I pretend not to notice, but as it goes on, I start to feel conspicuous—and angry.

The last time I dared to confront anyone in this schoolyard it spectacularly misfired. I recall Eleanor's puzzled look, the relief, as well as the smug satisfaction, that passed over her face when Kieran found his invitation in his backpack. Had she been at least a little worried that there hadn't been one put in his bag? I'm not sure if I'll ever get to know her well enough to ask.

But this time...

I walk over to the woman I'm pretty sure is Jennifer Evans—the mastermind behind that awful petition. I feel calm, almost, bizarrely friendly, as I approach her. I know she saw me coming, because she looked away quickly, but now that I'm standing right behind her, she's pretending I don't exist. It's so obvious, it's almost funny.

I tap her on the shoulder. She tenses, then turns around, her expression a parody of surprise.

She raises her perfectly arched eyebrow. "Um... yes?" No friendliness in that tone.

"Do you have a problem with me or my son?" I ask her pleasantly. I'm even smiling. "Because I've heard that you started a petition to get him expelled."

She draws herself up, glancing around for support, but

everyone around her is silent and wide-eyed. I think of Natalie's comment about people passing the popcorn as they watched her separation unfold and I'm pretty sure I know what she means. I also have the surprising sense that people might not actually support Jennifer Evans and her nasty petition as much as she thought they did, and it gives me courage.

"Do you know he wasn't actually the one to push her?" I ask her. "Not that it even matters, because what happened was an *accident*." I pause for emphasis before continuing in the same steady voice, "I know Kieran's had some behavior issues since he started here, but we were going through a tough time as a family, and of course this is also a new school, new home, new town... well, you get the picture." My smile widens, but I know the expression in my eyes is flinty. "You can imagine, maybe, how challenging it can be for someone to settle in, how important it is to feel welcomed."

"Look—" she begins, all bluster, but I cut her off.

"I'm going to talk to Mrs. Bryson about the illegality of the petition. I'm pretty sure it constitutes harassment, so considering the school's policy about bullying, I have a feeling she's not going to want to support it. But in any case..." Again, I pause. Make sure she's listening, which she is, and looking decidedly uneasy. "Maybe have a hard look at yourself, and your own actions, before you go pointing the finger at other people." I glance around at the other mothers, who are watching me avidly, a look of horrified fascination on their faces. "And that goes for everyone here, myself included. I know I could have made more of an effort. I'm not all that great in groups. But not one mother here, save Toby's mom, even tried to welcome me. Not one smile, not one hello. Do you know how that feels? Can you *imagine*?"

No one responds, but I see their sideways looks, more embarrassed than snide.

I wait a second, and then I give a nod. "Well, I'm still here, and so is Kieran. And I'm always happy to chat." And then I turn away and walk back to where I was standing. My legs are shaking with nerves, but I'm actually smiling—still. That felt *good*, crazily enough, and I'm glad I did it... even if I can hear the furious whispering from all the way across the playground. I realize I don't even care.

Well, not much anyway.

"That was *amazing*."

I turn to see Rachel standing beside me, smiling, and I manage a shaky laugh.

"Amazingly stupid, maybe," I reply on a half-laugh, "but I'm still glad I did it."

"Jennifer Evans deserved it," Rachel declares. "I don't know if anyone actually likes her. She's always trying to act like she's the queen bee—"

"I thought that was Eleanor," I can't help but say. That was the sense I got—Eleanor, president of the PTA, gracefully bestowing her favor on the adoring populace, but maybe this whole thing has knocked her from her pedestal, which, really, is no bad thing.

"Eleanor *is* the queen bee," Rachel concedes with a smile. "Jennifer's just a try-hard."

I laugh, shaking my head, even though talking about the other moms like this makes me feel sad. Doesn't anyone ever grow up? "It feels like we're still in junior high."

"Aren't we?" Rachel only half-jokes. She touches my arm. "Look, would you like to get Toby and Kieran together one day, maybe at the park? Just for a run-around? Nothing, you know, too stressful."

I hesitate for a millisecond, or not even. I am thinking of the therapies I read that can help kids with Conduct Disorder. One of them is supervised playdates.

"That would be great," I say, and Rachel grins.

The door to the third-grade classroom opens and kids

tumble out into the crisp fall day. I wait, the fresh breeze blowing right through me, an expectant smile on my face. I realize, maybe for the first time, that I don't feel anxious about what Kieran might have got up to, or what the other parents might be thinking or gossiping about. It's not because I'm naïve enough to think he didn't get up to anything; I think he probably did. But if we get a diagnosis, we can learn how to live with it, and that feels like a huge step forward.

As for the other mothers? Well, I'm not sure they matter as much as I thought they did. Maybe I can take a page from Kieran's book and be a little more indifferent to them. The ones that matter, like Rachel, and who knows, maybe even Natalie, will accept me—and Kieran—for who we are.

I see Kieran come through the door, and I smile and wave. He doesn't smile or wave back, but he gives a little nod as he heads toward me, and right now, that feels like enough.

More than enough.

As Kieran stands in front of me, I ruffle his hair ever so briefly, and then we fall into step together as a few leaves drift lazily down.

"I thought we could get ice cream after school," I tell him, and he looks surprised, and then pleased. He looks like any other little boy.

"Okay," he says, and I smile.

TWENTY-FIVE

NATALIE

It is Friday before I make it to Hartford to see Bella, which makes me feel guilty, but I simply had to work, after all the time off I've taken. And then there was adjusting to Matt moving back in, and making sure we spent some time together, just the three of us. Or so I told myself...

But the truth is, I don't know where I stand with Eleanor anymore, or really, where she stands with me.

We've exchanged texts throughout the week, but they've been perfunctory, and I haven't seen her at all. I have no idea how Bella is doing, besides that she's awake and "recovering well," and Eleanor has no idea about my life, that Matt wasn't having an affair like she'd thought, and we're back together.

In a different situation, another life perhaps, I would have been over at Eleanor's every day. I would have been helping take care of Lizzy, dropping off meals, throwing in a load of laundry. And if our roles were reversed, Eleanor would have done the same for me. She basically did do that for me, after Matt left.

So a week of near-silence feels weird. Wrong. And yet the truth is, I can't imagine it any other way.

But I'm here now, with a bouquet of flowers from the florist in Wetherby, looking a little limp in their hand-tied, eco-friendly wrapping. I've also brought a dozen muffins from the artisan bakery, in a variety of flavors, but my gifts feel like cheap, pathetic offerings, considering the enormity of what happened. Still, I can't go empty-handed. Part of me doesn't want to go at all. I haven't *missed* Eleanor this last week. I don't know what that says about me, or her, or the state of our friendship, but it's the truth. Being apart has been something of a relief... not that I'd ever tell her so.

And, like I said, I'm here now.

I stiffen my spine and straighten my shoulders as I head into the hospital and up to the neurology ward. The corridor is quiet, the only sound the occasional squeak of a cart wheel and the persistent beeping of various monitors as I pass by rooms, doing my best not to rubberneck and look inside.

When I get to Bella's room, I find Eleanor alone, standing by the window, staring out at the trees; they've really changed color, I notice, and are a sea of scarlet and gold. To my surprise, Bella is not in the bed, and for a second, I feel a terrible frisson of fear.

"Eleanor..."

She turns, smiling when she sees me, although she looks incredibly tired. "Natalie."

"I'm sorry I didn't come before..."

She brushes my words aside. "Don't be. I feel like we haven't had a moment's rest, to be honest. Bella's just in physio right now. Sometimes I go with her, but I can be a distraction, so..." She shrugs, smiling and spreading her hands.

"She's in physiotherapy?" I can't keep the surprise from my voice. I expected her to be bedridden, and, let's face it, barely sentient. "That's... I mean, that's..."

"It's great," Eleanor says firmly. "She's doing great."

I brandish the bouquet and box of muffins before putting them on a side table. "Just a little something..."

"Thank you."

I take a few moments to arrange the items, and to compose myself. Eleanor and I are talking like acquaintances, not friends. It's disconcerting, but also unsurprising. Finally, I straighten and turn to face her. "So."

"So," she says, like an agreement. Then: "Do you want to get a cup of coffee? There's a restaurant on the ground floor that's not too bad. Bella's going to be another half-hour or so, at least."

"Okay," I say, and we head out.

We don't speak as we walk to the elevator, wait for it, and then step inside. We're still silent as we soar downward, and Eleanor leads the way to the café. I'm starting to feel nervous, like she's going to level me with something I have no way to expect. She's walking with purpose, a swing in her step, almost like the old Eleanor... but different. Less bouncy and optimistic, maybe, and yet she seems *settled*, in a way I wasn't anticipating. How could so much change in less than a week? Then I think of my own life, and realize that, yes, of course it can.

We get our coffees—a latte for her, a cappuccino for me— and then sit at a table by the window. For a few seconds, both of us just sip.

"How are you?" Eleanor finally says, putting down her cup.

"I'm fine..." I hesitate. "But I think the more important question is, how are you? And how is Bella? Physio sounds like a positive step..."

Eleanor glances down at her coffee cup. She's wrapped her hands around it, like she's seeking its warmth.

"It is," she agrees after a moment. "Bella started waking up on Tuesday... by the evening, she was more or less conscious, but sleepy. She definitely knew us, and she was able to speak, although her speech was—and still is—a little slurred." She has started speaking in rote, and I realize she must have given this spiel many times. "They can't really assess the damage fully," she continues in the same brisk voice, "but it's something, obviously. The slurred speech, the physio... her gait is a little imbalanced." She gives a little shrug. "Time will tell. At her age, the neuroplasticity of the brain is pretty amazing. So a full recovery is not off the cards, and, of course, it's early days."

"Very early days," I interject, trying to sound hopeful even though I am quietly appalled. "Eleanor, that's—"

"I need to tell you what happened," Eleanor cuts me off. She sounds quietly, calmly determined, but the words alone make me tense.

"What happened..." I repeat, unable to hide the uncertainty in my voice.

"On the day of the party." She gives a little nod. "I know it all now, or almost all of it. Everything that's important, anyway." Her gaze is direct, unflinching, and I tense. Is Eleanor blaming Freya? It doesn't seem like it, and yet... where is she going with this? What has she found out?

"Okay," I say, because what else can I say? But I'm not sure I want to know.

Eleanor lets out a little sigh, then steels herself to begin. "There are so many factors," she states, "that contributed to what happened. But to start at the beginning, or close to the beginning, the reason I was so... agitated... that day was because I was afraid Brian was having an affair."

I can't help but goggle. An *affair*? And immediately chasing the heels of that thought is another—was that why she was so willing to believe the worst of Matt?

Eleanor glances down at her coffee cup. "I know it seems crazy, but the fact that he didn't come to the party... he changed his passwords..." She shakes her head. "Oh, it doesn't really matter, but there were a dozen little things that together made me freak out. I suppose it exposed the weakness in my supposedly strong marriage. Anyway." She looks up, direct and determined again. "That's where I was mentally and emotionally, on that day. And why I left you to basically manage all the kids, which was wrong and unfair, I know. He's not having an affair, by the way," she adds with a faint smile. "On the day of the party he was seeing his mother."

"His *mother*?" I stare at her in disbelief. I know Brian hasn't been in touch with his mother for about twenty years; the way Eleanor described it, he cut her out of his life as if he were wielding a pair of scissors.

"I know, right?" Eleanor smiles again, but sadly. "She got in touch with him a few weeks before the party. Wanted to reach out... to make amends for his childhood, all that. He started talking with her, meeting her... he didn't tell me about any of it."

"Why didn't he tell you?" I find I am fascinated by all the things I didn't know, all the contributing factors that somehow led to Bella being here, at this hospital. It wasn't just me and my phone call, or Freya internalizing Matt's absence. There were other things going on. *So many other things.*

Eleanor lets out another sigh, this one heavy, as she pushes a hand through her hair. "We're still working through that," she explains slowly. "We've started to talk about it, but the short answer is... our marriage wasn't as strong or great as we both thought it was. Or, really, as we both wanted the other person, along with the rest of the world, to think it was." At my look of confusion, she clarifies, "I was trying to be someone I wasn't for Brian. I think I always knew that on some level, you know? I had to be the perfect mother because his was so bad. I had to be the loving wife because he'd felt so unloved as a child. I had to be this paragon, and I needed everyone else to believe it too, and the truth is, it is so far from what I've ever truly felt or been. Family photos on the staircase aren't proof of anything, in the end, except that you can all smile and say 'cheese.'"

I must look even more confused, because she gives a wobbly

laugh and waves her hand in dismissal. "Sorry, that's another story. The point is, I've always felt totally inadequate, but I never wanted Brian—or anyone else—to know. If I end up having therapy, and I think I might, I'll probably learn it's because of my brothers. Heart surgeon and lawyer, captain of everything growing up, and I was just... me. Pretty enough but not super bright. That was basically what all my teachers said, if not that bluntly, and it's certainly what my parents have thought, and continue to think."

"Oh, Eleanor..." I can't believe I didn't know any of this. Admittedly, I knew some of it—about her brothers, for example —but not all the painful emotions underneath. I had no idea that Eleanor felt inadequate about *anything*.

"The thing is," she continues, glancing down so her hair slides in front of her face, "I didn't realize that Brian felt the same way. Like he had to be this big, strong guy for me. The protector and provider times, like, a thousand, when he never had anything like that, growing up. When he wasn't even sure what that looked like, so he felt like he was faking it all the time, and he was just waiting for me to figure it out." I am shocked, and also moved with pity for Brian. The big man who inside felt so small. Eleanor raises her head, tucking her hair behind her ear. "We were both playing roles for the other person, afraid that if we stopped, we'd let them down. It was all basically fake."

I hardly know how to respond. "And you discovered this...?" I begin delicately.

"This week, when he told me about his mom. He hadn't wanted to tell me before, because to him it felt like weakness. He'd made this decision to cut her out of his life, and now he was rowing back on it. And, I think, he didn't want to seem like he needed her, which he did and does... doesn't every child need his or her mother?" She gives another sad smile. "As to how this relates to Bella getting hurt... well, there's more. A lot more. I just wanted to explain why I was inside, leaving you to it. But you know how Bella was telling Freya and Kieran that they didn't have dads?"

I stiffen, even though I'm trying not to. "Yes..."

"Bella *wasn't* teasing them. At least, she didn't mean to be. She was worried for them—she'd drawn this picture, I found it up in her room, of Kieran and Freya with Brian, like they were part of our family, right next to Brian..."

I feel my mouth purse a little sourly. Bella the angel, again?

"But it wasn't Bella," Eleanor clarifies, "it was Lizzy."

I stare at her blankly. What on earth does *Lizzy* have to do with any of this?

"She told me all about it after I found that picture," Eleanor continues, shaking her head. "I knew she was struggling. I should have realized there was more going on. But at the party, Bella told Lizzy about Kieran and Freya not having dads. She'd overheard us... not saying that, not exactly anyway, but you know how children are." She sighs heavily. "Anyway, when Bella said that, Lizzy said something about mentioning it to Kieran and Freya. Tell them that since they didn't have their own dads, they could have Brian. I think Lizzy knew it would upset Kieran, but Bella didn't understand. And," she finishes quietly, "I think Lizzy was angry with us because she felt we favored Bella. She said it in anger, but Bella took her seriously."

I can only blink, trying to absorb it all.

"So Bella asked Kieran and Freya to come to the pond, according to Lizzy," Eleanor continues. "She said she was going to tell them a secret. And then she told them they didn't have dads and so they could share hers. But, because of Lizzy, it sounded like she was teasing them, and so Freya got angry, and then I guess Bella pushed her, and Freya pushed her back and ran off, without even realizing Bella had gotten hurt." Eleanor pauses. "Lizzy saw most of it."

My mind is spinning with all this new information. "She did...?"

"Yes, she told me she'd started toward Bella when I ran up to her, and then she stayed away because she was afraid. It's been eating her up inside this whole time. She's actually been self-harming—it doesn't help that she's fallen in with a group of friends who aren't the best. They stoked all the insecurity."

"But why was Lizzy so angry with you?" I wonder aloud.

Eleanor's face falls, and for a second, she looks as if she might cry. "Because, like I said, she felt we loved Bella more than her, and do you know, I understand why she felt that way. Sometimes it must have seemed as if our lives revolved around Bella, and Lizzy felt like an add-on. Her friends fed that whole idea, too, apparently... saying she was second best..."

Yet more people indirectly involved in this tragedy. "Why would they do that?" I am genuinely mystified.

Eleanor shrugs unhappily. "Why does a teenager do anything? To cause drama, or because they were angry about their own family situations, or both? Who knows? The point is, Lizzy was feeling forgotten. And we did—not forget her, but neglect her, at least a little bit. You know how long we tried for Bella..."

"Yes," I say quietly. Six years, four miscarriages, and three IVF attempts. It was a long, painful road for both Eleanor and Brian.

"I suppose that skewed our perception. And, to tell you the truth, as Lizzy got older, she became a bit more difficult, as any teenager does. Bella felt... easier."

She lapses into silence, while I continue to absorb all that she's told me. I feel as if my view of my best friend, of her whole world, has altered, like the swirl of a kaleidoscope, presenting me with an entirely new image.

"You know," Eleanor muses sorrowfully, "a few days ago, I'd convinced myself that Bella's accident—and I do believe it really was an accident—wasn't anyone's fault. I know Brian and I were acting like someone had to be to blamed at the start, but I think that was just out of fear. I'd moved on from there, and I'd decided that no one was to blame, and so I could absolve myself, along with everyone else."

She pauses, her expression hardening into determined lines.

"But then I realized the truth was not that it wasn't anyone's fault, but maybe that it was *everyone's*. We all played our part, didn't we? If Lizzy hadn't felt left out... if Brian had been honest with me, and I'd been honest with him... if Freya hadn't lost her temper... if you hadn't been on your phone... hell, if I'd agreed with Brian to remove that rock." She holds up a hand to forestall anything I'm going to say. "I'm not blaming you. I'm just saying, it was the perfect storm of events and attitudes and actions, and it resulted in where we are today. And maybe that's just what life is like... a dozen different situations and people contribute to any outcome. We need to accept responsibility for our part in it... however small, and then we need to move on. To *choose* to move on." She smiles faintly. "I'm sounding pretty philosophical, aren't I?"

I have no idea what to say. "Eleanor, I'm so sorry about it all." It feels like the most honest, and maybe the only, thing that I can say right now.

"I know you are. And I am, too. I'd never wish what happened to Bella on any child or mother, but... some good has come of it, you know? Brian and I are more honest with each other. I think our marriage will be stronger than ever. And getting this all out with Lizzy... that's been important, too. We're going to start therapy, as a family, I think."

"I'm glad."

Eleanor gives me a direct look. "As for you and me and our friendship," she says bluntly, "I don't know where we stand. With everything that has happened. I... I realize that maybe I wasn't as good a friend to you as I thought I was." She gives me a small, sorrowfully wry smile. "We didn't have a very balanced relationship, did we?"

This acknowledgment rocks me as much as anything she's said before. I never expected Eleanor to understand the dynamics of our friendship that caused me so much frustration. I never expected her to even be aware of them.

"And I don't think I was as a good friend to you as I thought I was," I admit. As I say the words, I know they are true. I thought Eleanor seemed smug in her superiority, but so was I, albeit in a different way. We were both wrong.

Eleanor nods slowly. "I don't know what the future holds," she states after a moment. "We have a lot of stuff to work on, and Bella is going to be in the hospital for another month, at the minimum. After that..." She shrugs. "I don't know. I don't know what her needs will be, or what will be best for us as a family. There's a small, progressive school toward Litchfield... we've thought about sending her there. And we've even talked about selling our house." At my look of blatant surprise, she laughs. "We don't need the perfect image anymore. We're not trying to prove anything to anybody now, or even—especially—to ourselves."

"Wow." I let out a shaky laugh. I am still reeling from everything she has shared. "You've done a lot of 'inner work,' as they say," I tell her with a small smile.

"Yeah." Eleanor gives an answering little laugh. "I've had to, and in a very short amount of time. There's more to be done, a lot more, but... it's a start." She takes a sip of coffee. "What about you? What's going on?"

I think of Matt moving back in, the three of us together again, a new hope for the future of our family. I'm not sure I want to explain all that to Eleanor now, on the back of her unburdening, but I will one day. One day soon. We might not have been good friends to each other, but maybe we can be, in future. In an entirely new and different way.

"I'm good," I tell her. "Things are actually really good. I'll tell you about it another time."

"Oh, yeah, jeez." Eleanor glances at the time on her phone. "Bella's going to be back in the room in a minute. Do you want to say hi to her?"

The prospect fills me with both apprehension and hope. "Sure," I say, and Eleanor smiles in understanding and gratitude. I think she knows exactly how I'm feeling... maybe for the first time, ever.

As we walk upstairs, I acknowledge again that there is a settledness to her that she didn't possess before. Before Bella's accident, Eleanor was always flitting about, full of enthusiasm and certainty that covered, I am starting to realize, actually a desperate need for approval. She's different now—more worker bee than butterfly, focused on what's ahead and not worried about what anyone, least of all me, thinks. It is, I decide, a good change.

As we come into the room, a nurse is helping Bella back into her bed. She's in a hospital gown, her movements painfully laborious and jerky, and for a second, I am appalled. Based on what Eleanor had been saying, I'd expected more of the Bella I once knew. This little girl is Bella—but gaunt, uncoordinated, *different*.

When Eleanor swoops in to give her a hug, Bella's arms struggle as they close around her mother. When she speaks, her voice is noticeably slurred.

"Hey, Bella-bee, look who's here to see you?" Eleanor exclaims. "Freya's mom!"

Hurriedly, I compose my features into a beaming smile of welcome. "Hi, Bella," I say, as, with Eleanor's help, she smiles at me. There is a bit of drool on her chin, and I try not to notice.

"Hi, Mrs. West," she says, forming the words slowly and with care.

The ensuing silence feels painfully awkward. I struggle to

think of something to say. "Look at you, up and about," I finally land on. My voice sounds cringingly jolly, the forced good cheer of someone who doesn't know how to handle this moment. "You'll be running races in no time!" Ugh. I feel so woefully ill equipped.

Bella doesn't reply, and Eleanor helps her back into bed, giving her a kiss on the cheek before she turns to me. "Thank you so much for coming," she says, and it's clearly a goodbye.

"Of course. I... I can come again." I don't sound like I want to, and inwardly I cringe. Again. I want to be better than this. I *will* be.

"I'm sure Bella would love that," Eleanor replies, "but she'll be really busy. She's moving to a rehab facility next week, anyway."

"Oh... right..."

"It was good of you to come." Eleanor takes my arm and, gently but firmly, steers me out of the door.

Out in the hallway, I turn to her. "I'm sorry..."

"For what?" Eleanor asks in a tone of steely challenge. "She'll get there, Natalie," she adds. "You don't realize just how far she's come. She'll get there." I see the fierce light of determination in Eleanor's eyes, and I believe her.

"Of course she will," I say, and then, to my surprise, Eleanor hugs me.

It isn't until she steps back that I realize how final a farewell it seemed.

As I drive back to Wetherby, I can't untangle how I feel—grief and hope mixed together, along with regret and gratitude. Has my friendship with Eleanor ended? Do I feel sad about it? I'm not sure.

Maybe every friendship has its course to run, I reflect, no matter how long or short, how straight or twisted. And what is important is not to dissect the past, but to look toward the future. And maybe I can have another, different kind of friendship—one where I am not the deputized sidekick. For some reason, this makes me think of Joanna. There is always possibility, I think. There is always hope, if you just choose to look for it. To find it... wherever it can be found.

As I turn off the highway for the small town where I've spent most of my life, I find I am smiling.

EPILOGUE

KIERAN

One year later

It's therapy day today. My dad likes to pretend we're just going somewhere to play, as if I don't know what it really is, a room with carpet on the *walls* and all these soft toys piled around, but I do. I know so much more than anyone thinks I do.

My mom, at least, is more honest with me.

"Dr. Andy can help you think about your feelings," she tells me sometimes. Her smile looks like it might slide off her lips.

I know I'm different from other kids. I've always known that, and I haven't cared. But maybe now, I do, at least a little, after talking with Dr. Andy.

Things are so different now—Bella has left the school, to go somewhere smaller, my mom said. My mom and I have seen her in town. She looks the same, but she walks slowly, like she's hurt one of her feet. Once, I heard her speak, and the words came out really slowly. I know it's because of the accident, but my mom and dad say she's getting better all the time.

Riley and Cooper have left too. I know their mom hated me. Once, when I was going into school, she grabbed me by the elbow and told me I was a little monster. I didn't tell anyone about it. I thought *she* looked like the monster, with her face all screwed up like that. I'm glad she's gone, even if Riley and Cooper weren't *that* bad.

The biggest difference, though, is I have a best friend. I'd do anything for Freya. I didn't tell anyone that she was the one who pushed Bella, and I still won't tell anyone the other part of the story—that Bella didn't push her first, like she said she did. I watched the whole thing. I saw how Bella lifted her hands like she was going to push Freya, and then she didn't. She looked sad, not angry, but Freya was too mad to stop herself. I know how that feels. She pushed her anyway, and I watched Bella fall. I wondered what would happen to her, if her head would stop bleeding, or if I'd be able to see her skull.

Dr. Andy says it's okay to have thoughts like that, but it's important to *do* something, too. That's what he's supposed to help me with—to remember to do something, because I just don't think about it.

I'm trying to do that now, though, because it seems to make people happy. I didn't used to care about that, and I still don't always, but sometimes I do. I want Freya to be happy. I know she still feels bad for pushing Bella. Sometimes she cries about it when she thinks no one is looking. She's not friends with Bella anymore, and she told me their moms aren't friends, either, although sometimes they say hello when they see each other. Our moms are friends, though, like we are.

"Hey, Ki," my dad says. His smile reaches his eyes now, in a way it didn't before. He takes my hand, and I let him, because I know he likes that. "Ready to go?" he asks, and I nod.

I'm looking forward to seeing Dr. Andy now. I didn't used to, so maybe I've already changed, at least a little.

"Yes," I tell him. "I'm ready."

A LETTER FROM KATE

Dear reader,

I want to say a huge thank you for choosing to read *In the Blink of an Eye*. If you enjoyed it, and would like to keep up to date with all my latest releases, just sign up at the following link. Your email address will never be shared and you can unsubscribe at any time.

www.bookouture.com/kate-hewitt

This story was somewhat inspired by my own experience—minus any tragedy or mean mothers!—of the dynamics of the school gate. How mothers relate, and how their children relate, is fascinating to me, and I wanted to create a situation and story where everyone had a part to play. While what happened at the party might seem grim, I do always want to end my stories with hope, and I hope that is how this one ended for you, too.

I hope you loved *In the Blink of an Eye* and if you did, I would be very grateful if you could write a review. I'd love to hear what you think, and it makes such a difference helping new readers to discover one of my books for the first time.

I love hearing from my readers—you can get in touch on my Facebook group for readers (facebook.com/groups/KatesReads), through X, Goodreads (goodreads.com/author/show/1269244.Kate_Hewitt) or my website.

Thanks again for reading!

Kate

www.kate-hewitt.com

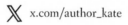 x.com/author_kate

ACKNOWLEDGMENTS

As ever, there are so many people who are part of bringing a book to fruition! Thank you to the whole amazing team at Bookouture who have helped with this process, from editing, copy-editing, and proofreading, to designing and marketing. In particular, I'd like to thank my editor, Jess Whitlum-Cooper, as well as Laura Deacon, Sarah Hardy and Kim Nash in publicity, Melanie Price in marketing, Richard King in foreign rights, Sinead O'Connor in audio, and Imogen Allport in editorial.

I'd also like to thank all the mothers I've encountered at the school gate—don't worry, none of you inspired the character of Jennifer Evans! She's pure imagination, but special thanks to Jo Walker, Cat Barker, and Amanda Endicott, as well as all the mums of the current Year 6. You may not have known it, but you all inspired me. It will be bittersweet to move on from primary school and the daily school run!

Thanks also to the current Year 6 class, and especially my budding writer Charlotte, who during a creative writing workshop all suggested character names and story titles. I hope you all like the final choices. Good luck in secondary school! You are all amazing!

PUBLISHING TEAM

Turning a manuscript into a book requires the efforts of many people. The publishing team at Bookouture would like to acknowledge everyone who contributed to this publication.

Audio
Alba Proko
Melissa Tran
Sinead O'Connor

Commercial
Lauren Morrissette
Hannah Richmond
Imogen Allport

Cover design
Alice Moore

Data and analysis
Mark Alder
Mohamed Bussuri

Editorial
Jess Whitlum-Cooper
Imogen Allport

Made in the USA
Las Vegas, NV
27 July 2024